THE ZODIAC COLLECTOR

Laura Diamond

SPENCER HILL PRESS

Spencer Hill Press

Contact: Spencer Hill Press, PO Box 247, Contoocook, NH 03229, USA
Please visit our website at www.spencerhillpress.com
First Edition:July 2014
Diamond, Laura
Zodiac Collector : a novel / by Laura Diamond - 1st ed.
p. cm.
Summary: On the eve of the Faire, Anne, along with her reluctant twin sister, Mary, conjures up a spell that will make their sixteenth birthday party a whirlwind event.

The author acknowledges the copyrighted or trademarked status and trademark owners of the following wordmarks mentioned in this fiction:
Alien, Band-Aid, Converse, Formica, Google, Hello Kitty, Junior Mints, Little Orphan Annie, Mickey Mouse, Mountain Dew, Nike, Peter Pan, PS3, Raid, Red Bull, Sauron, Scooby-Doo, Snow White, South Park, Spam, Spider-Man, Thermos, Tupperware, Twizzlers

Cover design by Lisa Amowitz
Interior layout by Jennifer Carson and Marie Romero

ISBN 978-1-937053-63-5 (paperback)
ISBN 978-1-937053-71-9 (e-book)

Printed in the United States of America

*This book is dedicated to all the people who
dare to pursue their dreams*

Chapter One

The Renaissance Faire wrecks my birthday every year. A month before the actors and merchants arrive to transform Hopewell Falls Park into a sixteenth-century towne—yes, with an "e"—Mom stops taking her lithium. Within forty-eight hours she's higher than a prom queen accepting her crown. As the best seamstress east of the Appalachian Trail, she thinks it's her duty to stay awake for days, surviving on double espressos and cigarettes, to make the royal court's costumes. She says mania makes her more productive, but all it does is turn her into a raging beast that puts Sauron, the Basilisk, and the Kraken all to shame.

Her internet business, *Devans's Dazzling Dresses,* caters to the Renaissance crowd and occupies her all year long, but our local faire gives her the most sales.

"These orders came in months ago. Why wait until the last minute to finish them?" I hover near the doorway to the living room—a.k.a. Mom's studio—and try not to choke on the stagnant air. A wheeze plays at my lungs. I finger the inhaler that I always carry in case I have to take a puff.

The room has the best natural lighting in the whole house. A large bay window, stretching from floor to ceiling, is the envy of every do-it-yourself crafter on the block. I dream about curling up on the seat cushion with a book and a cup of hot chocolate, but Mom never lets anybody in there. No. Matter. What.

I'd need to wear a gas mask, anyway, to prevent an asthma attack.

Heavy-metal music throttles my eardrums. I resist the urge to clap my palms over my ears. Mom says she can draw energy from the sound waves. She thinks the bands create their music specifically for her. No amount of lithium makes that go away.

"What else am I supposed to do? This is how I create." Her blue eyes spark with fury as she takes a drag on her cigarette. Two inches of ash hang on the end. It's beyond me how it doesn't fall off and burn the fabric she's working on. At least the dry cleaner can erase the smoky stench from her masterpiece after it's done. She throws a pincushion at me and returns to her ironing. "Now get out of here. Don't you have finals to study for or something?"

"But Mary's and my birthday is coming up and I wanted to talk to you—" My voice squeaks and tears burn at my eyes.

Her head snaps up, sending wild-colored curls swaying with agitation. "I'm. Working."

I can't even get two sentences out and she's in attack mode. My stomach twists on itself as instinct claws at my chest, begging for clean air. *Ask quickly and get out.* That's the plan. I lick my dry lips. "We're turning sixteen. It's important."

She plucks the cigarette from her mouth and pulverizes it in a nearby ashtray. Her nicotine-stained fingers shake, fumbling to light another one. It takes two flicks for the lighter to ignite. Her cheeks hollow out as she sucks in a long drag. She holds it in for a few seconds, eyes closed in fleeting bliss, and blows it out. The lines of her face—webbing crows' feet, jagged wrinkles across her forehead, arcs from her nose to the corners of her lips—deepen. Pale gray fog surrounds her like she's a smoldering dragon working up to the big explosion of fire.

"Everything's about you and your sister, isn't it? Well, did it ever occur to you that the work I do helps pay the bills around here? I don't see you bringing in a paycheck."

"Whatever." Like a defenseless knight who's lost his courage, I retreat. I storm upstairs, my ever-ready puffer in one hand while I wave away the haze of smoke with the other. The whole house smells like stale nicotine and my asthma is flaring like Jenny Johnson's face that time she farted in gym class. I slam the door behind me.

"You interrupted Mom, didn't you?" My ever-perceptive twin, Mary, guesses right. She removes her earbuds and sets aside her biology textbook.

"No." I take a hit from my inhaler and flop on my paisley bedspread. Doesn't matter that I stare at the ceiling. Her accusation crashes over me like a tsunami. I roll on my side to face her. "Yes."

She runs her hands through her curly espresso-colored hair and glares at me with her jade eyes. "Why?"

"Why not? We've never had a real, disaster-free birthday party because of the Renaissance Faire. Isn't it about time?" I refuse to surrender to her disapproval. She'd never challenge Mom. At least I try. My Papillon dog, Castor, leaps on the bed. The fringe of his sable ears flutter like streamers as he licks my cheeks.

Mary averts her gaze and picks up his brother, Pollux. It was Mom's idea to name them after the Gemini twins. She called it "kitschy." Pfft. Amazing she didn't name *us* after them.

"Well?" I sit up. Castor's and Pollux's dark eyes stare at me with sympathy. The cozy bedroom is their safe haven as much as it is ours.

"The more you bother her, the less likely it is we'll get a party. I bet she won't bake a cake this year, either." She presses her chin against Pollux's head.

"So it's my fault we won't get a party?"

She winces. "I didn't say that."

Regret presses on my shoulders and slides down my spine to nestle in my gut like a snake. It coils in my stomach, tail rattling with agitation. "I don't mean to make things worse."

"I know," she barely whispers.

I take a deep breath and imagine the regret snake spontaneously combusting and evaporating into nothingness. Better than having it strike and lodge its fangs into my liver. "What kind of cake would you want?"

"It would be cool to have a tiered one, with piping and flowers. Maybe even edible pearl candies or something." The corner of her mouth hitches up.

Mary likes pretty things. I prefer edgy. "What about one with a knight beheading a dragon on top? Blood-red icing can trail down the sides and pool around the base."

She scrunches her nose and scratches behind Pollux's ear. "Gross. Maybe we can get a Papillon cake. It'd be so cute."

It's not a bad idea.

Her half-smile fades. "Doesn't matter. Mom won't go for any of it."

"It's so unfair." Amped on the pain of injustice, I launch myself to my feet and pace our bedroom, from our window overlooking the wooded park across the street, to the desk we share on the other side. The braided rug between our twin beds massages my bare feet.

"Yeah, and what are you going to do about it? Nothing, that's what." Mary cradles Pollux in her arms and carries him to his doggie bed. After gently lowering him to the round cushion, she stares at her closet, gaze scanning every inch, and taps her chin. Sucking on her bottom lip, she falls into an OCD trance, and I've lost any chance at wrangling her back into the conversation about Mom.

She rips all her shirts out and slaps them on the bed, hangers and all. One swift sweep of her arm slides her pants to the left. She goes back to the bed and fishes out every red shirt, top, tank, and sweater. Next, orange. After that, yellow.

"Mary, please. There are better ways to deal with this." I try to block her, but she shoves past me to hang up all her green garments. Castor barks at her, then goes to his own bed and gives his best sad-puppy-dog expression.

"You put a lime cardi at the end, after forest green." I shouldn't encourage her compulsions, but if it gets her talking again…

"And I suppose you getting Mom even more upset is a better way to handle it?" She sighs and moves the cardigan next to a lemon-yellow tank. It reminds me of the yellow roses in Gamma's yard. As a kid, I couldn't pronounce "Grandma," so I called my grandmother, Edith, "Gamma." It stuck and I call her that to this very day. Mary calls her "Grandmother." A complete, well-rounded word. Stable. Precise. Makes me roll my eyes every time.

"What do you do with brown?" I fold my arms and sit in my chair, tapping my foot against the bookcase. My math book mocks me. It's sitting there, closed on my desk, waiting to scramble my brain with impossible algebra problems. I'm never going to ace the SAT, but I have to if I want to compete with Mary and get into the same college, avoid Mom's snarky comments about how stupid I am for not keeping up, and land an all-expenses-paid scholarship to a far away, competitive university.

"It's neutral. It goes at the end with tan, white, gray, and black. In that order." She holds up two similarly colored shirts, one a button-down, the other a pullover. "Which one's darker?"

"Does it matter?"

"Anne." Her tone matches her scowl.

"The button-down."

She nods and places them in order, navy after royal blue. "At least I'm organized. Really, you should let me fix your train wreck of a closet."

I shake my head. "It's not that bad."

"A complete and total mess. Then again, there's not much to organize since you only own black."

"That's not true," I pout.

"Only because you borrow my clothes half the time." She glances at me over her shoulder, then turns back to stare at her work. The pause is good. She might be done with this round. On the other hand, she could decide to start over. "Anne, why'd you have to bother her?" This time the accusation is gone, but the pain remains.

Knights would have a lot fewer problems if they let sleeping dragons lie. I shouldn't have provoked the one downstairs. There has to be another solution. I step between her and the rainbow of clothes. "We could plan our own birthday party."

"Duh. We do that every year." She continues to fidget with a hoodie.

"No, I mean, we can make our own cake, decorate however we want, and make it all on our terms. Forget Mom. She just ruins everything, anyway." I ease the garment from her fingers and hang it up.

Mary smirks. "Yeah, remember last year when she sprayed everyone with the water hose because they didn't like the cupcakes she made? Like it was their fault she put in salt instead of sugar."

"Right." I blush at the memory. Mom blamed us for the mistake because we dared to disturb her. We got weeks of pity glances and hissing whispers behind our backs at school. Only my best friend, William, stuck it out with us. He has his own parental malfunctions, so he understands what it's like.

"Do you think we can get away with it?" She eyes the heaping laundry pile covering the steamer trunk at the base of my bed. If brains had gears and hydraulics, I'd hear them grinding in her skull.

I leap in front of the leaning stack. I still have her patchwork scarf that I used for a belt two weeks ago. With my luck, it's sticking out of the pile like a hair in a bowl of mashed potatoes. "Of course we can. She's so busy, she won't even notice. And if we have it at Gamma's or something, she won't have to know anything about it."

"Grandmother's?"

"Why not?" I shrug. "It's as good a place as any. She has a great garden in the backyard. We can turn it into a fairytale land or something. Garlands, lights, butterflies, candles— it'll be so cool!"

Her eyes widen. Oh yeah, that's right. Pretty gets her every time.

"What do you say?" I bounce on my heels and tuck Castor under my arm. His little tail whacks my back rapidly. Happy doggy. "We can dress the pups up like sprites or something."

Her mouth twists to the side.

I sweep my hands back and forth to erase the idea. "Okay, forget dressing up the dogs."

"Let me organize your clothes and I'll go along with your birthday idea."

"Low blow!"

She grins. "What are sisters for?"

"Okay, but you have to promise to keep it a secret from Mom." I hold out my pinky finger. Mary wouldn't voluntarily let the secret out, but no one withstands Mom's inquisitions.

She winces. "Mom's heinous when she's in interrogation mode. You won't be able to keep it from her if she grills you, either."

I dropped my hand. "We need something more, then."

"Like what?"

For as long as I can remember, Gamma's house has been a safe haven for us, like an enchanted garden protected by wish-granting fairies and good witches. It's been too long since she's opened her spellbook, lit candles around us for the elements, and chanted a good-luck charm. I miss dreaming about her happily-ever-after stories starring twin girls with dark, curly hair and green eyes.

I grin at Mary. Maybe it's time to break out the magick.

Chapter Two

"We could dress the dogs up in chain mail, or as unicorns." I can't resist jabbing at Mary with corny ideas. It's better than fighting and it's better than not talking at all.

"Unicorns?" She tucks her chin in and purses her lips. It makes her look like a baby mid-poop.

When Gamma's house comes into view, Castor and Pollux yip and hop over each other, tangling their leads like foxhounds honing in on a kill. In this case, they get home-baked treats rather than a fox.

"Release the hounds," I exclaim, rushing ahead with Castor while Mary hangs back, correcting Pollux for his eagerness.

Gamma's front door is open, so I knock on the screen door's frame. "Gamma? It's Anne and Mary."

The TV is blaring in the living room. Sounds like a Seventies game show. Ick.

"Gamma!" I glance at Mary. She's still at the base of the steps, hands gripping Pollux's lead tight, chewing on her bottom lip. Absolutely no help. With a sigh, I yank open the screen door and slip inside. The door slaps shut behind me. Castor whines, his tiny toenails tapping and skittering on the hardwood floor.

There's a scratching at the door. I peek over my shoulder.

"Pollux!" Mary picks him up and hugs him to her chest. He wiggles in her grasp and licks her face, his tail wagging like a pinwheel in a tornado. She comes inside and sets him down next to Castor. They greet one another like long-lost brothers separated by famine and hardship only to be reunited in the land of plenty.

I unhook Castor's leash. Hardships forgotten, he sprints away, heading down the hallway that slices through the center of the cottage. He slides around the corner, colliding with the wall before catching enough friction to steady himself. In the kitchen, he yips and whines.

Pollux barks in reply, pained at the immediate abandonment by his brother. We all suffer trials and tribulations, Gamma would say.

"Shh," Mary taps his nose.

"Let him go," I say.

"He needs to learn how to behave."

"He's a dog. You can't expect him to be as perfect as you."

"I'm not perfect," she murmurs. Rushing by me, she sets him down farther into the hallway. He scrambles behind Castor.

Gamma shuffles out from the living room, carrying a stack of magazines, and pauses. "What's all this ruckus? Oh, hi, girls. Didn't hear you come in."

"The TV is too loud." I point to the living room.

"Eh?" She peers up at me, then turns to Mary. "Mary, love, turn the TV down, will you?"

Mary tries to suppress a smile. "Okay."

I follow Gamma into the den. Bookshelves line the walls, filled with knick-knacks, books, pictures, and drawings that Mary and I did when we were kids. A pair of wingback chairs flanks the window, their pale blue fabric paling on one side from years in the sun. Gamma's desk is covered with stacks of papers and a tray of candles, some short, some tall.

We used to call this our conjuring room. It's where Gamma told us stories while we drank tea and ate cupcakes. The smell of aging paper, leather, and wax ignite memories of chanting rhymes and studying plants with magickal properties. It's hard to remember when things changed, when I decided it was fake and let go of my faith. I can still have fun imagining, but that's what it is—fiction, fantasy, a way to avoid reality.

Avoidance. That's what Mary does.

Gamma heads to the corner of the room and bends, head turning left to right, as if she's taking a mental inventory of the odds and ends littering the floor. Magazines, paperbacks, newspapers, and old mail stuff the bulging woven baskets. Several stacks stand alone, filling the spaces between them.

We shouldn't have come here for a solution. Gamma can't help us with a silly spell or luck charm. She can't even decide where to store her junk. *Wake up to reality, Anne.*

Gamma hums like she's serenading her stockpile of useless stuff.

"Need help?" I ask.

"I got it, dear." She files her magazines in a row of baskets. *Gardening With Gloves* in one, *Herbs For Today* in another, and *Fruits and Veggies* in the last. All are addressed to Edith Cripper, my Gamma. She used to subscribe to magick magazines—*Fae and Fantasy, Modern Spells, Quick Chants*—and read them to me while I colored. It's been so long that I've forgotten most of the rules and tricks I'd learned.

Finished with her chore, she looks me up and down, her brown eyes enlarged by the magnification of her dollar-store glasses. Their fire-engine red frames span from above her eyebrows to beneath her cheekbones. "What brings you by?"

Mary's voice echoes down the hallway. She's trying desperately to tame Castor and Pollux. With her occupied, I have the perfect opportunity to talk to Gamma, but my lips won't move. Truth is, I'm not a knight fighting a dragon. I'm a little girl pretending to be greater than I am. My mother may rival the rage of mythical beasts, but she's all too human and there's no magick trick that'll cure her. The fragile bubble of hope collapses in my brain like a startled soufflé.

"What is it, Anne?" Gamma smoothes a strand of hair behind my ear.

I turn away from her and run a finger along the bookcase shelf. My journey leaves a wobbly trail in the fine layer of dust. "Mary and I turn sixteen this year."

She laughs softly and edges in front of me so I can't avoid her. "When did you grow up? I remember when your mom toted one of you in each arm, wee little babes." She brings her hands together and holds them a few inches apart.

"We want a special party." I wander to the candles and peel some of the melted wax off the tray.

"I don't blame you."

I wipe my hand on my jeans. "Mom won't let us."

Her mouth puckers in sympathy. "Oh, I wouldn't be so sure of that."

I blow a raspberry. "She said so. She's *working*." I air-quote the word.

"It is almost faire time. I don't know how she does it, making all those dresses every year." Gamma twirls a bangle on her arm and heads out of the room. "Let's get a snack."

I shuffle behind her to the kitchen, eyeing the flowered wallpaper and wondering who in their right mind would combine mustard yellow, olive green, burnt orange, and candy-apple red. In the kitchen, the black and white checkerboard linoleum tiles are worn in the corners and the cabinets are pale oak, covered in what seems like at least an inch of varnish.

Mary's sitting at the chrome and speckled Formica kitchenette table, holding Pollux and leaning over to scratch Castor's chin. Pollux wiggles out of Mary's grip and jumps to the floor. He scrambles to Gamma's feet, sliding like a hockey puck into Castor. Gamma laughs.

"I suppose you two want a treat?" she teases, sliding her feet inch by inch, herding the twins toward the pantry. She reaches for a Tupperware container on the second-highest shelf and peels open the cover. It gives a soft *pop*. She hands one bone-shaped peanut-butter crisp to each dog. "One for you and one for you."

I slump into the turquoise vinyl chair next to Mary.

Gamma returns the treat container and selects a package of double-stuffed chocolate cookies. She joins us at the table, tearing at the plastic seal. "Help yourselves, girls."

Mary slides out of her chair and collects three glasses from the cupboard. She sets them on the table, then fetches the milk and pours a glass for each of us.

"Cookies and milk. Nothing like it." Gamma takes a big gulp of her one percent and chomps on a cookie. Crumbs settle on her chest and the table. Mary eyes them and squirms. I wonder if Gamma will get the whole cookie eaten before Mary's cleaning the bits left behind with a napkin.

I separate the chocolate wafers and lick the vanilla-cream filling. "Mmmm."

Gamma reaches for a second cookie and Mary's out of her chair again, dousing a towel in the faucet. She wrings it out and wipes the table down.

I dip the wafers in the milk and let them soften for a minute. While the cookie soaks, Gamma's comment digs deeper inside me. She defended Mom. Pretty much blows any chance of planning a secret party with her. Disappointment prickles at the base of my neck, itching and gnawing its way through my body like a nest of termites. My leg jitters in response. We're here to talk about important stuff, and we're dipping cookies into milk like kindergarteners.

Mary gets Gamma a plate. "You can catch the crumbs."

Gamma pats her hand. "Thank you, dear."

I can't stand it anymore. "So, about our birthday…"

"I remember my sixteenth birthday. It was the same night as the school dance. I wore a purple dress with a satin sash. Momma had given me her sapphire hair clip. It was costume jewelry, of course, but it was so beautiful I worried about losing it all night. Well, until Billy Hatchfield asked me to dance. Oh, he was so handsome. Tall, crystal-blue eyes, and the warmest smile. Warm enough to thaw winter snow on the Adirondacks." Gamma gets this far-off look to her eyes, like she's traveling in time to that specific moment. She blinks a bunch of times and removes her glasses. Tugging on the hem of her shirt, she wipes the lens clean. "I should've married him, but your grandfather asked me first. No one said no to Mitchell Cripper."

"A school dance on your birthday." Mary chews the heck out of a bit of cookie.

Being on June twentieth, our birthday generally falls after school finals, so there are no convenient school dances to latch onto. Generally, we don't have homework—awesome!—but this year is different. We're taking the SAT, the review course falls during the faire days, and the test is on our birthday. A trifecta of pain. I slide deeper into my seat. Mary can only focus on one thing at a time, two tops. One: studying. Two: the faire. Yet another strike against my grand idea of a smash-hit sixteenth *bon anniversaire* bash.

"What do you girls want this year?" Gamma slides her glasses on and brushes extra crumbs off her chest. They fling around the room, and Castor and Pollux compete for them. Opportunists.

My gaze darts to Mary. She swallows loudly.

I sigh and run my hands through my straightened hair. "A normal mom."

"Anne!" Mary gasps.

"Well, it's true, and don't say you wouldn't wish for the same thing." I smack my palms on the table. The noise startles the dogs. Their wing-shaped ears perk up.

Her eyes widen. "She's not normal and she never will be, so there's no point in wanting it. Wishes are for kids."

"Consider this, love. Giving up on dreams means you've abandoned creativity and magick." Gamma pats Mary's hand.

Magick? I sit up straight. She hasn't mentioned magick in *forever*.

"What does that mean?" Mary's alarm seeps into her voice.

She shakes her head. "Amazing how everyone forgets at such a young age."

"Huh?"

Gamma sighs. She stands and rushes—kind of a half-walk, half-slide—out of the room.

Mary and I look at one another. "Do we follow her?" I ask.

She shrugs. "Dunno."

A couple minutes later, Gamma ambles back in, carrying a rectangular box and a smaller, square box. She plops the bigger package in front of me, then hands the other one to Mary. After pecking the tops of our heads with kisses, she sits down. "Go on, open them. I'm not getting any younger."

"But it's not our birthday yet," Mary says.

I don't bother hesitating for formalities and tear into the silver metallic wrapping paper. Rainbows shimmer across its surface as I expose the gift beneath.

A leatherbound book, twice the size of my laptop. The edges are rough to the touch, but the cover is soft. A Zodiac wheel is inlaid on the front. I draw my fingers across the surface. "*Gamma.*"

She chuckles. "I take it you like."

"I can't take this." I clutch the Zodiac spellbook to my chest. It's been years since I've flipped through the pages and scanned the spells and potions inside. Cold embers of a long-extinguished belief rekindle. I smile.

"I want you to have it." The skin around her eyes crinkles with her smile.

The flattened soufflé of hope lodged in my diaphragm puffs up a bit. My chest swells and tears blur my vision. "Thank you."

Her smile fades. "I never told you, but this book belonged to my twin, Eneaz."

"You have a twin?" I launch to my feet and set the book on the table.

A shadow crosses Gamma's face. Her gaze cuts to the floor. "It's not an easy thing, losing a sister. Be sure to hold onto one another, my dear granddaughters, no matter what. Do not let anger, jealousy, or any outside forces divide you. It's the bond you share," she laces her fingers together, "in unity, that will help you overcome whatever adversities you face."

Mary fiddles with the ribbon on her gift. "Grandmother, what happened?"

Gamma's eyes widen like she's choking on past regrets. Then she coughs and shakes her head. "She had a mind of her own and wouldn't settle for a simple life. Her thirst for power became an obsession. It ruined her in the end."

"Did she die?" I ask.

Mary flinches at the word "die."

"No. She just…left." Gamma points a crooked finger in my direction. "I don't want you trying any spells until we get a chance to review the rules, got it?"

The blossoming hope stokes the young, tentative fire of belief tickling my belly. "I promise."

"This is important, Anne. There's a lot of good magick in that book, but if done incorrectly, bad things can happen."

Her warning threatens to blow out the flames warming my heart. "I swear." I slash an "X" across my heart with a finger.

"All right, then." Gamma directs her attention to Mary. "Open yours."

Mary bites her lip and carefully peels the tape holding the edges in place. She unfolds each corner, creating a little paper placemat. The box is white and unmarked, so she untucks the lid and pries it open. A delighted squeal blazes from her. "Grandmother, it's exactly the one I wanted!"

Gamma laughs.

She lifts the mini-digital camera from its tissue-paper bed with both hands and turns it this way and that.

"I already put a battery in it. The original packaging is in the living room. It has instructions. I wanted to surprise you, so I put it in this old thing." Gamma picks up the box and closes the lid.

Mary taps the power button and immediately starts clicking photos of Castor and Pollux. They try to sniff the camera and practically knock each other out of the way to be the first to investigate it.

She pauses in her photo shoot and fiddles with more buttons. "Whoa. I can do so much more with this camera than my old one. Thanks, Grandmother!" She hooks an arm around Gamma.

"I'm glad you like it." She pats Mary's arm, then turns to me. "Now, I have some things to tell you about that book."

I lean forward to listen, still clutching the leathery treasure to my chest.

"Magick can be tempting. And it's not a simple thing. There are consequences."

"I won't do any dark stuff, I swear."

"That's not what I mean. All spells can be dark if done wrong. I'm serious when I tell you not to chant any of the spells or make any of the potions until I teach you."

"I promise. No spell stuff until you teach me."

Gamma wags a finger in the air. "This is different from regular magick. It draws on Zodiac power. Be mindful of your sign. Do not take the Gemini twins' energy willy-nilly. What you take must be given back."

"What do you mean?"

"Read the book. Then we'll talk." She stands and ushers us to the front door. Castor and Pollux follow obediently.

We snap on their leads and direct them outside.

When we get to the sidewalk, Gamma calls to me from the front porch. "And don't think you can change people with magick, Anne. Your mother is your mother."

Her words haunt me all the way home.

Chapter Three

I run the flat iron over my hair what feels like a hundred thousand times. Mary plays with her new camera while she waits. She's probably filled most of her memory card with snapshots of Castor and Pollux. Knowing her, she'll spend the next several weeks analyzing each shot, editing and tweaking, before choosing one to add to her wall of art. Her art teacher, Mr. Weaver, loves her "eye for composition." His favorite shots—a macrophoto of a lily, a black and white photo of Dad's blacksmith shoppe, a mess of Tarot cards flung over a table—capture a different part of the faire.

Section, clamp, drag. Repeat. I love the sheen of straight hair. Too bad I was born with the tightest curls since that Orphan Annie kid.

"You almost finished? We'll miss the movie." Mary slides off her bed and into the desk chair.

I check the clock. Seven. William is meeting us at the theater in a half-hour. "The movie doesn't start until eight."

"Do you have to be late for everything?" She plugs the camera into our laptop. The thing is so old that the letters on the keyboard are all but worn off and there's a crack in the case. Gamma gave it to us on our thirteenth birthday. Mary—always the organized one—set up a schedule for us to share it. It keeps fighting to a relative minimum.

"Do you have to be early to everything?" I nestle a sparkly headband into my hair and check for lumps one more time. My T-shirt has a rhinestone flower on the mini breast pocket, playing off the design on my headband. I tuck my feet into silver flats, completing my outfit. Hope is sparkly, and I'm the embodiment of it. "Okay. Ready."

Mary finishes downloading her photos and unplugs her camera. She tucks it in her jeans pocket and grabs her purse. The red piping on the purse matches her red polka-dot shirt.

We kiss Castor and Pollux goodbye. Before leaving the room, I tuck Gamma's spellbook into my pillowcase. The chances of Mom leaving her gowns to toss our bedroom are slim, but I just can't leave the thing out. Mary will have to keep her new camera hidden from now on, too. If she ever puts it down, that is.

Mom hates it when Gamma gives us things. Says it spoils us too much and makes us lazy. Of course, no one can match her energy during a manic episode, so she thinks *everybody* is lazy. To her, sleeping is a waste of time. So are things like showering regularly, eating ice cream—it's frivolous—and watching TV.

Dad drives us to the mall in his pale blue, rusted-out pickup truck. The name of his smithy shop, *Devans's Forgeries*, is painted on each door. Mom and Dad slap our surname on everything—T-shirts, business cards, mugs, pens, and tote bags. They send flyers to all our neighbors, take out ads in the high-school yearbook, and buy full-page spreads in the newspaper. They make overkill seem mild.

Dad's hands and clothes are all black from smelting. As the faire's blacksmith, he creates metal sculptures, weapons, horseshoes, gates, light fixtures, even furniture like benches and tables. The faire opens the day after tomorrow—Sunday—and runs for two weeks. Our birthday is smack dab in the middle of it, on the summer solstice and right on the cusp of Gemini.

"Call me when the movie gets out." Dad pulls the truck up to the curb.

Mary hops out first and I follow.

"Thanks, Dad," I say.

Inside, the air conditioning smacks away the early June humidity. The smells of salty, fatty, good things from the food court surround us and set my mouth to watering. Easy-listening music filters through the speakers. I don't know why the mall gods bother with that. Probably costs a lot and there isn't one person I've met who actually likes the sound of it.

We find William lingering by the box office. An easy slouch defines his calm style. So do his V-neck T-shirt, low-slung paint-stained jeans, and flip-flops. His dark hair forks in several different directions, carefree and untamed, framing his melt-my-heart blue eyes. My heart flutters. How he can make I-don't-care-how-I-look hot is beyond me.

I hesitate. I've known William since before kindergarten. We used to play in the sandbox together at the park. We shared buckets and mini-shovels and knocked over each other's sand castles. In first and second grade, we shimmied into the same tractor tire planted in the ground and told stories to one another during recess. In third grade, we shared crayons and colored pencils and created our own faire-based cartoon story. By the time we reached fourth grade, we had a system down for tag-teaming each other in gym, and in fifth we split our money to share snacks from the vending machine. It wasn't until sixth grade that we begged to have our lunch periods changed so we could eat together. In seventh, we had the same study hall and helped each other with homework. In eighth, we swore to take the same high-school classes and have continued the tradition each year since.

We're inseparable. Well, we were, until about six months ago. Right before winter break, William surprised me with a Christmas present—an autographed copy of *Watership Down* by Richard Adams. My most favorite book ever.

That moment changed everything. It sparked a war of Operation Fuzzy Confusion and Mission Sharp Excitement in my head. Operation FC would fire a he's-just-a-friend rocket to blast Mission SE to bits. Mission SE would retaliate by launching a see-that-spark-in-his-eyes-means-he's-into-you missile at Operation FC. Each camp, entrenched in its own stubborn side, raged on day after day, leaving me dizzy from casualties on both sides.

Mary hooks her arm around mine and drags me ahead. "Something wrong? William's over there, by that bench."

"Hey." He waves at us and smiles. Darn his dimples.

I return the smile on reflex, fully supporting Mission SE. "Hi. Been working at the faire?"

"Yeah, the jousting arena needed some touching up." He scratches some yellow paint off his arm and sits, angling his body away from me.

"Ready to get tickets?" I stuff my hands in my jeans pockets and roll from my heels to my toes. My heart's pumping faster than usual, carrying me to the Operation FC side.

"Got 'em." He holds up four tickets.

"Four? Who else is coming?" Mary asks.

"Evan." William tips his head and focuses his gaze behind us.

On cue, Evan Wu jogs up to us. "What's up?" He's taller than Mary and me by four inches—two of which are made up by his spiked hair. His navy polo shirt is the exact same shade as his dark-wash jeans and Converse sneakers. Navy hipster glasses round out his monochrome look. Evan has a pair of glasses to match every outfit. On anybody else, it'd be totally weird, but it works for him.

And it works for Mary. She drives her toe into the floor and fidgets with her hair, twisting a curl so tight it folds in on itself.

I raise an eyebrow at her.

She glares back at me and lowers her hand. "Let's go."

We take the escalator up to the theaters and make a pit stop at the concession stand. Chatter from families, groups of friends, and kids surge around us. It's a lively Friday night crowd. I bet most of them are heading to the same flick we are.

I yank on the hem of William's T-shirt. "Why don't you get the snacks while Mary and I save some seats?"

He gives me two tickets. "Good idea. What do you want?"

I fork over a twenty. "Nachos and a blueberry Slushee."

"Junior Mints, please," Mary squeaks. She's still positioning herself as far away from Evan as possible—making sure William and I are between them—regardless of the constraints of the folks pressing behind us.

He folds the money and pins it between his index and middle finger. "You got it, but it's my treat, okay?" He holds the bill out to me.

I flip back to Mission Sharp Excitement and accept the Andrew Jackson, flashing him a broad smile. "We'll try for the upper level, first row." I scoot out of line and rush to the theater with Mary in tow.

Since we're early—yes, I managed to get my hair done with time to spare, much to Mary's surprise—we get the seats we want.

"Where should we put the guys?" I ask.

"William should sit next to you and Evan can sit on the other side." Mary's leg is shaking so hard I can feel the tremors in my butt.

"What's wrong with you?" I extend my legs and prop my feet on the bar in front of us.

"What do you mean? Nothing." She slouches down and folds her hands across her belly, staring straight ahead.

"You're acting totally weird around Evan."

"You should talk, the way you flirt with William."

"I'm not flirting with him."

"You totally are."

"Whatever." It's my turn to study the expansive white screen. Dark red curtains frame the thing and line the walls. Speakers and dim, rectangular sconces hang every few feet.

"William's a good guy," Mary says softly.

"So's Evan," I counter.

She goes back to futzing with her hair.

"You should talk to him."

"Don't push me."

I roll my eyes.

The boys arrive, arms laden with popcorn, nachos, drinks, and candy.

William sits next to me and Evan takes the open seat next to him, just like Mary wanted. Avoid, avoid, avoid. She'll go to her grave avoiding things. Doesn't make her any safer.

"You bought enough to feed the whole theater." I take my nachos and hand Mary her Junior Mints.

"I'm hungry." He shrugs and sets my Slushee in the cup holder between us.

Evan tears into a package of Twizzlers with his teeth and chomps on three at a time. Mary steals glances at him while delicately opening her candy.

The theater goes dark and the previews start. I focus on my nachos. *Crunch, crunch, crunch*. So cheesy, salty, *yummy*.

I lick my fingers clean and reach for my Slushee. My fingers circle around…

…another hand.

"Eek!" I let go and nearly toss my food.

William starts laughing. "Sorry," he snorts, "forgot that was yours."

"Y-yeah, it's okay." I pick up the drink and suck on the straw until my mouth fills up with sugary ice. While the opening credits roll, I replay the moment in my mind. All I can think about is how slippery my fingers are and how disgusting it is that I slimed his hand with my spit.

I shudder. It's hard to tell if it's from the Slushee expanding in my stomach or the panic rising from my spine. Did I gross him out? No. He laughed. If he'd been turned off by it, he'd have yelled, or something.

Searing pain stabs my eyes. "Dang!" I spit out the straw and pinch the bridge of my nose.

Mary elbows me. "What's going on?"

"Brain freeze." I lean forward and plop the cup on the floor. Pinching the top of my nose, I pray for the agony to subside. Instead, it intensifies. "Ow, ow, *ow.*"

"Hey, you all right?" William's breath tickles my ear.

My leg kicks out in reflex, lobbing the Slushee under the railing and to the footpath below. "Crap!" I groan, squeezing my eyes shut.

"You should try out for the soccer team."

"Shut up," I whine.

He laughs, rubbing circles on my back with his palm.

I wish I could savor the sweetness of it, but the jabbing in my head is ridiculously distracting. I open my mouth and breathe out, hoping to funnel warm air to my palate.

William is there the whole time, rubbing and leaning with me.

Finally, my nerves settle and my brain thaws. I sit up straight.

He removes his hand. "Better?"

"Yeah," I sigh, relieved the pain is gone and bummed that William's no longer touching me.

A huge explosion bursts on the movie screen. Typical action flick. Blow up something important and let the big hunk lead a mission to set things right.

I can't pay attention no matter how hard I try. Every so often, I rub the sweat off my palms onto my jeans and remind myself to breathe.

After the movie ends, we wander out of the theater and hang around the food court. A few other kids from school do the same. We acknowledge each other briefly, like different species meeting at a watering hole, then huddle in groups around the larger tables. The goths are like stuck-up zebras, the nerds are nervous gazelles, and the jocks are hyenas—ready to crack up when the outcast giraffes trip over their own feet.

I sit on top of a table. "Did you like the movie?"

"Yeah, you?" William turns a chair around and sits on it backward. At least he's facing me this time.

"Yep." I glance at Evan. "What'd you think?"

He leans back into his chair and runs a hand over his spiky hair. "I've seen better, but the CGI was pretty good."

"The dialogue was kind of lame, though," Mary adds.

Evan chuckles. "Totally."

She smiles.

"*'I'm not just taking you down, I'm taking you down to your graves,*'" he mimics the main character's deep, meathead voice.

William snorts. "That was so lame."

"And what about, *'They didn't destroy our Capitol, they destroyed our heart.'*" I fake-stab myself in the chest with a fist.

We all laugh.

"Guess we should call Dad." Mary pulls out her cell and dials home.

"I'll walk you outside and wait with you." William hops up and tucks his chair under the table.

Evan pops from his seat. "Yeah, uh, me, too."

He and Mary walk ahead of William and me. She glances back at me once, her eyes wide.

I grin at her, the best nudge I can give under the circumstances. I want to say, "Go on, talk to him. He totally likes you," but I can't.

She bites her lip and settles in next to him. Evan chats about the special effects in the film, how they're made, and what the director could've improved on, and Mary nods emphatically, hanging on every word.

William and I don't talk. Ordinarily, it'd be a comfortable silence, but ever since his wicked awesome gift…well, let's just say both sides—Operation Fuzzy Confusion and Mission Sharp Excitement—are on full offensive strike. A good friend would give him something equally as cool. A more-than-a-friend would…would…crap. Operation Fuzzy Confusion is winning this round. I can't think of anything super fantastic enough to give him.

On the ride home, Mission SE launches another campaign.

I've got Gamma's spellbook. There must be something I can use inside those worn, yellowed pages. Inspiration climbs from its hidey-hole deep in my spine to the battlefield in my brain.

Gamma doesn't want me to chant, but if it's for a good reason then it should be okay. Besides, how much damage can one teensy-tiny spell do?

Advantage: Mission SE.

Operation FC raises the white flag of surrender for this round.

Chapter Four

By the pale yellow glow of my clip-on book light, I open the Zodiac spellbook and dive into its mysterious depths. A brightly colored Zodiac wheel marks the first page. Red for the fire signs, yellow for air, green for earth, and blue for water. In the center is a five-pointed star. The next ring shows the constellations, with an image of the corresponding sign superimposed on top. The final ring depicts the symbol of each.

Gemini is yellow. The constellation looks like two stick figures with the stars Castor and Pollux making up the head of each twin. On top of the outline is a drawing of long-haired boys dressed in tunics standing next to one another with their temples touching. The symbol in the outer ring looks like the Roman numeral two.

I trace my fingers along the image. This is my sign. Where I get my magickal energy from. All I have to do is figure out how to call on the stars.

"Castor and Pollux, are you listening?" I whisper. I hold my breath and listen really hard, as if expecting an answer.

"Who are you talking to?" Mary asks.

I yelp. "I thought you were sleeping."

Mary fluffs her pillow. "Nope. Grandmother said to be careful with that."

"She also told me to study it."

She purses her lips.

I blow a raspberry at her.

The dogs think I'm playing a game. They rush out of their doggie beds and hop on top of me, yipping for pets.

"Guys, easy. Go back to bed." I lift the book so they can't scratch at the pages.

"Pollux, come here." Mary snaps her fingers and the little Papillon scrambles to her bed.

Without competition, Castor can relax. He settles onto my lap, rolls over, and waits patiently for a belly rub. "You're such a ham."

His tail wags like crazy.

"If you're going to study something, why don't you prepare for the SAT?" Mary prods.

"Hey, you played with your camera. I'm playing with my present."

"Want me to snap your photo now? I'll use the flash," she snarks.

I huff. "I want to look at the spells."

"You need to wait for Grandmother."

"Yeah, you said that already. Message received."

She rolls her eyes. I dip my nose toward the spellbook and ignore her. Her mattress creaks. I glance in her direction. She's facing the wall. Good. I can immerse myself in the book's beauty, wonder, and mystique in peace.

I ease Castor to the end of my bed and balance the book on my lap, ready for another swim in the deep pool of magick Gamma presented me with. To test the parchment waters, I dip my toes in the front index. Each sign draws me in by degrees. Then I wade through page after page of spells for good luck, healing, sweet dreams, protection, truth, peace, even air fresheners. Some pages are islands of potions for rejuvenation, love, and warding off evil energies. Toward the back is a treasure chest of chants calling on spirits, invoking the Zodiac signs, and phasing into astral projection. I surf the swirly script, float on the star and curlicue designs in the corners, and navigate the key on the bottom of each page outlining the matching signs.

When I come up for air, sandy grains in my eyes force me to stop exploring and pull me toward sleep. I click the light off and huddle under the sheets, holding the book in my arms.

♐ ♈ ♊ ♏ ♓

It's so lame being at the library on Saturday morning, surrounded by towers of crowded bookshelves instead of trees and frayed carpets instead of soft grass. Mary and I should be hanging out at the faire grounds, spying on the early-bird vendors. I should be fighting off asthma attacks triggered by pollen rather than dust. But no, we have the SAT coming up.

Mary diligently studies biology while I stare blankly at my math textbook and tap my pencil against my notebook so fast it blurs. *Taptaptaptaptaptap...* My leg bobs up and down in rhythm.

There's no way I'm focusing. Besides, whatever I study today will be withdrawn from my crappy memory bank, leaving me with a negative balance by the time our exam comes around.

My gaze shifts to my backpack. Inside is the cool waters of the spellbook. Its refreshing aura tempts me. *Pick me up*, it says. *Quench your thirst.*

"Shh," Mary glares at me.

I drop my pencil, tearing my gaze from my backpack to raise my eyebrows at her. "What?"

"That tapping is annoying."

I shrug. "Nobody's here."

"*I'm* here, and you're bothering me."

"Sorry." I bite my lip and resist the spellbook's siren call. My eyes close like an unfurling sail. I take a deep breath. My heart pounds with want and my fingers tingle with need.

Mary clears her throat.

My eyes fly open.

She jabs my textbook with a finger and goes back to studying.

I sigh and make a valiant attempt at making sense of letters with exponentials and equal signs and brackets and—oh my!—X's. My eyes cross by the time I get halfway down a page.

I "grrr" under my breath and slam the book shut.

"Anne."

"*What now?*"

"Never mind." Mary juts out her chin and slides to the other end of the table.

The spellbook pulls at me like an anchor. I tumble after it, snatch it out of my backpack, and lay it on the table over my textbook. The pages greet me with friendly crinkles and swishes as I turn them, like secrets whispered between best friends.

Mary's finger slides under my nose and shakes back and forth in a no-no motion.

"Geez!" I gasp and jerk back.

"What are you doing?" She uses the same voice she scolds Pollux with.

"I'm taking a break. You?" I yank the book toward me.

She slaps a palm over the spell I'm reading. "You're supposed to be studying for the SAT."

"I don't need you telling me what to do."

Her lips thin. "Why do you have to be so stubborn?"

"Why do you have to be so controlling?"

"*Anne.*" She leans over the table.

"*Mary.*" I meet her in the middle until our noses almost touch.

She growls and retreats to her biology book. A few minutes later, she says, "I'm not trying to fight with you." Her eyes remind me of a neglected puppy, hollow and ripe with pain.

My guts writhe like a mass of worms and heat flares into my cheeks. I know she's trying to help and I have no right to snap at her. "Sorry for being such an ass."

She smiles, glowing from the nourishment of my apology. "Sorry for being so controlling."

"I would never pass the SAT if you didn't keep me on track." It's true. Mary can pull off an A+ GPA like it's as easy as breathing. My brain, like my lungs, betrays me and I have to eke out every percentile bit by bit. The only reason I placed in the same class as her this past year was because she stayed up half the night quizzing me. She's a blessing I don't deserve.

"How can we be twins and yet be so different?" A cloud of puzzlement darkens her face.

"Maybe we're like Yin and Yang."

"More like Frick and Frack." She scrunches her nose.

I close the spellbook and point to Gemini. "Maybe it's our Zodiac sign."

"What do you mean?"

I flip to the index and read. "Special power is granted to twins born under Gemini. Their astrological ancestors, brothers Castor and Pollux, were the closest of friends, until Castor was killed in battle. The distraught and grieving Pollux beseeched the gods for immortality and his wish was granted. The twins were transformed into stars and reunited once more in the night sky."

"That's a great story, but what does it have to do with us?"

"There's more. Some Gemini twins are unaware of the bond they share and are fractured, likely to bicker, and risk losing one another. Because of this, it's the only Zodiac sign prone to division. However, Gemini twins who embrace their power and join together can become some of the most powerful magicians in the world."

She eyes the book warily, full of mistrust and suspicion, sort of like how the dogs react to a thermometer—like they know nothing good will come of it. "That has nothing to do with genetics."

"But it has everything to do with our sign. You can't deny how accurate horoscopes can be."

"Those things are so vague they fit everybody."

"Just because you can't scientifically quantify something doesn't mean it doesn't exist."

"I'm just saying, you don't really know what you're playing with."

"So you *do* believe."

She props her elbows on the table and drops her face in her hands. "No. I don't."

I grin. "Yes, you do, or you wouldn't be so worried about it."

She huffs. "Whatever. Can we get back to studying?"

I pout. "I don't wanna."

Mary peers between her fingers and giggles. "You look like Castor when he's about to puke."

Slipping the spellbook into my backpack, I reply, "Math makes me nauseous."

"Okay, Gemini twin, why don't we work together? We can review equations, logs, and exponents. After that, we can do a few practice questions, then take a break."

Things go better when she coaches me, that's for sure. On the other hand, I know she'd prefer working on biology—it's what she had scheduled for the morning. I give her a sideways glance. "What's the catch?"

She puts up her hands in surrender. "No catch. I'll study bio this afternoon while you work on memorizing history facts. Remember your flash cards?"

"Oh yeah, those were helpful." I slump in my chair. "I lost them."

She hangs her head to the side. "No, you didn't. I put them in a safe place."

Relief bathes me in sunny warmth. "You're too good to me."

"Don't forget it."

We settle into our work. My brain hurts almost as bad as when I got brain freeze at the theater, but Mary helps me through it and by noon—three hours later—I'm able to find "X" all by myself, like a *boss*. I fist my hand and puff my chest, ready to take on the Descartes Dingoes and Rithmetic Rangers single-handedly. (Seriously, those are the names of our Nerdtastic—ahem, I mean Scholastic—clubs, coined by the king of geeks and math teacher extraordinaire, Ms. Sutters.)

On the walk home, Mary tries to rope me into a discussion of *To Kill A Mockingbird*. It's what she considers a break. I love the book, but I'd rather talk about *Watership Down*, even if it is about killing innocent, fluffy-tailed bunnies.

"What happened in that book is sickening. The court convicted an innocent man." Mary shakes her head.

I can't disagree with her. "But it's fiction, right?"

She nods. "Yeah. Okay, let's discuss vocabulary and grammar."

I groan. Forgot about that. "I don't have enough room in my head for all this crap."

"You'd have more room if you stopped stuffing it with star magick."

"*Zodiac* magick."

She whips out a pile of flashcards. "This is real, Anne. So is the SAT. If you want good scores, you'll need to embrace reality and stop dreaming about *Zodiac* signs and constellations."

I groan again.

Ignoring my protest, she quizzes me on the definitions of words like "harbinger," "extrinsic," "fastidious," and "iconoclastic."

I'm practically brain dead by the time we get home. "You're 'inexorable,'" I say as we climb the front steps.

"And you're 'impertinent.'"

"Yes, but I'm 'ebullient' to try a spell during our break." I trot upstairs, ignoring the growing wheeze in my lungs. Less than a minute in the cigarette-smoke-laden house and my asthma is flaring.

Mary trundles up behind me. "That's not the correct use of that word."

"Why not?" I drop my backpack on my bed and pull out my inhaler from my pocket. After a puff, I can feel my lungs open and the tingly fire of tightened airways subsiding.

Mary fetches my history flashcards from her desk. "Actually, I don't know."

Our fleeting laughter is as precious as shooting stars.

I take the cards and set them next to my backpack. Then I retrieve my spellbook and flop on the mattress.

"Aren't you hungry?" Mary asks, laying out her morning texts and swapping them for her afternoon pile.

"I want to try something first." Even though we keep our bedroom door shut most of the time, smoke from Mom's cigarettes still filters through. It's the dregs of a dragon's poisonous breath. I'm sick of smelling it. I'm sick of sucking it in. I'm sick of having asthma attacks because of it.

"You don't mean a spell." Her eyes widen.

I shrug. "What can be so hard? We just read the spell and that's that."

"No way. Grandmother said to wait. She said there are consequences."

I search the pages for a purification spell. "Gemini is an air sign, which means we might have better control over it."

"Over what, air?"

"Yeah."

She sits on the edge of her bed, wringing her hands. "I don't know."

"It won't hurt to say the words." I lean over the book. "Ah! Here it is."

"Anne."

"I need your help. It'll work better if we chant together." I jitter from a shockwave of anticipation. We can totally do this. It'll be a small spell and Gamma won't even have to know.

She bites her fingernail. "But..."

"Please? If it doesn't work, then I won't bug you anymore, okay?"

"Promise?"

"I swear." I hold out my pinky.

She pops up and slides to my bed, hooking pinkies with me as she lands. "What do we do?"

"We say the spell together."

"Don't we have to light candles or make a salt circle or something?"

"Uh, yeah, we can do that." I hop off the bed and paw through my junk drawer. Collecting four tea lights and a match, I light each wick and anchor a candle at each compass point. "North, South, East, West."

"I hope you know what you're doing."

I pick up the spellbook and drag her to the center of the room. I hold the book up for both of us to see the chant.

"Four elements of life,
Earth, fire, water, air.
Four corners of the earth,
North, South, East, West.
Four elements of the Zodiac,
Purify, purify, purify!"

Mary scans the room. "Nothing happened."

I take a deep breath and immediately start coughing. The air is heavy with scruffy dog and stale smoke smells. "Must've screwed it up."

"Or maybe this stuff isn't real."

I stuff down the scratchy, dry idea that she's right and herd the dogs out of the room. "I'll take the boys for a walk."

To Gamma's house.

Chapter Five

Gamma's in her fairy garden when I arrive. It stretches along the length of the house. Stone gargoyles perched on either side of the front steps cling to their guard posts, silent watchers of the comings and goings around them. Fairy statues nestle between the Roses of Sharon, hibiscus, asters, double-headed marigolds, and daisies. Some sit on mushrooms, others lounge on the ground, and some hover on hooks so they look like they're flying. One has her nose stuck in a geranium blossom. Her gossamer wings flutter in a soft breeze.

Gamma's on her hands and knees, pawing in the dirt with a trowel to eject an invading dandelion. Next to her is a wicker basket overflowing with puffy, purplish-blue hydrangea blossoms. A pile of weeds, wilted flowers past their prime, and browned leaves fills a black wheelbarrow.

"Hi, Gamma. Need some help?" I tie the pups' leashes to the porch railing. They yip at me as I walk away, probably disappointed I haven't taken them directly inside for a treat.

Gamma cranes her head around. Her red-framed glasses cling to the tip of her nose like a mountain climber realizing she's afraid of heights. "Anne, hello. Take that barrow and dump the weeds on the compost heap, would you?"

"Sure." I take the evicted dandelion from her and drop it on the pile. It's a fairly short walk to the backyard where Gamma keeps her compost. I tip the wheelbarrow over and shake it a few times to make sure all the bits fall out. When I return, she and the dogs are gone. The clipped flowers are still there, so I return the wheelbarrow to its spot in the garage, then pick up the basket and go inside.

Gamma's washing her hands in the kitchen sink, humming an off-key tune. The dogs are sprawled on the area rug next to the stove, crunching on their treats.

I set the basket of organic pom-poms on the counter next to her.

"Find my blue vase, dear." She plugs the drain and lets the faucet run to fill the sink.

"Okay." I head to the pantry and spy the vase on the top shelf. I have to stand on my toes to reach it.

"Do you know the magickal properties of hydrangea?" Gamma asks, already re-cutting the stems under water to prevent air bubbles from entering and blocking the flowers from sucking up enough water. Steam hovers above the sink like a warm fog.

"No." I set the vase on the counter.

"You used to."

Those three little words bore into my chest, opening a wound I'd stitched shut a long time ago. The gaping, hungry beast of disappointment tunnels inside, searching for crumbs of memories devoured by neglect. "I don't remember."

She hands me a bunch of discarded leaves. "Breaks curses."

"Yeah?"

She nods, filling the vase with lukewarm water. "Arrange the flowers as I hand them to you, dear."

I add cutting after cutting to the vase. The tight clusters compete with one another for space and crowd the rim. Soon, I struggle to find a place to stick in another stem. "Mary would love to photograph these."

"Where is she?"

"Home."

Gamma glances at me. "Had another fight?"

"No," I answer too quickly. Defensively.

She pins the nosepiece of her glasses to the bridge of her nose and stares me down. "The magick won't work right if you're divided."

"We're not fighting. I decided to take Castor and Pollux for a walk, that's all. They wanted to come here." I tip my head toward the dogs.

She chuckles. "I'm sure they did, but what brings *you*?"

I carry the bouquet to the kitchen table. "Well, I wanted to talk to you about the Zodiac spellbook."

"Have you read it?"

"Yeah." I slide into a chair. Castor trots over to me and climbs up my leg. I pick him up and hold him on my lap. "How do the spells and chants work?"

Gamma sits next to me. "Getting ahead of ourselves, aren't we?"

I shrug. "I want to try something."

She leans against the counter and crosses her arms. "Have you been chanting?"

"No." I shake my head until I'm dizzy.

Her lips purse like she's sucking on a thousand lemon sours. "You have to invoke the twins first; otherwise the spell won't work."

I sit up straighter. "How do I do that?"

"You don't. Not by yourself." She wags a finger at me. "And don't you try to do it on your own."

My throat goes dry. "I won't," I croak.

She shuffles to the table and sits in the chair next to me. "You didn't bring the book."

I shake my head.

"No matter. We can go over the basics without it."

I lower Castor to the floor and prop my elbows against the table.

"The first step is making sure you and Mary are united."

"United how?"

"Both of you need to work together. Realize the power of being sisters—of being *twins*—is greater than any magick."

"What do you mean?"

Gamma whips her glasses off and wipes them on her shirt. "I shouldn't have let you girls lose your connection with the Zodiac magick. This'll be so much harder now."

"What'll be harder? I'll practice all the time and Mary will help, I swear." I'm on the edge of my seat, swallowing down the swells of panic erupting from my gut like a soda-fueled belch.

"You can't force someone to believe, Anne." She slips her glasses back on.

I slump over the table and dig my fingers into my hair, falling into the pit of lost screw-ups. "We used to believe, didn't we?"

"Mary and you?"

I nod.

"You sure did. Don't you remember chanting with me? We'd set up candles in the four corners, invoke the Zodiac signs with an offering, and read from the book."

The memories pick at me like hundreds of little teeth. I close my eyes, rolling back the scroll of time, unraveling the days, weeks, months, and years. The pungent tang of a freshly sparked match, the cloyingly sweet scent of vanilla candles, and the bitter aftertaste of bergamot tea mingle together, creating a foundation on which I can plant my feet and anchor my soul.

My eyes fly open. "We invoked the Gemini twins."

Gamma claps her hands and laughs with glee. "That's right. You remember!"

"We made butterflies sparkle."

"And flowers glow." She fiddles with a strand of my hair. "Mary won't want to remember."

"Why not?" I lace my fingers with hers.

"The Zodiac power is wild, strong, and unwieldy. Mary likes consistency and certainty."

I sigh. "When I tell her about our chants, she'll remember."

Gamma uses her free hand to pat mine. "Of course she will."

A "to be continued" silence settles over us.

It's up to me to figure out how to get Mary on board. Roadblocks with signs screaming "she'll never believe" pop up in my mind instead of ideas. I change the subject. "What kind of offering should we give?"

"The twins are warriors, first and foremost. They like weapons."

No problem. I've got an arsenal in my closet. *Not*. I lean back in the chair, deflated by another obstacle. "Oh."

"They were also skilled equestrians. Untamable horses would bend to their will."

My shoulders slump. "Where do I get a horse?"

She taps my temple with an index finger. "You should *remember*. All you need is a symbol, dear. A figurine, statue, or toy."

"Oh!" Excitement courses in me like a power surge. "Where do I put the offering?"

I dodge Gamma's finger. She draws an "X" in the air. "Intersect the lines between the candles, of course. In the cross section is where you place the offering. That's where you stand, too."

My eyes glaze over a bit. Sounds a lot like algebra to me. "Okay. When do we get started?"

Gamma pushes off the table with her hands and groans as she stands. "Not today, dear. Your Gamma is old and needs her rest. Go on home and get back to studying. Work on your sister, but don't push it. *Belief in magick can't be forced.*"

I scrunch my nose. So that's where Mary got her nag gene.

$$\nearrow \ \Upsilon \ \mathrm{I\!I} \ \mathrm{m} \ \mathrm{\mathcal{H}}$$

I grab a slice of cold pizza and chomp on a bit of cheese as I climb the stairs to my room. The dogs try to knock me over to get a bite. I shoo them away and sit on my desk, out of reach. Mary frowns at me—the potential for rogue crumbs must be blowing her mind—but doesn't say anything.

"I won't leave a mess."

"Because Castor and Pollux will suck up anything you drop."

"Furball vacuum cleaners—the perfect backup plan."

"Where'd you go, anyway?"

"Gamma's."

Mary gapes. "Why?"

"Why not? I wanted to talk to her about the spellbook."

"Did you tell her what we did?"

"No."

"Good."

I arch a brow at her.

"You heard me. We weren't supposed to do anything yet."

"Well, she gave me some tips on how to do it right."

Mary groans. "You're not thinking of trying again, are you?"

"Why not? I know how to do it now." I wipe the grease from my hands onto my jeans and hop down.

William gave me a jousting-horse figurine last summer during the faire. I snatch it off the bookshelf. It's the size of my hand. The horse and knight are black and the shield is painted in yellow and blue. The knight holds a tiny lance. A horse and a weapon. Bingo! I align myself in the center of the "X" like Gamma said.

Mary sets aside her textbook and rises from the bed. "Grandmother said it was okay?"

"Yeah."

"What're you going to do?"

"Invoke the twins."

"Huh?"

"You don't remember chanting with Gamma when we were little, do you?"

She squares the stack of books on the bed.

"Mary?"

"I remember. Just like I remember wishing Mom would be normal." She tucks her hair behind her ears. "We tried chanting it. Remember that?"

I exhale, expunging the hope of rekindling Mary's belief while the memory trickles in one drop at a time. It was so long ago that it doesn't seem real. "Yeah, I remember."

"Why are you holding onto this kid stuff?" She waves her hand at the figurine, then glances at my pillow and the spellbook hiding underneath it.

"It's not kid stuff. It's real. I'll show you."

She shakes her head, whipping her tight curls back and forth. "How?"

The only way to get her buy in is to pick something she'll go for. An idea perches on my shoulder and whispers in my ear. "I'm going to make sure we have a great birthday, without Mom interfering and ruining it."

"With magick?"

"That's the idea." I pull my hair into a ponytail.

"It won't work." She sounds like Penny Archerson snarking at Katy Nelson when she tried to do a special backflip in gymnastics. Penny was right and Katy twisted her ankle on the landing.

"Yes, it will. I wasn't doing it right before, so it didn't count." She can't argue with my foolproof logic.

"Please, don't."

"You sound scared," I challenge.

She folds her arms across her chest. "I'm not scared."

"Then we can try again."

"Don't be silly. Magick isn't real, Anne. Science and physics are."

Funny how she doesn't remember the chants that worked. And by funny, I mean convenient. "Thanks, Professor Knowitall. You tell me how Mom knew when we tasted the ale last year at the faire? She wasn't anywhere near us and no one saw us, either."

"So, you think she has her own Zodiac spellbook? She doesn't. She's just crazy."

"I'm not saying that. I'm saying that there's more out there than we think. Things with no rational, logical explanation."

"Whatever. Anybody could've seen us and then told her. Everybody knows everything around here."

"That's small-town living for you." I offer her the figurine. "Hold this."

She plucks the thing from my hand and bites her bottom lip.

I spin and grab the spellbook. Standing there, in the middle of my bedroom, I flip through the pages, searching for the invocation spell. Anticipation sharpens its talons by raking them up and down my spine. The oily scent of ink mixes with the bitter leather and teases my nose. I take in a deep breath and smile. Yes, this will work.

"Ah, found it."

"Great. Now what?"

"Now I chant it." I set the book on the floor and gather my collection of pillar candles. So much better than tea lights. Within seconds, I have them arranged on the rug, one for each direction on the compass, like before.

"Do we really have to do this?" Mary joins me on the floor, folding her legs under her.

"Yes." Any scientist will tell you there's no better way to prove something is real than to demonstrate it. Therefore, if Mary sees magick, then she'll have to believe it. I strike a long stick match. The tang of sulfur tickles my throat. I light each wick, calling out each name as I go:

"North, south, east, west. Earth, fire, wind, water."

Pollux and Castor stare at us from Mary's bed. They don't like fire, even if it's from a small candle flame.

Mary fumbles with the figurine. "What's this for?"

"It's an offering to the Gemini twins. We have to invoke them first, then we can do the spell." I blow out the match. Smoke streams from the tip in a serpentine dance.

She places the horse and knight statue between us. "Invoke? Oh, gawd."

"It'll be okay. Take my hands and read it with me. Gamma said it'll work better that way, if we do it together." I rest the book on my legs and extend my arms.

"Oh, all right. We'll chant, it won't work, then you can drop it so we can focus on the exam." She leans toward the book.

We chant:

> "Four elements of life
> Earth, fire, water, air
> We invoke thee.
> Four corners of the earth
> North, South, East, West
> We invoke thee.

Four elements of the Zodiac,
Earth, fire, water, air
We invoke thee.
Four bodies of the cosmos,
Planets, stars, moons, comets,
We invoke thee.
Gemini twins,
Castor and Pollux,
We invoke thee!"

Mary squeezes my hands. Sweat slicks my palms. I swallow the growing lump in my throat. I didn't bother to ask Gamma how I'd know if the invocation worked or not.

"Is that it?" Mary asks. She's breathing fast and her forehead is wrinkled from worry.

"We have to actually chant a spell to keep our birthday plans a secret."

She nods. "Hurry up."

My stomach jitters. I don't have a specific spell, so I have to modify an old story Gamma told us about once. A witch had made a pact with her diary to keep her secrets. She'd messed up the wording and ended up losing her ability to speak. She could only write in the dairy, but whenever anyone tried to read what she wrote, the pages became blank—an unexpected consequence and a mistake I won't fall into. If I word things correctly, I can weave a chant allowing us to keep our birthday party a secret. It can't be too hard. Mary and I are working together, the Gemini twins are invoked, and we're not trying to change anybody. Really, we're only asking for a blessing. Nothing wrong with that.

"Anne?"

"I'm just thinking how to phrase it."

Her gaze ricochets from me to the book and back to me again. "You're not using a spell from the book?"

"Hold on." I search the pages and find the Secret Spell. "I'm using this one."

She squints at me. "*O-kay.*"

I chant:

> "Four elements of the Zodiac,
> Earth, fire, water, air.
> Gemini twins,
> Castor and Pollux.
> Hear our plea.
> Let our sixteenth birthday
> Be a great party."

"Is that really in the book?" Mary's mouth twists to the side.

"Shh. I'm personalizing it."

She sighs.

"Close your eyes." I continue:

> "Castor and Pollux,
> It is our wish, it is our plea,
> That our birthday planning
> Stays under lock and key.
> Castor and Pollux,
> It is our wish, it is our plea,
> That our birthday
> Is filled with magick and revelry!"

"Say it with me," I say.

"I don't remember what you said."

I let go of her hands with a sigh, collect a notepad and pen from the desk drawer, and write down the chant. I pass the bubble-gum-scented paper to her.

She studies my quick scribblings. "Your handwriting is terrible."

"Focus, or something will go wrong."

She throws up her hands. "Oh, great. Now you're telling me something bad will happen."

"Just say the spell with me." I hold out my hands. "Three times, then we're done."

Her hands are cold and clammy, though the room is warm.

We chant the spell:

> "Castor and Pollux,
> It is our wish, it is our plea,
> That our birthday planning
> Stays under lock and key.
> Castor and Pollux,
> It is our wish, it is our plea,
> That our birthday
> Is filled with magick and revelry!"

At the end of the third round, I open my eyes and let out a long breath. "Wasn't so bad, right?"

"Yeah." Mary nods. She rubs her hands together. "So, is that it?"

"I—"

Goosebumps erupt on my arms as the temperature suddenly plummets. Everything in our room shakes—beds, desk, chair, light fixtures. Our cell phones ring and the alarm clock buzzes. A gust of wind whips our hair into knots and sends a stack of loose papers swirling in circles. The candles blow out, throwing our room into twilight. Castor and Pollux both howl from under Mary's bed.

"Oh, crap, we did something wrong." Mary's voice trembles with fear.

"Ack!" A paperback novel swoops toward my head. I duck. It ricochets off my mattress and slides toward Castor. He scrambles deeper under the bed. Pollux barks at him, then the book.

"Stop it, Anne!" Mary swats an airborne sweater before it wraps around her face and smothers her.

"I don't know how." I grab her arm and drag her toward the door. "Let's get out of here!"

We huddle by the door and Mary keeps watch for random projectiles while I jiggle the handle. I twist and twist, but the thing won't turn. "It's locked!"

By now, the swirling wind, wonky electronics, and yelping dogs have fried my brain. I can't think beyond *please stop, please stop, please stop.*

"Anne? Mary? Knock off that racket! I need to concentrate." Mom is louder than the commotion in our room. "I mean it. Don't make me come up there!"

I can't decide what is worse—a poltergeist or Mom.

I stand and put my hands up. "Castor and Pollux, hear our plea. Stop destroying our room, I beg thee!"

The chaos intensifies. The dogs go crazy. Mary starts crying.

"Castor and Pollux, shut up!" I stomp my foot.

The wind stops. Everything falls to the floor as gravity once again takes over. Our phones stop ringing. The alarm clock dies.

I smooth my tangled hair—like it's possible—and try to catch my breath. Mary is still whimpering by the door. I kneel next to her. "It's okay. It's over."

Whatever "it" was.

"Anne," she stares at me with a white face, "what have we done?"

Chapter Six

"Girls! The power's out. Did you do something?" Mom's voice is muffled, like a hoarse bleat from a tuba. The brash percussion of her heavy stomps follow, vibrating the walls. Knickknacks and lampshades tremble in terror, much like my bones.

"Oh jeez, she's coming upstairs!" I dash around the room, gathering the candles and tucking them under my bed, along with the spellbook.

A rapid series of bangs pummels the door. "Anne! Mary! Answer me!"

Mary retreats to her bed and clutches her bio notebook to her chest like a shield.

I bellyflop onto my bed and pry open my math book a half-second before Mom bursts in.

She looms over us, eyes wide and teeth bared. The dragon is awake. "Well? What have you done?"

Mary picks at a fingernail. "N-n-nothing."

Mom props her hands on her hips. I picture a thin layer of leathery skin stretching from her shoulders to her wrists—dragon's wings. "Nothing? Nothing! How am I supposed to use my sewing machine without electricity?"

"We didn't knock the power out. We were studying," I say.

Mom stomps farther into our room and steps on the figurine. It breaks with a sharp *crack*. She scoops it up like a bird of prey snatches a field mouse with its claws. "What's this doing on the floor?"

Mary tucks her hair behind her ears. "C-c-c…P-p-p," she pauses, eyes darting. "The dogs were playing with it."

Mom chucks it into the wicker trash can under the desk. "This isn't a dog toy." She points to my pile of laundry. "Clean this up."

I nod and try to hold my breath. Hopefully the shroud of bitter cigarette smoke surrounding Mom will prevent her from smelling the subtle—but potentially traitorous—odor of a freshly blown-out candle.

Mary glares at me while Mom storms out of the room and marches downstairs.

"What?"

"Why's the power out?"

"Dunno."

She springs to her feet, crosses the room in a millisecond, closes the door, and leans against it. Her eyes pinch shut and her mouth puckers. Makes her look like a constipated supermodel. "It was the spell."

"We don't know that."

She shoves off the door and pads to my bed, pinky finger extended. "Pinky swear and cross your heart that you'll never make me do another spell *ever*."

I sit up and extend my arm in ultra-slow motion, puzzling over what could've gone wrong. We'd followed Gamma's instructions. We'd given an offering to the twins. Hooking fingers with Mary, I promise to myself that I'll

figure out what happened and correct it for next time—
with or without Mary's help.

"You're not planning something, are you?" She holds
onto my finger as if touching me will let her identify
insincerity like a lie-detector machine.

I waggle free and bend to scoop Castor up into my arms.
"No way."

"Right. I can hear the wheels turning in your skull."

That evening, I head downstairs to fix dinner, even
though it's Mary's turn. It's the least I can do, and it should
be easy considering the power's out, so there won't be any
actual cooking involved.

I creep downstairs, keeping an eye on Mom's studio
door. A burst of curses rattles the paintings hanging in the
hallway—sounds like she pricked herself with a needle.
An odd assortment of sketches, dress patterns, and Dali
landscapes huddle together like islands in a sea of robin's-
egg-blue walls. The collection pretty much covers all of
Mom's tastes. Except for the very first sword Dad forged. It
marks the center of the display, as if he is claiming a piece
of an otherwise Mom-dominated world. Maybe that's the
type of weapon I need for a spell to work. Maybe I pissed
off Castor and Pollux with my five-dollar faire trinket.
Maybe they didn't like the idea I'd "re-gifted" it.

A drum solo drowns out Mom's riff of swears. She must
be using her battery-powered radio.

I round the corner and slip into the kitchen. I don't
know why I sneak. She can't hear me over her own noise.
Yet it seems like angry eyes are shooting javelins at me from
another dimension or something.

Like in all the horror books I've read, the hairs on the
back of my neck stand on edge and my stomach sours. A
shiver rips down my spine and the nagging feeling of being
watched heats my skull. A presence is definitely behind me. I
clench my jaw, fighting the urge to run. I'm being ridiculous.

It's probably nothing. I shiver again. Pressure builds behind me and a shadow darkens the room.

It's the sun going behind a cloud.

Except it's not.

The air thickens and grows heavy. Something suffocating is closing in.

I spin around, ready to confront whoever or whatever is lurking behind me.

The hallway is empty.

"Stupid. Stop freaking yourself out."

I shrug off the chill and head to the kitchen. Nothing happens when I turn the switch. I huff. Right, the power is out.

"I wish I could just chant a spell and voila, dinner's on the table," I mutter.

Even though I'm alone, I can't shake the worry willies that keep skittering across my shoulders. I wipe the sweat from my palms onto my jeans and head to the pantry. Unlike at Gamma's, our pantry is a large, built-in cabinet dividing the kitchen and dining spaces. Inside, I find a loaf of oat-nut bread, peanut butter, grape jelly, and baked vegetable chips. I dump the items on the table and check the fridge for fruit. Pre-washed strawberries and blueberries—score! I toss them in a bowl with some sugar. There's pound cake in the pantry. Drizzle on the fruit and *bam!*—dessert.

Outside, an arc of lightning flashes across the dark, heavy clouds. Thunder grumbles like an old man awoken from a nap. Rain spits on the roof.

Poor Castor and Pollux. They hate thunderstorms.

The dogs, I mean. The Gemini twins, I can't say.

Dad has a sixth sense where food is concerned. As soon as I have the table set, he appears, a smile on his face. "No power, eh?"

"What happened?"

"No idea. Flipped the circuit breakers to see if there was a short somewhere in the house, but no go."

Old Man Thunder grumbles some more, but a slice of sunlight spears the ground. All talk and no bite.

"Could it be the storm?" I ask.

He shrugs, lathering his greasy hands with hand sanitizer. "Yeah, if it hit a transformer."

There. A logical explanation. It has nothing to do with the spell.

"You excited for your birthday?" Dad pours himself a glass of milk and sits at the head of the table.

I join him. "Yeah."

"What are you and Mary going to do?" He drinks half the glass in one gulp.

I inhale, ready to tell him…and my brain flashes the blue screen of death. There's no sense in telling him about our bloated wishes of a birthday blowout to end all birthday blowouts, because, well, he's Dad. "I dunno."

"You could see a movie with William, or hang out at the faire." He finishes his milk and gets up to pour another glass.

I rest my case. He doesn't get it. "Yeah."

Mary joins Dad and me for dinner. Mom doesn't. Her empty place setting is a stark reminder of what it's like when she's manic. I stuff down tears of anger and sneak a glance at Mary. She cuts the crust off her bread and nibbles on a clean edge like a squirrel.

I push the chips toward her.

"No, thanks." She takes a sip of water.

Dad shovels three sandwiches down his gullet in a matter of minutes. He'd give the funnel-cake-eating contest competitors a run for their shillings. Bits of crumbs and mini-globules of jelly litter his bushy moustache. He wipes his mouth on a discount paper napkin, finishes off his glass of milk, and belches. It used to make us laugh. "Thanks, girls. Great dinner. I'll be in my workshop. I'll also see if I can get the generator going so your mom can work through the night. How 'bout you? Got your costumes ready for the faire?"

We nod.

"It helps your mom's business when you wear her gowns, you know." His hooded emerald eyes volley between Mary and me. He always looks so much older when Mom is manic. It's as if she drains his energy to accelerate hers.

I bite my tongue. I hate being a walking advertisement, but that's what Mary and I are. Every year, we parade around in her creations and never get to explore or enjoy the faire on our own.

Mary smiles. "We know, Dad."

He carries his dishes to the sink, then heads to the fridge and drags out a six-pack. "Tell your mom I'll have the power on soon. That should cheer her up."

"Right." I grimace behind his back. Why can't he tell her?

He cradles the beer and leaves.

I put the leftover food away while Mary clears and wipes the table.

As we work, the lights flicker to life and a happy "Whoop!" echoes from Mom's studio all way to the kitchen.

"We should see if she's ready for us to try on dresses now, while she's in a good mood." Mary shakes the dishtowel out over the trash can and folds it over the bar mounted onto the cabinet door under the sink.

"Good idea." I suck in a puff of my asthma medicine. If I go in without pre-medicating, I'll end up in a full-blown attack within a minute.

Mom's rocking out to her favorite band while she irons. Her hips sway left to right and her hair bounces around her head like a lion shaking out its mane.

I slip into the living room and Mary stays close beside me. "Hi, Mom. Hungry?"

She whirls, a lopsided grin on her face and a cigarette tucked into the corner of her mouth. "Girls! You're just in time. The lights came back on. Now I have proper lighting to finish your dresses." She sashays to two dress forms by the bay window. Both gowns are green—one is dark emerald, and the other reminds me of light grass.

"These are really pretty, Mom." Mary tracks around the edge of the room to Mom.

"I think you should wear this one, Mary. Anne should wear the jewel-toned one." She removes the lighter-colored dress from its form and holds it up to Mary, who stands as still as a statue. After a short inspection, she says, "Yes, this one. Go put it on."

Mary clutches the gown to her chest and heads out of the room to change.

Mom gives the other dress to me. "These will be perfect. Well, hurry up. I want to see how this looks on you."

I follow Mary to the den, where we change clothes. We have to help each other lace up the gowns. They weigh at least twenty pounds and we don't even have our corsets on. A layer of sweat slicks my skin. Wearing this thing outside all day is not going to be fun.

Mom gushes like a fairy high on unicorn glitter when she sees us. "Oh, so beautiful. My best work ever." Her gaze travels over the gowns, but never to our faces. It's like we're mannequins and our only purpose is to make her dresses look good. "Turn around."

We rotate slowly on imaginary skewers so she can see every angle. Her eyes burn hotter than any campfire. My flesh sizzles under her gaze.

While she pins various bits to fix, I ask, "We don't have to wear these on our birthday, do we?"

She freezes, holding a pin inches from the hem of my bodice. Her hand shakes a bit. A flurry of rapid blinking stokes the blaze in her eyes. "You know how important it is for you to show these gowns around the faire."

"Yeah, but our birthday is toward the faire's end, anyway, and it's only one day."

"It's not 'only one day.' Don't forget, you're in school this year during the day for your SAT review *and the test itself* and most people are gone by evening, so you're already doing less." She shoves the pin in the fabric, almost stabbing me with the tip.

I shy away on instinct.

She winds her wiry fingers around my upper arm and gives a socket-tugging yank. "Don't be such a baby."

"Can you give us the evening off, maybe?"

Mary whips her head back and forth, warning me to drop the subject.

"Why?" Mom shoves us out of the room.

"It's our birthday."

"Change out of those and give them back to me so I can make the alterations." She slams the door in our faces.

Mary slugs me in the arm. "Why'd you piss her off?"

I rub my arm. "I didn't do it on purpose."

"Thought you wanted to keep everything secret."

"I do."

She rolls her eyes and heads down the hallway to the den.

The doorbell chimes, and Mary halts.

I walk to the door and pry open the curtain. William and Evan stand on the porch.

William waves at me. "Hey."

"Hi." A smile instantly erupts on my face. I open the door and step outside. Mary crowds behind me and I shift to the side so she can come out.

"Wow, you guys look awesome." William checks out our dresses. He checks out mine more than Mary's.

Heat flames my cheeks from his attention. "Thanks."

His gaze meets mine and his dimples flash. "Makes your eyes look super green."

"Yeah?" I twist a strand of hair around my finger.

Evan coughs. "Uh, Mary, I like your dress, too. Reminds me of the color of Mountain Dew. Did you know the term used to refer to moonshine?"

Mary giggles and fluffs the skirt a bit. "That's cool."

Evan smiles. "Yeah. Another term is white lightning."

I have to cut this off before they both get their nerd on. "What brings you guys by?"

"Ev and I are watching B-list sci-fi flicks. Wanna join?" He hooks his thumbs through his belt loops. For the love of all that's Elizabethan, he smells *so* good. Clean and fresh, like the park after a warm rain. Or fresh laundry. Or the forest on a scorching summer day.

Let's see—an evening out of the house, away from Mom, plus hours with the cutest boy I know? Tough decision. "Sure. Let us change."

Chapter Seven

Morning sun strikes through my bedroom window, searing my eyelids. Birds chirp in a random chorus, fighting to keep their territory. I want to duct tape all their chipper little beaks shut. A torrent of emotion swirls inside me. I ride the wave, floating on the memories of sitting next to William for hours on end, paying more attention to his breathing, laughing, and yummy clean smell than to the movies we watched. Then I sink into a whirlpool, smacked in the face by the eddies of goofed birthday chants and failed negotiations with Mom. Disappointment lingers over my shoulders like a damp wool cloak.

I roll out of bed, disturbing Castor. Poor thing stuck out the night with me, despite my kicking him in the head a dozen times. He hops off the bed and sneezes. I chuckle as he wags his tail and yaps at me. Really, I have no other choice than to pick him up and pet him.

"Where are Mary and Pollux, eh?" I coo into his ear. His tongue laps at my chin. "Let's go find them."

Castor hops around my legs all the way downstairs, through the foyer, and outside to the front porch. Mary's sitting on the wrought-iron bench Dad built out of scrap metal. White paint flecks off every time someone sits on it because of the years of neglect. Refinishing it is on his to-do list, but everything's on hold until the faire ends. Pollux hovers at her feet—most likely praying for her bowl of cereal to spontaneously capsize so he can snarf it down.

It's a blessedly normal morning, no weirdness in sight. I tell myself a new day means a fresh start.

"Hey, what's up?" I use my *hunky-dory, everything-is-great* voice and sit next to her. A cool breeze rustles the leaves and rattles the rusted wind chimes hanging from the porch roof. It reminds me of the tornado that took over our room yesterday. I shiver, chilled more by the memory than the temperature.

Mary swallows a mouthful of frosty flakes and points with her spoon. "The caravans are here."

Pollux wags his tail, ever hopeful. Castor joins him and yips a greeting.

A line of cars, vans, and trucks hauling campers whizzes past in a constant stream. Each vehicle is at least twenty years old. Some have duct tape holding bumpers and windows together. Others are painted in patchwork-quilt patterns. An epic fantasy battle between wizards, dragons, and ogres decorates the side panel of one van. It's followed by a van with a haunted cemetery scene. Half the cars are burning oil, and the acrid stench turns my stomach and burns my nose. I should've grabbed my inhaler.

"More cars this year," I say, stealing a sugary corn flake from Mary's bowl.

"Hey, go get your own. It only seems like more because you're up early enough to watch the whole procession." She peers at me out of the corner of her eye. "Why are you out of bed, anyway? You tossed and turned all night."

I shrug. "I had trouble sleeping."

"Why?"

"Dunno." Staring at the traffic helps me lie. If I look at her, then I'll have to tell her about my nightmares about pissed-off warrior stars and Mom attacking me with lance-sized sewing needles. Then she'll have more reason to pick on me about the magick spells.

"Uh-huh. Right."

"And I suppose you slept just fine?" I can't keep the accusation out of my voice. Guilt wags its accusing finger at me, saying I shouldn't be getting angry at her simple question. I should be mad at myself for making Mom angry, for chanting before Gamma taught me how, and for freaking Mary out.

Pollux barks. His patience has expired. Castor simply lies on my feet. He's pretending to be laid back, little faker. Mary surrenders the remains of her breakfast to Pollux. Castor swoops in like a piranha. Pollux doesn't complain. "Look, what happened yesterday—"

"Is my fault. Just like everything else." I stand and fold my arms.

"Everything else?"

"Yeah, making Mom mad, fighting with you, pretending magick will work...all of it."

She clears her throat. "You need to chill out."

"*I* need to chill out?" I point to my chest, eyes bugging out of my head. "You're one to talk, Miss Everything-Gives-Me-a-Panic-Attack."

Her leg bounces up and down like a seismometer pounding out the quaking in her brain. "I'm not trying to fight with you." Pain tightens the angles of her face, pinches her mouth, and hoods her eyes. The aftershocks radiate out to me and my anger crumbles from a slab of granite to pebbles and dust.

I sigh. "Yeah, I know."

"Why do you get mad all the time?"

"I'm not mad *all* the time."

"Yes, you are. Sometimes you act like Mom."

"That's so unfair! At least I'm not a coward. You want a birthday party as much as I do, but I'm the one who has to do something about it." I pick at her, unable to leave alone the festering pimple that is our oozing, infected relationship.

"Not wanting to make Mom mad doesn't make me a coward. Sometimes I think you enjoy it when she's angry."

"You calling me a chaos boss?"

"No, I'm calling you a drama llama." She snatches the empty bowl from the dogs and heads inside, fleeing like a jackrabbit running from a coyote.

"Hey, we're not done." I follow her straight to the kitchen.

She scrubs her bowl with a hypoallergenic sponge. "I don't have anything else to say."

"You didn't want the spell to work."

She smacks the bowl on the drying rack and goes at her spoon, rubbing it so hard sparks might start flying. "You're not saying what happened was my fault, are you? Because it's not. You don't know what you're doing. Grandmother said you shouldn't even—"

"I know what she said." Heat flares into my cheeks and I fist my hands. The pinch from my fingernails digging into my palms shocks me almost as much as her accusation.

It's so unfair. I'm not an idiot. And I'm not like Mom. I just get mad sometimes. Doesn't mean I'm crazy.

I head to the shower to cool off. As I lather my hair, I vow to myself to learn how to chant properly. Then I'll show Mary that it works and I can do it. With any luck, I'll figure it out before our birthday and we can still have an awesome party.

Forty-five minutes later, I'm finishing straightening my hair. Mary's sitting on her bed studying, as usual.

She stays quiet. And she will as long as she has nothing to say.

Mary and I fight like tectonic plates sliding over and under one another. We have to be together all the time, but sometimes the pressure builds up and we blow, causing an earthquake. After, everything settles down again. It bothers me—a lot.

I can't stand the silence any longer.

"I'm going to check out the jousting arena. Maybe William needs help setting up or something." If I act like nothing's wrong, maybe Mary will, too. I pull my flat-ironed hair into a ponytail, praying it stays somewhat smooth. I have to use six different products to get it to stay straight. Maybe I should embrace the natural curls, like Mary. Somehow, she makes them look good and I just look scruffy. I don't know how that's possible, since we're identical twins, but it's true.

"You guys should just admit that you like each other already." I catch her playful smirk in the mirror. Maybe some of the built-up pressure between us is blowing off.

"I don't know what you're talking about. We're just friends." I whirl, elated she's not giving me the silent treatment anymore. I slip into my favorite silver ballet flats and smooth my green-striped polo shirt, a strategic choice on my part. William *had* commented on Mom's green dress bringing out the color in my eyes, after all.

"You are such a bad liar." Mary closes her textbook, hops off the bed, and crowds the mirror to check the collar of her white blouse and apply her grape-flavored lip gloss.

The only thing similar about our outfits is our jeans—dark wash, skinny cut.

"Well…you wouldn't be all dressed up if you didn't think Evan would be there!" I tease her back.

"Shut up." She tosses a Robin Hood hat at me.

I catch it mid-air and toss it on the desk.

"What, you don't want to wear it? Then you can say to William, 'does this hat make my eyes look greener?'" She bats her eyelashes.

"Shut. Up." I narrow my eyes at her, but smile.

She laughs and slips her camera into her pocket. Always on the lookout for some random snapshot.

I affix a pin in the shape of a Gemini symbol to my lapel. We wear them on opening day every year. I forget why we started doing it, but now it's tradition and we have to.

She puts on her own pin, then holds out her hand for a fistbump. "We cool?"

Warmth seeps from deep in my soul, down my limbs, and kindles a smile. A truce. A connection. A reboot to factory settings. I extend my arm. "Always."

Our knuckles collide, and a clap of thunder almost snaps me out of my shoes.

"Holy crap!" Mary dashes to the window. "Weird. There isn't a cloud in the sky."

My stomach goes all wobbly. "Yeah. Weird. Come on, let's go."

Before things start flying around the room again.

♐ ♈ ♊ ♏ ♓

The park is close, so it only takes a few minutes for us to walk there.

We present our merchant passes to the security guard. He examines them for a full minute before waving us through. His executioner's mask hides his expression. His chainmail shirt does *not* hide his gut. I try to ignore the fact that he's wearing pale gray tights. Yikes, what a sight!

We follow the dirt trail marking the outer rim of the grounds toward the jousting arena. To our left is the forest. To our right is a "street" of merchant shoppes and tents. Some buildings are sided with dark-stained planks, and others are Tudor-style plaster and timber. The gypsy tents are thick canvas stretched over wooden stakes pounded into the ground. Layers of brightly colored fabrics line the fences nearby. The only stone structure is the one-story castle replica that provides a backdrop to the arena. Its central gate is arched and decorated with Dad's wrought-iron designs.

Mary veers left along a trail winding into the trees. Multi-colored streamers hang from several branches. A wooden sign nailed to a trunk reads "Enchanted Forest." She reaches for her camera while her head tips back to the canopy above.

"Hey, where are you going?" I follow her. Though I've been in these woods dozens of times, it's different during faire weeks. Like the collective imagination of the actors, patrons, and period players primes the trees, making them take on the role of a magick-laden dark forest. My skin erupts in goosebumps and my breath hitches. I reach for my inhaler and try to shrug off the heavy, oily sense that someone's watching.

"This is neat," she calls, already focused on whatever it is she wants to photograph.

"What's neat? We should be looking for William." I scan the area, searching for anything remotely unique. Then again, through her eyes, something ordinary could become extraordinary in the correct lighting or at the best angle. Veined leaves, mushrooms growing out of bark, birds' nests made of string—who knows what will trigger her inspiration? The sooner she finds it, the sooner we can get back to the main path. I squeeze the inhaler, almost to the point of cracking the plastic.

She pauses. "Shoot, I must've scared it off."

"What are you talking about?"

She twists to me, eyes wide. "I saw a fairy, but it flew away."

I blink. "Uh, are you making fun of me?"

She blows a raspberry and snaps a photo of me. "It's the Renaissance Faire. The only place where magick really is real."

I scrunch my nose at her.

She grins and clicks another pic.

"I'm going to hold you to that and make you chant here, on the faire grounds."

Her smile fades. "You never let anything go."

"What do you mean?" I reach out and yank a leaf off a nearby maple.

"You're not giving up on this magick thing, are you?"

I stare at the leaf's veins. "It's real, Mary. You said you remembered..."

"Yeah, that it didn't work. We've already talked about this and we had a fight. I don't want to discuss it again." She palms her camera and walks toward the main path.

"Why can't we talk about it?" I stomp after her, huffing with every step. The pollen mixed with the frustration of Mary dodging yet another important conversation inflames my lungs. I pause long enough to use my inhaler.

Mary twists to face me. Her brow furrows, shifting her from avoidance mode to overprotective mode. "Anne, are you okay?"

I lean over and prop my hands on my knees. The trail's entrance—and the freedom of open air—is so close and yet so far. Oxygen is oxygen, but magickal, dark-forest air has a decidedly heavier quality than sunny field air.

She rushes over to me. "You sound wheezy. I'm sorry, all right? Don't go into a full attack because of me." She rubs my back like it'll open my lungs or something. "Focus on breathing."

"Yeah, I'm doing that." I close my eyes and visualize cool, clean air opening my airways and expanding my lungs. The tightness eases some. The confusion about Mary thinking the asthma flare is her fault doesn't. Asthma is asthma. The only person that brings it on is me—when I'm upset, it's worse. No one can control my emotions, except me. And I suck at it.

"Are you girls lost?" A dry, gravelly voice interrupts us.

We spin to face an old woman standing just a few feet away. Dressed in a black, hooded cape, she looks a lot like the witch in Snow White. Without the warts and hooked nose, but with twice the wrinkles.

"Twins. How lovely. The bond between twins is so much stronger than that of other siblings." Intense black eyes scour over us. Her jagged smile slashes at me like the tines of a rusty rake.

"Where'd you come from?" Mary asks, trying to sound polite. Her fingers digging into my arm, however, tell me she's feeling anything but friendly.

The woman's gaze locks onto mine and my mind splits open, leaving me raw and exposed. My heart races in a rush to heal the assault of her cleaving stare. "I have a shoppe at the end of the trail. I sell trinkets, love potions, herbal teas, talismans, and the like."

"That's nice." I cough and suck on some albuterol, telling myself she's an innocent, old woman dressed up as a witch to sell her goods, not some sorceress wandering a forbidden, magickal forest.

She stretches a crooked index finger and points at my pin. "The Gemini symbol. Wonderful!" She laughs, but it comes out as a half-cackle, half-grunt. "I collect Zodiac symbols. I could show you. Come take a look. You might find something you like."

"Maybe later. We're meeting someone." Mary bites her lip.

"It won't take long. This way." She waves her arm and limps along the footpath, deeper into the woods.

I glance at Mary. The asthma attack is fading, otherwise I'd get the heck out of there, but... I can't let an old woman freak me out. Someone famous somewhere—or some "when"—said you have to confront your fears and, well, this seems like a good opportunity. We'll look at her shoppe, see how lame her stuff is, and go about our business without the fear of running into her for the next couple of weeks while the faire is open. Besides, I've faced Mom a million times, and she's a dragon. I can take on a little, aged witch. "She's an old lady. Let's take a look to make her happy."

"You're okay?"

"Yeah."

"Okay." She stays close as we walk.

"I am Zeena, the Zodiac Collector," the old woman tells us when we get to her little shack. It's situated in the middle of a little clearing, on top of a small hill. With the sun beating on it, it almost seems quaint. Like the gingerbread house that Hansel and Gretel got lured into.

Zeena opens the door. It creaks loudly. Inside is packed with all kinds of things, and a dusty, moldy scent occupies the empty spaces from months of non-use. If she opens the window and keeps the door open—and maybe lights a few dozen scented candles—the smell might evaporate by the end of the faire.

She shuffles to a wooden chair and side table tucked into a corner. The floorboards moan and creak under her weight. Shelves line all the walls. Candles, jewelry trees filled with necklaces, pins, rings, and earrings, glass bottles of various colors and sizes filled with powders or liquids, books—you name it, she has it.

She swings her arm in an arc, the sleeve of her robe billowing. "See something you like?"

Mary and I scan the room.

"You've got lots of stuff," I say.

"Here's my favorite collection." She pulls a velvet-covered, notebook-sized plaque off a shelf. On it are trinkets for each zodiac symbol—waves for Aquarius, an arrow with a line through it for Sagittarius, a circle with a curlicue tail for Leo. All of them are there except for Libra, Aries, and Gemini.

"Oh, we're not interested in buying anything." Mary smiles sweetly, softening the blow of saying no.

"I'm not selling these, dear. I'm collecting them." Her eyes shift to my pin.

I cover it instinctively. "This was a gift," I blurt.

"Are you Gemini?"

We nod in unison.

Zeena's mouth quivers. "Do you know the original Gemini twins?" The room darkens, as if the sun has gone under.

"Castor and Pollux. Our dogs are named after them," Mary replies.

A rush of wind comes up and swirls around the shack. It chatters under the pressure and the door slams shut with a *bang!*

Mary yelps and clutches my arm tighter.

The old woman's gaze darts to the single window. "Such a smart girl."

"We should get going. Thanks for showing us around." Mary edges toward the door.

"Hold on. I want to give you girls something." She cradles the plaque in one arm while drawing her fingers along a shelf of potions. She taps a bottle with her fingertip and picks it up. The white powder inside shimmers. "Here it is."

"What is it?" I ask.

"This is stardust. Sent from Castor and Pollux themselves." She extends her arm.

"No, we can't take that." I hold up my palm in a no thanks gesture.

"Oh, but you must! Make an old woman happy." She shakes the bottle and winks. "Wouldn't want to upset the Gemini twins, either."

I accept the bottle. "Erm, thanks. What do we do with it?"

"Sprinkle some on a candle the next time you light one."

"And then what?"

"It'll be a surprise!" She grins and claps her hands.

Oh, good. Just what we need. More surprises.

Chapter
Eight

"You sure you're okay?" Mary frets over me as we head to the jousting arena, walking elbow to elbow with me.

If there's anything I hate, it's someone hovering in my personal space during and after an asthma attack. As if I can claim all the air around me as my own. There's plenty for everyone. "Yes, I'm fine." I take a deep breath to prove it. My lungs seize a tiny bit, but I keep a smile plastered on my face, trying not to let it show.

"That lady was weird." She gives me a little space by putting a couple feet between us.

"Beyond weird." I shake the bottle of glitter, daintily labeled "Stardust." White wax seals the cork. I'm tempted to sprinkle it on a candle or an offering during my next chant, even though stuff like this is totally fake. A real witch wouldn't sell her magicks. She'd keep them secret. Unless it's a front. But then that would still make the dust a sham.

A flutter of stubborn belief tickles my stomach. Doesn't hurt to try it, right? Mary won't have to know. I'll wait until she's sleeping.

"You're not going to keep that, are you?" She eyes the bottle warily.

I shrug. "Why not? It's kind of pretty."

"Hmmph." She puts another foot between us. It's as if the distance marks the extent of her disbelief.

"Come on. It's not like it'll spontaneously cause the earth to tilt off its axis and dive into the sun."

Her eyebrow arches.

"It's probably fake anyway."

"Oh, so that's fake, but your Zodiac magick is real? You can't have it both ways."

"All science isn't true." I tuck the bottle in my pocket and walk ahead.

The smells of dirt, warm grass, and leather mingle together. Chatter from early faire actors and vendors caresses me. I soak it all in, filing away each sensation like a camel hoarding water. The faire only runs for two weeks, then I have to wait another fifty for it to return. This year is even worse because of the SAT. Bittersweet longing tarnishes my fragile happiness. One of these years, I'm going to enjoy the faire and just do what I want to do. No heavy dresses to wear in the hot sun, no marketing of Mom's business, no exam to study for, and no ruined birthdays.

William is at the stable behind the arena. He's shoveling wood shavings into a wheelbarrow. Lord have mercy, he's not wearing a shirt. His skin is darkened from the sun. Sweat slicks his chest, back, and arms. His hair is soaked at the edges. And, oh man, his jeans hang low on his lean hips. He's all muscle.

My tummy does the squee tingle—the funny nausea, swirly-gig thing that happens when an elevator comes to a stop and you're weightless for a nanosecond. Except this is a million times stronger.

"You're drooling," Mary whispers, nudging me with her elbow.

"Shh." I clear my throat. "Hey, William."

He stabs his shovel in the pile of shavings and turns to us. "Hi." His dimples flash and I want to melt right there.

"Whatcha doin'?" I dig my toe in the dirt and smile, but stop short of twirling my hair around a finger.

He snatches a navy-blue kerchief from his back pocket and wipes his face. "Getting the stalls ready. Shequan's dad is bringing the horses today."

"Awesome." I try not to stare at his ripped abdomen. Jousting is one of my favorite parts of the faire. Horses are gorgeous animals, and the excitement of the knights charging full-tilt at one another jazzes me up every time. I keep telling myself I'm going to start riding lessons and join the knights. I don't know if they'd "allow" a girl in the band, but whatever, I suck at taking "no" for an answer. A vision of me knocking the Red Knight off his chestnut stallion with a lance and the crowd bursting into cheers briefly takes over. It would be *so* cool.

"Dude, hurry up, we still have four stalls to fill." Evan jogs up to us. He waves at me and grins at Mary. "Hey."

Mary giggles. She *does* twirl her hair. "Evan. I didn't know you were here."

"Yeah. This guy bribed me into it." He tilts his head at William. His gray shirt has deep sweat stains around the neck, pits, and back.

William laughs. "Bribe? You mean I'm splitting my pay with you."

Evan grabs the wheelbarrow handles and spins it toward the barn entrance. "Right. That's what I said."

"You guys need help?" I ask.

Mary kicks my heel.

William shakes his head. "Nah, if I split my money any more, I won't be left with anything."

"I don't mind. I don't need any money." Gawd, how desperate do I sound?

His mouth twitches with amusement. It's the same look any boy gives a girl when they know the girl is totally into them. A flash of heat burns my cheeks and his grin widens. I'm like a slice of toast that's fallen butter-side down—a complete and total loss. "Okay, well, do you want to put some hay in each of the stalls? There's a rack. Just put a flake in each one."

Is it a pity chore, something to make me think he's not rejecting me? I huff, following him to the stack of hay just inside the barn. At least he's not taking full advantage and making me do all his chores. A lock of hair drops into his face as he bends to cut the double set of twine wound around a bale.

He pulls at the edges with his long fingers, sectioning the bale. "See? The flakes separate on their own. Super easy."

Evan walks by with an empty wheelbarrow. "Need a refill," he says, his gaze lingering on Mary more than anyone else.

"Cool." William follows him outside. He pauses just beyond the threshold and peers back at us. His gaze locks onto mine and the heat in my cheeks intensifies.

I go into full on nuclear-core meltdown when he flashes his dimples at me.

Mary watches until they're out of sight, then sighs. "Thanks for volunteering us."

"It won't take long. Besides, you can earn points with Evan for being here to pitch in."

"Is that why you offered to help? To 'earn points' with William? You don't need to do that, you know. He already likes you." She pulls her hair into a low ponytail and then grabs two flakes. Bits of loose hay shake off to the floor as she walks to the first set of stalls.

"We're just friends." It's a good thing her back is turned to me. Even I can't pull off the lie to myself, let alone someone else.

"Yeah, right. And I'm the High Queen." She circles around for another load of flakes.

We fall into silence. There's twelve stalls and it only takes us a few minutes to distribute the hay.

The guys have one stall left to prepare by the time we're done. Mary and I linger while William fills the barrow with shavings.

Evan sidles up to Mary. He leans against the barn, super casual. "I had fun last night."

Mary tries to mime his posture. "Me too."

"We should hang out again some time."

"Totally." She yanks the elastic from her hair and shakes out her curls. Definite mating behavior.

A buzz of pride tingles along my spine. This is a big step for her.

He smiles so sweetly my teeth ache. "Cool. When?"

She twists her mouth in thought. "It's kind of lame, but do you want to study for the SAT together?"

He angles his body toward her and I want to cheer like Marcy Stucky did after her quarterback boyfriend scored a touchdown during overtime at the All Stars game. The girl nearly peed her pants, and several people around her had to clamp their hands over their ears. "No, it's not lame. How about tomorrow afternoon?"

"Okay." Mary gives him a time and location and seals my fate as the third wheel.

I angle away from them and toward William. He's almost finished filling the wheelbarrow.

"Hey, Anne. I'm heading in. Walk with me?" He lifts the handles.

"Sure."

When we get to the last stall on the right, he says, "*They're getting along.*"

I chuckle. "Evan's nice. I like him."

William nods, driving the wheelbarrow into the stall and lifting the handles to tip it forward. "He's had a crush on Mary the entire year."

"You're kidding!" She's had a crush on him, too, but I keep that to myself.

"Yeah." He walks backward, shaking the wheelbarrow along the way to distribute the shavings.

I grab a rake and spread them out some more. "I'm glad they're finally talking, then. Although I may have lost my studying partner." Without Mary prodding me along, I might not be able to focus enough on studying for the exam.

He drives the barrow out of the stall and gestures for me to give him the rake. "We could study together."

I dig my nails into the stall door as I shut it. Hanging out with William would make studying less like torture. On the other hand, it'd also be harder to concentrate. But, heck, I'm willing to risk it. "I'd like that."

♐ ♈ ♊ ♏ ♓

Dad's smithy shop is kitty-corner to the arena. Its vertical clapboard siding is painted black. Above the entrance is a wooden sign. Its iron lettering reads: *Devans's Forgeries.*

A silly play on words, but it gets Dad a lot of comments.

Shequan and his dad, Marcus Whitaker, are inside when Mary and I arrive.

"One horse already threw a shoe. She balked at the trailer and hit her foot just right on the edge. Bent the metal." Marcus is dressed in a white T-shirt, jeans, and boots. Over six feet tall, he towers over everybody. He yanks a misshapen horseshoe out of his pocket and shows it to Dad.

"No problem. I'll come fix it right now, if you like." Dad's leaning against the counter that runs parallel to the far wall of his shop. A couple beer cans are at his elbow. As usual, his clothes are stained with soot and dirt. He wears a thick leather apron when he works, but it doesn't seem to keep him clean.

"That'd be great. Thanks, Dan." Marcus claps Shequan's shoulder. "Ready?"

Shequan lifts the front of his orange button-down shirt to stuff his hands in his jeans pockets. "Bet the horses are ready to get off the trailer."

All the guys notice us when they turn toward the door.

"Hi, girls." Dad greets us with a smile.

"Anne, Mary, hey." Shequan gives us a nod. "Ready for the SAT?"

Shequan is one of the few students giving Mary competition in the grades department. Evan is the other. William and I, well, we're happy to be second-string as long as we're doing well enough to keep our parents happy and to score into a good college.

Mary and I groan in unison. Mary doesn't have problems acing exams, but they rev her nerves and she hates the feeling, hence her uber-study schedules.

"Me neither. It's too bad the faire runs at the same time," Shequan says.

"Yeah, if the test was later, we'd be able to enjoy it more." I should work on a spell that could alter time. It'd be so awesome to create a portal to another dimension so I had time to study and do boring stuff, but could spend as much time as I wanted here, at the faire, or with William. I'd have to check the Zodiac spellbook for a time-weaving spell.

"Right?" He scratches the back of his head. "History is going to kill me."

"Math will annihilate me," I mutter.

He snorts. "Annihilate. That's funny."

"Coming to see the horses, girls?" Dad carries his farrier tools in an open wooden box with a handle.

"Sure." Mary takes his chaps from him and folds them over her arm.

"I'll meet you at the barn. Gotta bring the truck around. It has the anvil and forge in the back." He heads outside with Marcus.

Shequan leads the way to the horse trailer, chatting about how much it sucks to memorize dates and people and events that'll have no impact on his future. I can't say I disagree, but memorizing is easier than finding your way through a math problem, in my humble opinion. With my warped sense of mathematical direction, I take the wrong turn at Albuquerque every time and end up somewhere in the Netherlands rather than Santa Fe.

The size of a semi truck, Marcus's livestock trailer carries up to fifteen horses. Sunlight reflects off the shiny metal like a lens flare. I hold a hand over my brow, creating some shade for my eyes.

Dad is already there, firing up his forge. Marcus drags the anvil off the truck bed and drops it nearby. Shequan unlocks the trailer door and extends the ramp so the horses don't have to hop. The scent of tangy horse sweat and manure oozes out.

I peek into the windows, catching glimpses of velvety noses and watery eyes. One pale horse flares its nostrils and snorts. A moment later, her face disappears. I bet it's the one who threw a shoe.

A steady stomp rocks the trailer and Shequan appears with the buckskin mare in tow. She has a white blaze down her nose and stocking feet. Her white mane is super long, almost reaching her chest.

The poor thing rushes down the ramp and spins around Shequan. He holds fast to the lead while reaching up to pat her neck. "Easy, girl."

Marcus helps Shequan attach the lead to a fence post. "Grab some hay. It might distract her."

Shequan jogs to the barn and appears a moment later with a flake. The mare's ears perk up, locking onto him. She paws at the ground.

Dad's able to approach her and pick up her right front foot without too much protest. He examines her hoof and files it a bit. "This'll be no problem to nail back on."

"Good." Marcus pats the mare's hind end. "This is her first joust. Should be interesting."

Her tail flicks at the flies and she chews in a steady rhythm, pulverizing the hay strand by strand, previous anxiety forgotten.

"She's beautiful." I run my fingers along her smooth neck and fiddle with her mane.

"You should come to the stable sometime. Take her for a spin." Marcus grins.

"That'd be great…if I knew how to ride." I scratch under her chin and she extends her neck, closing her eyes with contentment.

Dad heats the horseshoe in the forge and pounds it into shape. Fixing the mare's hoof between his legs, he sets to nailing the thing on. "Girls, how about I pay for some riding lessons with Marcus? It'll be an early birthday present."

"Really?" I bounce like a five year old getting a megaton of her favorite candy.

Mary hands the mare another handful of hay. "Sounds fun."

I'm not sure I believe her, but she's too polite to disagree.

"What're you guys doing for your birthday?" Shequan runs his fingers through the mare's mane, loosening the tangles.

Mary and I glance at one another.

I shrug. "Haven't really planned anything yet."

"Hard to with studying."

"Yeah."

He scrunches his face like he's working out an algebra problem in his head. "Let's see. Your birthday is in late June… That makes you guys Gemini, right?"

"That's right. You into the Zodiac?"

He shrugs. "A little. I play this Zodiac-based RPG and the characters traits are based on their sign and constellations. Each sign has its own power—water, air, fire, earth—and Pet System. Like the Gemini are pretty good warriors. They use windstorms, and their Pet System is a horse." He pats the mare's neck.

"You know a lot about Gemini."

The corner of his mouth ticks up. "It's important for strategy."

"Which sign are you?"

"I stick with Aries. It's a cardinal fire sign. I get lots of extras with that one."

"Is that your real sign?"

"Yep."

"Cool."

Mary, who's been quiet so far, nudges closer. "Anne's an expert on the Zodiac. Once you get her started on it, she can't shut up. Seriously, she can tell you any fact you'd never want to know."

I frown at her. "Very funny."

"I'm just saying." She tips her head so her hair hides her face from Shequan's view and gives me a what-the-triple-*heck*-are-you-doing look.

I glare at her.

"Bet I can out-talk you." He gives the mare more hay and adjusts the noseband of her halter.

Mary tucks her hair behind her ear. "Please, don't give her a dare."

Shequan laughs.

I open my mouth to lob a comeback and Mary gives me another look. The snark dies on my lips and coats them like sticky gloss. Geez, one flirt fest with Evan has given some sort of super power—Confidence Girl with the power to steal retorts and fizzle arguments with one stare.

For once, I let Mary cart me off. Though I'll admit, I'm so curious to ask her why she freaked about Zodiac chat, getting her one on one will give me an opportunity. I wave 'bye to Shequan. "So…I guess we'll see you around the faire."

"Sure." He unties the mare, who's now sporting a fourth shoe, and walks her toward the stable.

"Meet you girls at the shoppe?" Dad snuffs the fire in his forge and helps Marcus lift the anvil into the truck bed.

"Yep." Mary nods.

I wait until we're out of earshot. "What happened back there?"

"Why do you always have to go on and on about Zodiac stuff?"

"Just like you go on about photography?"

She pouts. "Touché."

"Besides, Shequan brought it up."

"I don't want you wrangling him into this." She twists her arms and wiggles her fingers.

"Wrangle? He's not a wild bull and I'm not a cowboy."

"You know what I mean." She tucks her hands into the rear pockets of her jeans.

"Actually, I don't. What makes you think I'm going to ask Shequan to chant with me?"

"Forget I said anything." She turns toward Dad's shoppe.

I make a beeline for her and bump shoulders. "Hey, if I knew so much about the Zodiac, I'd be able to make a chant work. I'm not going to drag anyone else into this, I promise."

She nods, sucking on her bottom lip. "Good. It's best if you leave this stuff alone."

"Why?"

She rolls her eyes. "Because it isn't real."

"Then how do you explain what happened in our room?"

She slows. "I don't know. But I don't want to try again to find out, either. We pinky swore, remember?"

"I'm not saying we should chant again." I leave off *right away*. Guess I'd have to practice on my own for a while. It'd make spell casting harder. Like Gamma said, we needed to work together for full power.

Unless I can find a substitute.

♐ ♈ ♊ ♏ ♓

I *have* to take a break from studying. It's Sunday night, after all. Lots more studying is lined up for tomorrow. I need my strength and I find it in surfing the Internet.

"I thought you were studying." Mary lies on her stomach, her upper body propped up on a pillow. Her knees are bent and her lower legs are crossed, sticking up in the air. Her history textbook is open in front of her. She must memorize the pages somehow. I have no other way of explaining how easy straight A's come for her.

"I am." I log on and scroll over my favorite website. New pics from the Magicks page take up most of it. Some are funny, some are inspirational, and some are simply pictures of misty woods and mythical creatures.

An instant message tab pops up in the bottom right corner. It's William. My heart digs its heels into my rib cage and makes a leap up my chest.

He writes: *The stars are out tonight.*

I smile, biting my lower lip, and reply: *Yeah?*

We should meet and look at them. I'll bring my telescope.

I almost squeal. My fingers hover over the keys, humming with eager glee. I want to snap back a "yes" immediately, but don't want to look desperate like I had at the stable, so I make myself wait. One-one thousand, two-one thousand, three-one thousand… I clench my fists and sit on them until I hit thirty. Then I type: *Where should we meet?*

The park by the fountain. Twenty minutes?

It's a farther walk for me, but I don't mind. *See you there! Okay.*

I power down the laptop, my mind whirring. "William wants to meet me in the park."

"Now? Why?"

"To look at the stars." I skip to my closet, hyped on girly giddiness, and yank a light-blue hoodie from its hanger. The days are warm, but the nights cool down. Maybe I should bring some hot chocolate.

"How romantic," Mary croons, flopping onto her back and resting a hand on her forehead in a fake faint.

"Yep." I lace up my sneakers and give Castor a jovial scratch behind the ears. "See you later."

She rolls her eyes, but her smile says she's happy for me. "Don't stay out too late."

♐ ♈ ♊ ♏ ♓

I clutch the Thermos to my chest and savor the weight of my backpack against my spine. My heart is pounding between my lungs like a magic jumping bean. William and I hang out all the time, but this is different. A nighttime rendezvous, alone, to look at the stars. Like Mary said, it's romantic. My lips feel dry. I lick them, thankful that the minty sting of my toothpaste still coats my tongue.

I find William in the middle of the park, near the water fountain like he'd said. It's not running, so the night is quiet—except for the chirping of crickets. I wonder what they're saying to each other.

"Hi, Anne." William greets me with his signature dimple-laden smile. He's got the telescope set up already. A lantern sits next to it, casting a ring of somber yellow light around him. It edges along the fountain's wall and to the grass on the opposite side.

I wave. Lame. "I brought some hot chocolate." I pause. "But I only have the lid for a cup."

"No worries. We can share."

Right. No big deal. Two friends sharing a cup. We do it all the time. "Cool."

He dips his head to the telescope and points it west. "I found Libra. Wanna see?",

"Sure." William's birthday is in October, making him a Libra. True to his sign, he's laid-back, levelheaded, diplomatic, and just. He always finds a way to get people to compromise and get along. On the flip side, he can't make a decision to save his life. I peek in the viewfinder and stare at the mass of white dots speckling the black sky. If I trace a line between the stars in the constellation, it looks like a lopsided house drawn by a five-year-old.

"Wouldn't it be cool to travel to other galaxies, visit other planets, and feel the heat of different suns?" There's awe in his voice. It carries wonder and adventure. The shockwave of it blasts me, inspiring me to dream.

"We could visit the stars of our Zodiac signs. Alpha, Beta, and Gamma Librae." I step away from the telescope and point to each star in the constellation. "Then Castor and Pollux." I have nowhere to point because they're not visible from our location.

"They say a planet in the Librae system could sustain life." He grins.

"We could inhabit another world."

"Yeah, one without SATs."

We laugh. He stares at me so intently I squirm like a butterfly under a microscope. Heat rushes to my cheeks and anxiety pools in my belly.

"Er, you seem deep in thought," I croak.

"You looked really pretty, wearing that dress."

Right there, without warning, my heart melts. The lack of blood flowing through my body creates a sharp ringing in my ears. I press a shaky finger to my temple as if it'll stop my brain from exploding. He'd commented about how Mom's dress brought out the color of my eyes, but he hadn't mentioned anything about looking pretty.

"Are you okay?" He drapes his hands on my shoulders. So gentle. His touch shatters me.

"Y-yeah." I lie. I mean, I'm not complaining about him being so close to me that I can smell his soap or feel the heat of his breath on my cheeks. It's one hundred percent, completely what I want. Which is what makes me not okay. We're best friends. Have been since we were in diapers. This is new territory and I don't know how to act.

Maybe there's a spell for that.

♐ ♈ ♊ ♏ ♓

I slip my backpack off as soon as I reach the top of the porch stairs. Slinking to the far corner, past Dad's rusty bench, I drop to my knees and steady my breathing. Mary would flip out if she knew what I'm about to do.

Huddling in the dark like a robber planning a break-in, I unzip my backpack and draw out a candle and book of matches. It takes three tries to get the wick to light. I scrape the wax off the stardust bottle's top with my thumbnail. The cork sticks and I have to wiggle it back and forth. It comes free with a soft *thunk*.

My stomach tumbles like an Olympic gymnast. I still haven't had a chance to practice spells with Gamma and the last one was a mess. This would probably go better with Mary, but she doesn't want any part of it. I take a deep breath and begin.

"Four elements of the Zodiac,

Earth, fire, water, air.
Gemini twins,
Castor and Pollux.
Hear my plea.
Help me figure out
How to make William and me be!"

I tip the bottle toward the flame, my hand shaking. Am I really doing this?

Yep.

With a flick of my wrist, a flurry of glitter rains down. It sizzles on contact with the melted wax and the candle almost goes out. Then the sizzling grows louder and the fire brightens, at first to a pale yellow, then a bright white.

I expect it to die down, but it doesn't. Instead, the light keeps getting more dazzling, more blinding, more…*star*-like.

I lean back, squinting. This isn't normal. I gulp. The old woman, Zeena, couldn't really have given us *real* stardust. She couldn't be a real witch. A kooky chuckle gurgles up my chest and past my lips.

The candle starts wobbling all by itself. There's no wind, no earthquake, no reason whatsoever for the thing to move on its own. Except for magick.

"Holy Castor and Pollux," I blurt. Had I listened to Mary and tossed the stuff away, I wouldn't be here, crouching on my front porch, caught in a spell beyond my control.

With a loud crack, the candle explodes and…

…disappears.

I'm surrounded by all-encompassing darkness, like the sky without stars.

Chapter Nine

Ms. Sutters, Math Teacher Extraordinaire, goes at the whiteboard with her marker like a butcher hacking into a rack of ribs. Red ink smears across the surface in symbols and letters that are supposed to make some sort of sense. Maybe they do to a smart person. Me, on the other hand, I can't organize a math problem from start to finish, even if my life depends on it.

The teacher walks us through the problem and adds another for us to practice. I copy the wonky mess and stare at it, mouth slack. I squeeze the daylights out of my wizard's-staff-shaped pencil. There's no way a solution will come out of this. Maybe the ghost of a math whiz will possess my hand and scrawl something across the page and help me out, 'cause I sure as heck can't.

After five agony-filled minutes, I drop my pencil and smash my cheek against my notebook with a groan.

Mary jerks and the tip of her pencil snaps off. She purses her lips and glares at me.

I wince. "Sorry."

"Quiet," Ms. Sutters wanders down our row. She pauses between Mary and me. Vanilla and cinnamon drift off her, and my nose tingles with a sneeze. Her brown bob ends precisely at her jaw, straight and boring like her boxy, plain white shirt and navy pants. She peers down her aardvark-like schnoz at me.

"I was apologizing for startling my sister," I explain.

Her thin lips grow thinner. "Why don't you go up to the board and solve the equation?"

My head whips back and forth. "No way, I can't."

Her arched brow climbs her forehead. "Try it. The class will help you."

Swallowing my pride and begging my knees to hold me up, I slide out of my seat and do the dead-man-walking march to the whiteboard.

My fingers curl around the red marker. I yank off the cap and raise the point to the space beneath the math problem. My vision blurs as I search for something recognizable. Surely, I can get the problem started. A wheeze shivers in my chest. I need to start writing. I need to save face.

Soft snickers trickle behind me. My ears combust and sweat bursts from my body.

Ms. Sutters claps once. "Let's be productive, class, not judgmental. Shequan, give Anne a hand."

I grind my teeth at the scrape of metal chair legs against tile floor. Quick footsteps move in and Shequan appears at my side. He picks up a blue marker, gives me an easy smile without any hint of pity, and explains the solution to me while scribbling across the board almost as fast as Sutters had.

"Can you take the test for me?" I whisper as he underlines his final answer.

His grin flashes brighter. "No, but I can teach you a trick to solving these problems. Come find me during lunch, okay?"

I nod. "Thanks."

He drops the marker on the rack and saunters to his desk.

I turn to follow him, but Ms. Sutters extends a hand.

"Wait. I'll put another equation on the board for you to practice on." Her clunky heels pound the floor, sealing my fate step by step.

I stand there, frozen to the ground, in front of the class, wishing I could melt into the wall and disappear.

There's no way I'm going to solve any equation, let alone pass the exam.

♐ ♈ ♊ ♏ ♓

"I think the girls would like riding lessons." Dad's voice carries from inside, through the screen door, to the porch where Mary and I halt, striking awkward poses—arms mid-swing and legs half in the air—like we used to while playing Red Light, Green Light.

"Horses are dangerous animals. Besides, we can't afford lessons," Mom says. They must be in her studio. I can't imagine she'd be anywhere else, considering she only leaves the room to pee or grab some food.

"Marcus is a good trainer. They'll be in good hands. It's for their birthdays. They deserve something nice; they're good kids." He's pleading with her. I gotta give Dad props for defending us.

"It's not happening!" she screams.

I catch Mary's gaze. Her shoulders square with rigid fear while mine slump with disappointment. Mom's heinous. There's no reason to hope she'll change. If I do get a spell to work, she'll find some way to ruin things, whether it's my birthday or something else. The proof is in the porridge, since we can't even go horseback riding. Other kids turning sixteen would be begging for a car. Mary and I wanted a nice party and riding lessons. Not a big deal at all, but in Mom's world both are impossible.

It's like she can't let us be happy. Or maybe she just doesn't want us to be.

"You're being ridiculous, Liz," Dad says.

Oh boy. He's essentially poked the dragon with a stick. My lips curl back from my teeth. Mary takes a reflexive step backward.

"What?" Mom's screech is like a handful of razor blades slicing down my spine.

"You're out of control. You need to take your medication." His words settle around me like a shroud. A heavy, confining, restricting shroud. More like a straightjacket, actually. My legs wobble under the weight of it. I tremble, aching to run, but my feet are rooted to the pressure-treated wood under my feet.

"How dare you!"

A jet engine would be quieter. Amazing all the glass in the house doesn't shatter. Something *does* smash with a jaw-clenching clatter. She must have thrown something.

"I've had enough of your insanity, Liz." Dad's heavy stomps fade deeper into the house.

Mary digs her fingers into my elbow. "We should go."

"Where?"

A steady scamper takes over for the deathly silence inside. Castor and Pollux appear at the screen door. Castor scratches at it and Pollux picks up his plea with a whine. They hate Mom and Dad's fighting as much as Mary and me.

"To Grandmother's." She retreats slowly, silently, gaze fixed on the door.

"Good idea." I open the door, snatching both dogs' collars before they can make a break for it. Mary takes over dog-handling while I slip inside to grab their leads. I paw at the wall like a cat scratching at a laser dot, gaze locked onto the living room door for any signs that the beast is moving. The first sign would be smoke. Second is the stream of fire.

"Anne, hurry."

With a frown and a lump in my throat, I grip the leashes and escape to the safety of the porch. I attach the clips to the dogs' collars.

Mary and I scurry down the driveway.

The dogs have no trouble keeping up. In fact, they rush ahead of us, quickened by the animal instinct to flee.

Mary's face is red. Vertical, wet tracks divide her cheeks.

"You okay?" I ask, handing Pollux's lead to her.

She rubs her eyes and accepts the leash. "I hate it when they fight. I wish things were different. I wish Mom wasn't such a..."

"Beast?" I scuff my heels as we walk, staring at the pebbles littering the sidewalk and avoiding the cracks. I don't believe that stepping on them really invites trouble, but why take the chance? Things are crappy enough.

"What's so awful about riding a horse?" Mary corrects Pollux for tugging too much on his leash, but it's half-hearted and he goes right back to yanking her along. He knows the route to Gamma's and I can't blame him for wanting to get there ASAP.

"There isn't anything awful about it. It's just Mom."

"I wish we didn't have to live there."

I almost trip over my own feet. We've talked about getting out of the house as soon as we graduate, but she's never brought up the idea of leaving now. "Maybe Gamma will let us stay for a while? She's got a couple spare bedrooms."

"Yeah." A small smile tugs at her lips.

"We should ask her."

Gamma's on her porch when we arrive, rocking in a rocking chair, sipping iced tea. Her big red glasses look like goggles. "Hi girls! Thought you'd be at the faire helping your father set up shop."

"Mom and Dad are fighting." I flop on the floor by her feet and pat my thighs. Castor hops onto my lap and tries to French kiss me. I turn my face to the side and scratch behind his ears until he settles down.

Gamma puckers her mouth, but says nothing.

Mary settles down next to me. "I love my camera, Grandmother. It does so much more than my old one. Thank you." Her eyes are a little red, but at least she's trying to act cheerful.

"You're welcome, honey." Gamma tosses her gardening magazine on the small table to her left. "What kind of pictures have you been taking?"

"I've got some early shots of the faire and some of Castor and Pollux."

A sudden breeze comes at us from behind. My hair blows into my face and I have to use both hands to keep it back. I twist to look up at the sky. Dark clouds stream in from the south, eclipsing the pale blue.

"Where'd that storm come from?" Gamma uses her hands to shove off the armrests and stands. She shuffles a few steps, then slowly straightens up and gains momentum. By the time she reaches the front door, she's upright and perky. "Let's get inside before the sky starts falling."

The dogs are more than happy to follow Gamma to the pantry, aka The Land of Tasty Treats. Although the kitchen is usually bright from the huge bay window over the sink, it's so dark from the heavy clouds rolling in that Gamma turns the light on. A flash of lightning blitzes across the sky and thunder rumbles a moment later.

Mary and I dump our book bags next to the table and slump into the chairs. Gamma joins us after doting on the pups.

"Why the long faces? Your parents will make up. They always do." Gamma smoothes the red gingham tablecloth with her palms.

"I hate living there," I blurt.

Gamma tut-tuts. "Now come on, Anne. Your parents give you a good home and good food. They work hard and they do it for you."

I can't stop myself from pouting. Gamma usually understands when I talk with her.

Mary leans forward on her elbows. "It's getting worse. Mom yells all the time. I'm getting sick of it too." She hides her face in her hands. Soon, her body shakes with sobs, and small whimpers leak out of her mouth. The sky releases its stores of rain, as if crying in sympathy with Mary.

Tears burn at my eyes reflexively. I want to reach out, wrap my arms around her, and hug the sadness away. But I don't. A hug won't change things. Instead, I clench my jaw and fists and sit there, mute.

Gamma's mouth puckers like a dying fish. Guess she can't decide what to do or say either. Finally, she clears her throat. "Mary..."

Mary shoots to her feet, sending her chair skittering across the floor. She drops her hands to her sides and dashes out of the room. I blink at the empty space where she just was.

I lean forward to stand.

Gamma points a finger at me. "Let her go."

"What are we supposed to do when Mom is like this?" I angle my chair to keep an eye on the doorway, in case Mary reappears. She doesn't. The screen door hasn't whined open or slammed shut, so I assume she's in the house somewhere.

"She'll get back on her meds and things will settle down."

I roll my eyes. "Why does she stop them in the first place?"

"She feels better off them." Gamma stands and scuffles to the cupboard. She pulls out three mugs, then fills a teakettle and sets it on a burner to heat.

I wander next to her. "Can we stay with you for a while?"

She leans back to stare up at me. "I don't think that's a good idea. You can visit every day if you like, but you know your mom needs your help. It's great advertising when Mary and you wear her dresses."

"What if we don't want to help her?"

"Sometimes we have to do things we don't want to. Wearing the dresses will help keep the peace, don't you think?"

She has a point. I chew on my cheek, eating the regret of asking to stay with her. It had seemed like a solution—a way out—minutes ago. But there's no escape from Mom. She'd come after us if we ran here. It wouldn't be fair to Gamma.

"Not only do we have to pick our battles, we have to choose when to have them. This is not the time to provoke your mother."

"Yeah, I got it."

Gamma sighs.

The teakettle whistles. She twists the burner knob to shut it off. I grab some mugs and tea bags—Earl Grey, so traditional—while she carries the kettle to the table and sets it on a potholder.

"When we graduate, we're moving away and never coming back." I add three heaping spoonfuls of sugar to mine and stir, watching the swirls of steeping tea infect the clear water. I breathe in the bitter scent of bergamot. Reminds me of stuffy sitting rooms, pipes and cigars, and stale, hot summer days.

Gamma squirts some fake lemon juice in her cup. "So you'd leave your Gamma?"

My stomach clenches. "I don't want to leave you, but I can't stay here. Not with *her*."

"Your mother loves you. Her illness makes it difficult for her to show it."

I want to bite back that it's a lame excuse. She has the chance to stay well by taking her meds and she chooses not to. She chooses mania over us.

"It's not her fault she has bipolar disorder, Anne. She didn't ask for it."

"But it is her fault that she isn't taking the lithium."

Her lips pucker again. After a long moment, she says, "Have you been studying the Zodiac spellbook?"

I blow on the tea. The surface ripples. "Yep. I want to practice, but Mary's not interested."

"Have you been dabbling in the chants already?" She dips her tea bag in and out of the water, then discards it on her spoon.

I slurp a scalding mouthful and choke. "What? No."

She squints. "I'm no fool, Anne Devans. This is an unnatural storm. Came out of nowhere. You've woken the Gemini twins, haven't you?"

"No." At least, I don't think I have.

"The storm came up when you said their name. Mary's upset. Emotions can be a trigger." Gamma lists off her proof.

Weird. I've said their names before without anything happening...except. I cringe. Last night's spell was different. The stardust. My throat goes dry. But Mary said their names not me.

"How'd you do it?" Gamma keeps pushing.

"I didn't!"

She leans over the table, her googly eyes bigger than those of most anime characters. "Don't lie to me."

"Gamma..." My stomach claws its way up my chest. If I don't keep my mouth clamped shut it might shoot out and skid across the floor.

"How?"

I suck on my lips. I have to come clean and tell her what I know. "Mary and I chanted and all hell broke loose in our room. I thought I'd messed up. Then I tried to chant by myself using some stardust a lady at the faire gave me. It was totally weird. The candle just disappeared!" I flail my arms. Like it even remotely demonstrates what happened.

Gamma's eyes widen. "What do you mean, 'disappeared?'"

"I don't know how, but it went poof. It was gone, like it never existed."

She slides her glasses to the tip of her nose and stares at me over the rim. "You said someone gave you stardust?"

"Yeah, but it wasn't real. It was some silly faire stuff. You know, fake." I nod as if I'll convince myself, despite what I saw.

"Who gave it to you?"

"Like I said, some old lady."

"Did she tell you her name?" She eases into her seat, but the intensity of her doesn't lessen, not one drop. It's like she believes the dust is real.

But it couldn't be. So what if a candle disappeared? It was dark and I lost my bearings during the weird blackout… Maybe the candle rolled off the porch. I never went looking for it after all.

"Spit it out, girl." Gamma waves her hand, urging me to spill the details.

"Mary and I were in the woods at the faire and this old lady came up to us. She brought us to her shoppe and gave us a bottle of stardust." I draw the bottle out of my pocket and show Gamma. "Said her name was Zeena."

"She new to the faire?"

"I think so. Never seen her before."

She grabs the bottle from my hand and holds it up to the light. Bits of hard wax cling to the neck and cork. Gamma shakes it, jostling the glitter inside. "Hmmph."

"What?"

"Tell me everything you know about this woman."

I review all the details I can remember. The way she embodied her role as sorceress. The way she coveted her astrological trinkets. The way she sniffed around Mary and I about our Zodiac signs.

"She was really interested in the Zodiac, eh?" Gamma slams the bottle down in front of me. "What possessed you to use this?"

I stiffen. "I didn't think it'd actually do anything."

"What was your chant?" An uncharacteristic hardness flows into her eyes, similar to Mom's when she's about ready to blow. Have I woken another dragon?

No, not Gamma. She's sweet and kind and gentle and always understands.

"Anne. Spill it." There's nothing sugar and spice about her tone.

I dip my head and pick at a hangnail. "It isn't the kind of thing you want to tell your grandmother about."

"Anne."

I suck in a breath and confess. "William and I, well, we've been best friends forever and things are changing. I really like him and I chanted for Cast—"

Gamma snaps her fingers to stop me. "Don't say their names."

"I chanted for a way for William and me to be...more than friends."

Gamma closes her eyes and sighs. "Oh, honey, you don't have to do that. William is such a nice boy. And you're a wonderful girl. You don't need magick to bring you closer. That'll happen all on its own."

The waves of embarrassment beating me finally decide to recede. A smile teases my mouth.

She pats the table in front of the chair Mary was sitting in, motioning for me to move there. "You should've waited to chant until I taught you."

"I know. I'm sorry." I trace a finger around the rim of my mug. "I've really blown it, huh?"

"Hopefully not. Anything you chant for will be short-lived. Seems you've invoked the twins, but if you leave it alone for a while, they should fade away." Her words are strong and confident, but the way she tugs at the hem of her shirt makes me wonder.

"Are you sure?"

She drops her shirt and pats my hand. "Of course I'm sure. Your Gamma knows magick and she knows the book. Don't you worry."

Who else do I have to trust but Gamma? She's the one who brought magick into my life. As far as I'm concerned, she's an expert. Relief tries to shine down on me like the sun on a winter day, but it doesn't warm me. We still haven't made sense of Zeena. "So you think that dust has some magickal properties?"

Gamma's cheek twitches. She stares at the bottle for a full minute. "Probably not. Best not to use it again though, just in case."

"I thought Zodiac magick was rare. What are the odds of this lady practicing it?"

"Hard to say. You said she had pendants of the Zodiac signs?"

"Most of them. Some were missing."

"Which ones?"

I close my eyes, constructing a snapshot of that day. "She didn't have Gemini or Libra. Another one was missing too." I open my eyes and tap my chin. "Aries, that's the one."

"She's collecting them."

"It's not that hard to find pins. You'd think she'd have tons of them, considering she's a vendor."

Gamma pours some water into the third mug and adds a tea bag. "Let's see how Mary's doing. Carry this for me."

I follow her down the hallway, careful not to drop any tea. "What about the spellbook? When will you teach me?"

Gamma shakes her head. "I don't think it's a good idea to teach you about magick yet. Hopefully, the twins' power will fade quickly and this'll all be over."

"But Gamma…"

"I told you not to mess around with it and what do you do? You chant without any instruction whatsoever, then you use stardust…"

"You said it probably wasn't real."

"That's beside the point. Chanting *is* real and you disobeyed me, after giving your word that you wouldn't." Her gaze pierces me with disappointment.

"I'm sorry. I won't do it again."

"That's right, you won't. I want you to bring the book back to me tomorrow. No more magick." She takes off again.

The bottle of stardust sits on the table. I should leave it, forget about it, fake or not. But I can't. Especially since I have to return the book and give up practicing magick on my own.

Birthday gift: Revoked. Disappointment level: Achieved.

I need a consolation prize. With a shaky hand, I reach out, pluck the bottle off the table, and stuff it into my pocket before heading off to find Mary and Gamma.

Mary's sitting on the couch in the living room, her legs drawn up to her chest. She's not crying, but she looks how I feel—gutted.

Chapter
Ten

I promise to bring the spellbook to Gamma after class tomorrow, so naturally I prepare to pull an all-nighter studying it.

After Mary falls asleep, I sneak downstairs, brew a ridiculous amount of coffee, grab a bag of chips and chocolate candies, and pack my book bag. The spellbook is already tucked inside, along with candles, matches, and the stardust. I'm not going to use any of it, but the items are a sort of security blanket, considering I'll have to give up my most bestest birthday gift *ever* in less than twenty-four hours.

The door to Mom's study is closed and it's quiet. Maybe she's sleeping. Could last a couple hours, could last fifteen minutes. I need to make my getaway ASAP or risk incurring the dragon's wrath.

With my stuffed book bag on my back and my arms full with a blanket, Thermos, and flashlight, I creep outside and make my way to the faire grounds. I can't think of a better way to study the book than on the hallowed land of my childhood adventures and dreams. The air is different there, as if permeated with the souls of 18th-century merchants, knights, princes and princesses, and fairies.

The night is cool and the moon is bright. I almost don't need my flashlight, but use it anyway to cross the street. Headlights appear at the bend in the road. The whoosh of speeding tires and a purring engine passing interrupts the squeaky chirp of crickets and burping croaks of frogs.

I slip under the chain that blocks the entrance and cut between two tents that'll be used for face painting and henna tattooing. At the jousting arena, I lay out the blanket and unpack. A candle goes in each corner and I sit in the center with the book and a notebook on my lap. I prop the flashlight on top of my bag, angling it to illuminate the book, and settle in to read.

First, I jot down notes on each Zodiac symbol, then I focus in on air sign chants and Gemini chants. After that, I search for Libra spells, which mostly call for balance and peace. Would be nice to try them on Mom. Might keep arguments to a minimum. Since Gemini and Libra are both air signs, maybe William and I can practice chanting together, since Mary doesn't want anything to do with it.

It's three o'clock before I stop to stretch and finish off the last of my coffee. The chocolate is gone and half the chips are left. My back pops and I groan, rubbing stiffness out of my neck. Time to call it a night.

A layer of dew molds itself to the grass and my shoes squeak as I walk. I hop over to the path and focus on the crunch of stones under my soles.

Snap! Something cracks in the woods. It's followed by a quick rustle of leaves.

I halt and peer into the trees. Two golden orbs blink at me and I yelp, swinging the flashlight. A web of tree branches is all I see. No eyes.

I swallow the lump in my throat and scurry on, telling myself it's only an animal.

The rustle matches me.

I halt.

It stops.

I walk a few steps.

The noise picks up again.

I whip the flashlight back and forth.

"*Anne.*" It's a whisper, nothing more. So soft, I have to wonder if it's my imagination.

"Who's there?" I call. My voice is shaky and weak.

"*Annnnne.*"

My heart drums a frenzied beat, launching adrenaline throughout my system. "W-what do you want?"

A malicious hiss responds.

Sparks of fear jolt my nerves, leaving an electric fire in their wake. It fuels my body. I thrust forward at full speed, digging my heels in the ground with each strike. The stretch of muscle over bone and burn of air rushing in and out of my lungs drags me down. I'm breathless by the time I reach the road, but I don't let that stop me. I take a hit from my puffer and keep on running.

♐ ♈ ♊ ♏ ♓

"You should've left your hair curly, Anne. It'd fit the costume better." Mom fusses at the lace of my sleeve and sets her disapproving gaze on my flat-ironed hair. "At least pull it back into a bun or something. And wear a headband of flowers, both of you."

"I will." And maybe I'll add some wings too. I have white gauzy ones with green dots and glitter that'll go nicely with this gown.

"Make sure to attach some ribbons to it and let them stream down your back."

"Okay." After last night's marathon study and freakout session, I have no energy to argue. I've just about convinced myself it was my sleep-deprived imagination that had dreamed up the slithery voice in the woods. And those yellow eyes? Probably an owl. The fluttering? Wings. Yep. All explained by rational logic. Mary would be proud.

"Help your sister with her boring hair." Mom dismisses us with a flick of her wrist and turns to her latest piece—the Queen's coronation gown. It's white and lacy and full of frills. A huge collar of folded lace looks like a dinner plate. The dress itself is shaped like a giant bell jar.

Ug to the ly.

"Okay, Mom." Mary smoothes the bodice of her lime-green dress and twirls the skirt. Her curls are fluffy and perfectly classic. Exactly what Mom wants.

Once my hair is sufficiently periodized and I've slipped into my fairy wings, we head to the faire. We flash our vendor IDs at the gate and begin the long afternoon of showing off Mom's work to the crowds. Anyone who comments on our dresses gets a business card and a pitch. Heck, anyone who looks in our direction gets a business card and a pitch. Mom expects us to hand out at least a hundred cards a day. The one time we dumped a bunch in the trash, Mom caught us and made sure we distributed double the next day.

Food shoppes are clustered along the central street. The scent of roasting meat, sweet-potato fries, and barbecue mingles nicely with the scent of spicy incense. I double-check my coin purse—about the size of a wristlet—to make sure my ever-ready inhaler is tucked inside. As long as I don't suck in the smoke directly, I'll probably be okay.

The distant rumbling of drums down the street clashes with the subtle vibration of a harp. The harpist sits in the shade of a maple on a circular Oriental rug. Coming in the opposite direction, a flautist plays a light tune as he wanders. He wears an anklet of bells around each boot and they chime with every step.

A vendor at the Kings Nuts stand waves his arm. "Good morrow!"

His greeting earns a nod and bow from the flautist.

The vendor plucks a peanut from a bag and tosses it at the flautist, who lowers his flute, ducks under the arcing nut, and catches it in his mouth. The vendor yells, "Huzzah!"

Nearby actors and vendors reply with a chorus of "huzzah." A couple dressed as pirates clank their flagons of ale. Faire patrons laugh and applaud.

The flautist resumes his playing and keeps wandering down the path.

"Here's a good spot." Mary directs us to a grassy patch at the corner of a crossroads. She twirls her skirts and fluffs her hair.

I smooth mine down, tucking a stray bit behind my ear. "'Tis a fine eve, is it not?" I use my diaphragm to project my voice. It makes me sound ten years older.

"Yea, dear sister."

"Hast thou seen the Queen?"

"Nay, I hear our Queen 'tis preparing for her feast."

A middle-aged woman with three little kids heads our way. She's got a grin on her face. The kids hop around her like the dogs do to us at dinnertime. The boy—he's gotta be around four—tugs on her shorts.

"Good even, Madame." I curtsy.

"Such beautiful gowns," she says, picking up her toddler. The little girl's blonde curls end in fine wisps. Her bright blue eyes stare at me with wonder.

"Our mother is a fine seamstress. The best in the land."

"Such a boastful maiden." A rich, masculine voice sounds behind us.

I whirl to see William sauntering our way. An easy smile brings out his dimples. He's dressed as a squire. A golden lion emblem covers the front of his blue and black tunic, showing that he's in service to the Knight of Camelot. Knee-high boots and a sword affixed to a scabbard on his belt finish the costume. He won't wear armor or chainmail until the joust.

"Thou'rt a fool, sir. Dost thou think me a liar?"

"Nay, my lady. 'Tis only a poor attempt to humor thee." He bows. As he rises, he reaches behind his back and, with a quick twist of his arm, offers me a pink rose.

A squeal of glee tickles my throat. "Sir, such a beautiful gift."

"For a beautiful lady." He dips his head.

My fingers brush over his as I accept the gift. "I thank thee." My face hurts from smiling so broadly.

"Wilst thou attend the joust?"

"Gladly, kind sir." I curtsy and hold the flower to my nose. Its soft petals tickle. I inhale the sweet, raspberry-esque scent.

He wanders off, calling now and then to the crowd, garnering interest for the joust. It doesn't start for another thirty minutes, so Mary and I have some time to kill.

"Let's find some shade." Mary hooks arms with me and we saunter to the forest, handing out Mom's business cards along the way.

We dodge a pair of flower wenches selling roses, lilies, and carnations. One of them—dressed in a red corset and blue skirt with a ton of glitter on her ample chest—waves a flower in a man's face. "Buy a flower for your fair maiden, fine gentle sir. Bosoms abound at the faire and a fine fellow such as thee can't help but to spy on them. This colorful little blossom is forgiveness on a stick! Four dollars for forgiveness on a stick. A fine deal, indeed."

The man chuckles and forks over his money. His lady—dressed in modern clothes—giggles and twirls the stem.

"Huzzah!" the flower wench calls.

It doesn't take long for us to come across Zeena's shoppe. The door is open and people are wandering in and out, pausing to comment on the gargoyle and troll statues littering the ground nearby. Some are grotesque, bodies and mouths tangled in painful positions, while others are fat with jovial grins widening their mouths.

"Didn't see those before," I comment.

"Must be new." Mary tugs me along the path.

I resist. "Hang on. Let's go inside."

"I don't know."

"Why not? She might have other stuff." And I can do a recon mission for Gamma. She hadn't mentioned wanting me to, but she sure was curious about Zeena. Getting more info about her is the least I can do for screwing everything up by chanting without her permission. Plus, if I discover some tasty tidbit, maybe Gamma will let me keep the spellbook and teach me magick.

"What, you need more stardust?" She untangles her arm from mine.

"No." I do a fish face at her and stomp inside. The skirt of my dress is so big that I have to angle in diagonally. Four other people are milling about, wandering along the walls, naming out various potions and fiddling with shiny crystals and polished trinkets.

Zeena sits in her chair, holding her plaque of Zodiac signs. Her dark eyes lock onto me instantly. Her smile is all yellow, crooked teeth. "Hello, deary," she croons. Her tone is different from the other day. She must be fully in character.

"Good even, Madame." I curtsy, staying in role.

"Such a pretty flower. A gift from a fine, strapping lad, I gather?" She rocks forward a couple times and stands, clutching the plaque to her chest.

"Yea, 'tis."

"How special, young love. And what sign is he?" The old woman sets her collection on the chair and strokes the frame like a new mother touches the face of her baby.

"Why, praytell, dost thou inquire?"

The other patrons pause in their shopping to listen.

"Ah, 'tis this old witch's fancy, is all."

Mary comes up beside me. "Good even."

Zeena nods her head. "Twins be a gift from the heavens, says I."

A woman giggles. Glad she's enjoying the show.

"Might I interest thee in a palm or tarot reading?" Zeena shuffles to the nearest shelf and collects a deck of cards.

"No thank you." Mary's quick to decline, not bothering to use the olde tyme lingo. She wraps a hand around my wrist and steps toward the door.

I twist out of her grasp. "Wait, sister. Wouldst thou not be curious to hear thy future?"

"Nay." She shakes her head. "'Tis almost time for the joust."

"It will only take but a minute." Zeena drags her side table to the middle of the tiny shoppe. She shuffles the cards and slaps them on the tabletop. "Split the deck."

I reach out with an unsteady hand and pick up half the cards. I set it next to the original pile.

Zeena taps the pile I split with her index finger three times. "Wouldst thou prefer to ask a question?" Her gaze strikes me. Like last time, it's as if she can see through me and into my soul. A flash of yellow glints in her eyes.

I blink and the illusion is gone. Must've imagined it.

"A question about thy love, mayhap?"

My throat's gone dry. I shake my head no.

"Let us try a simple reading then." She flips three cards over, calling out each one as she goes. "The past, the present, the future. Thy past is represented by the Chariot. It means thou must take control of thy emotions, lest they race away from thee. Thy present is represented by the High Priestess. It means thou be in a time of discovery, pondering thy own self. Thou stand on the precipice of change and transformation. The High Priestess acts as a moderator, giving thee the ability to see past the veil of consciousness into the unconscious. She allows thee to recognize the power within. It's already there, waiting, resting, until thee claims it. Thy future is represented by the Wheel of Fortune. It means change be headed thy way. The wheel turns, and so it shall be." She waves a hand over the cards. "Thou hast a powerful and demanding path ahead. Methinks thee be strong enough, but meeting thy destiny will challenge thee."

A heavy silence permeates the room. I scan the shoppe, catching the rapt expressions of the patrons. Tarot readings are mesmerizing, particularly when done by someone as commanding as Zeena. She's got to be more than a simple old woman selling fake magick and jewelry.

Gooseflesh erupts on my arms as a shudder of ice slides down my spine. I'm holding my breath and I exhale slowly.

A trumpet's call echoes in the forest and a collective cry followed by a round of applause sounds in the distance.

The joust is about to begin.

Chapter Eleven

At least a couple hundred people crowd the benches lining a sloped hill facing the arena. Others stand to the sides, clogging up the walking paths, and more people huddle along the forest edge, clinging to the shade. A lot of the patrons wave brightly colored flags, supporting their favorite knights.

The King and Queen are seated on a canopied pavilion at the top of the hill. To the King's right is an honored guest (in this case, it's a faire patron whose name was pulled out of a raffle) and to his left sits the Queen. She's wearing the coronation dress Mom crafted last year. Its deep crimson pops against her pale skin. Ruby lipstick accents the gown. The Queen's ladies-in-waiting crowd around her, serving tea and crumpets. One lady slowly waves a large feather fan in her direction. Standing off to the far right side of the King is the trumpeter. He generally kicks off the joust with a blaring toot and announces the end by repeating the song.

"We missed the King and Queen's introductions," Mary complains.

"We have two weeks to catch it. Besides, it's not like we haven't seen it before."

"I know, but I like to see the Queen's gowns." She flops onto the edge of a bench and I gather my skirt to squeeze between her and a Rubenesque wench. Seriously, her boobs are bigger than most watermelons. And her corset is so tight it turns 'em into torpedoes.

Two groups of riders cluster at either end of the tilt. They're dressed in armor and their horses' barding shows their colors—yellow, green, blue, red, orange, white, purple, and black. An even number of Knights for an even number of jousts. Some horses are docile, standing with their necks extended and relaxed, while others pace impatiently, feeding off the energy around them. The mare from the other day is particularly agitated. She prances in place, tossing her head now and then. Her rider goes with it, letting her blow off some tense energy. The actors shout at one another and call each other names. Laughter and random shouts of "huzzah" bounce around the crowd.

I crane my neck to catch a glimpse of William. He should be with the Blue Knight.

"There he is." Mary points and I follow her finger to the barn's entrance. William jogs out, carrying a bunch of narrow lances in his arms. Shequan is with him. He's dressed in red and black, matching his father's color. While the crest on William's costume is a roaring lion, Shequan's is a fire-breathing dragon.

"Cheer for thy Knight!" A young boy, dressed as a squire in training, waves a rainbow of flags in my face. "Pick your color. Fifty cents!" he shouts.

I flail my arms. "You don't have to yell."

Mary shakes her coin purse. Loose change jingles inside and the boy zeroes in on it. She pulls the mouth open and sticks her fingers inside, drawing out two quarters. "Blue, please."

The mini-squire grins. "Thankee, m'lady!"

Mary hands me the flag and the boy moves down the line, pushing his felt flags on the crowd.

William and Shequan pass around the narrow lances, one for each Knight. The riders cut and parry with them, circling their horses around one another. The play grabs the audience's attention and they hush.

The White Knight trots to the center of the arena, where I'd had my late-night study session the night before. His horse, a giant white Percheron, tosses its head. Two ponies ridden by colorful jesters trot behind him. One is dressed in yellow and red and the other in purple and orange. They flank him on either side and screech, "Huzzah!" while jutting their fists in the air.

The knight makes a big show of frowning at the wannabe jousters. He swings his arm to quiet them down. "Shush," he hisses, loud enough for all of us to hear.

Laughter cascades through the crowd.

The knight clears his throat like a disapproving parent. "Welcome, patrons, to the joust!"

In unison, the ponies extend their left front feet and bend their right front feet. Dipping their noses to the dirt, they bow. The jesters slump forward and tumble over the ponies' heads, landing in a heap. This gets the crowd roaring.

As the jesters dust themselves off and make a spectacle of mounting their short and stocky steeds, the knight gives the crowd a mini history lesson. "Here, you will behold the most popular sport of the Middle Ages."

He gestures for the jesters to demonstrate. They spin their ponies in a circle and split off, yellow-red cantering to the left end of the tilt and purple-orange trotting to the right. They hold their reins high and flop their arms—the exact opposite of how it's supposed to be done, but the comedy of it delights us.

"Jousting calls for the bravest of men—" The jesters "huzzah!" again and the Knight glares at them. "...to race at full gallop toward one another, holding twelve-foot long lances."

A squire gives each jester a fat, black and white striped, three-foot long stick. Yellow-red fumbles his lance, while purple-orange inspects his to make sure it's not warped or cracked.

"The goal is to knock the opponent off their steed." The White Knight gallops his horse to the arena's corner and halts. He spins his horse to face the tilt, extends his arm, and chops the air.

The jesters *whoop!* and charge at one another. Cheers volley through the crowd as yellow-red knocks purple-orange off his pony. Yellow-red takes a victory lap and promptly falls off his ride while coming to a stop.

Addressing the crowd for a final time, the White Knight announces, "The winner takes the spoils and earns a dance with the Queen at the coronation ceremony on the last day of the faire!"

The audience applauds and so do I, caught up in the moment. I don't give a crap about dancing with the Queen, and there's a heck of a lot more to jousting than he said, but nobody wants to hear it. They just want to see the action.

The knights kick off the games by charging from one end of the arena to the other and back. Then they take turns racing down the tilt, trying to catch small rings with their narrow lances. The rings are hung from ten-foot high poles and are spaced fifteen feet apart. Some of the rings are as small as a couple inches across.

When the Blue Knight rides, William does his best to incite the audience. I whip my flag around and scream, grinning more for him than for his Knight. William salutes me and gives me a bow.

I scream even louder when his knight catches all the rings.

The Purple Knight prepares to go next. His squire holds his shield as he tests the weight of his lance.

I elbow Mary. "Oh, my gosh, it's Evan!"

Evan rushes to the fence and shakes a fist in the air while displaying his knight's shield. A white unicorn, rearing up on its hind legs, pops out against the plum background.

Mary grins and waves.

"Go Evan!" I call.

He turns his head in our direction and shouts, "Huzzah!"

Mary and I echo his cry. "Huzzah!"

"I didn't know he was a squire." Mary has to shout in my ear over the cheering of the audience.

"He's so cute!" I holler back.

She futzes with a tangled curl, her gaze fixed on Evan. They're such a perfect match for each other. No magick required. I dip my chin, buckling under the pressure of shame. I'd chanted to make William like me more. Here I am, accusing Mary of avoiding everything when it's actually me who's the coward.

After the ring catch, the knights retreat to their respective corners and pair off for the joust. First, the Yellow and Green Knights face off. The Green Knight's bay gelding rears while the Yellow Knight's Appaloosa paws at the dirt. Each warrior lowers his lance so it's horizontal with the ground.

Their squires rouse the audience into a frenzy of screams and flag waving. A horn player bleats out a tri-toned tune, bringing the crowd down to an expectant silence. It's the pulse and surge, the rise and fall of energy that people thrive on.

"Charge!" The Yellow Knight cries and the pair spur their mounts to a full gallop.

I imagine what it would be like to be in the arena, riding a horse, staring down my opponent. How awesome would it be to ride on the back of such a powerful animal, armed with a lance and shield, swelling with the pride of pre-battle adrenaline?

I close my eyes and the world melts away. Instead of an arena and bustling crowd of faire patrons, I see Castor and Pollux astride a pair of black stallions, manes and tails flowing in the breeze. The twins give each other toothy grins, more for sport than war. In unison, they lower their spears and charge at one another.

The sharp *thwack!* of the Green Knight's lance impacting the Yellow Knight's chest plate catapults me into reality. But the vision is enough to ignite an ancient call. Something surges inside me, tingling along my spine like ghostly fingers. My muscles tense.

The crowd shouts when the Yellow Knight collides with the ground. A plume of dirt rises in his wake and his horse skids to a halt. The Green Knight canters to the end of the tilt, raises his lance, and shouts, "Huzzah!"

"Huzzah!" I shout, shooting to my feet and thrusting my fist in the air.

Mary grabs a fistful of my skirt and tugs. "Sit down." Alarm furrows her brow.

My butt smacks the bench. "What?"

"We've seen the joust a hundred times. What's got you so worked up?"

"This is way more exciting than seeing the Queen's gown, don't you think?" I slide my fingers across the edge of my flag and twirl it. "Castor and Pollux would enjoy this."

"Huh?" She tips her head to the side.

A gust of wind taunts the trees and a wall of charcoal clouds advances across the sky. Lightning flickers between the puffy ridges. Half a second later, a peal of thunder rips the air.

The Blue Knight's horse whinnies and rears. The mare twists, knocking William over. He rolls out of the way, narrowly escaping her hooves.

She rears again, despite her rider's yanking at the reins.

"William!" I leap to my feet and run to the arena. He'll get stomped to death if he doesn't move. The folds of my skirt slow me down. I hike the fabric up around my knees.

Shequan dives around the animal, tackles William, and rolls both of them away from the horses. They land a few feet from the fence.

I drop to my knees and stretch my arm through the rungs, but I can't reach them. "Are you okay?"

William plunks his head on the ground and exhales. "Thanks to Shequan."

Shequan hops to his feet and extends a hand to William. "No biggie, man."

William claps Shequan's hand and grunts as he rises. Dirt cakes their costumes and dusts their hair.

Lightning cracks the sky, powering yet another drum of thunder. Fat water pellets smack my head. One, two, a thousand drop on us in an instant. Rain falls so densely it creates solid sheets.

The Knight dismounts and drives the mare toward the barn. The rest of the troupe does the same.

It doesn't take the crowd long to figure out the show is over. They disperse to nearby shoppes and tents. Doesn't matter. Everybody is soaked anyway. Storms can crop up fast, but this is ridiculous.

William stares down at me. Water streams over his hair and down his face, but he doesn't seem to notice or mind. Right here, in this moment, all his focus is on me. And I don't mind one bit. He curls his fingers around the fence rung between us. His dimples make an appearance.

"That was really scary." I lay a hand over his. Our skin is slippery.

"That mare tends to spook." He flips his hand over to lace his fingers with mine.

I shiver, not from the cold rain, but from his searing touch.

"Anne! Our dresses!" Mary slops to me. Her hair is plastered to her head and her lime-green dress appears several shades darker.

Crap. Mom is going to murder us. So much for a romantic moment in the rain.

"I have to help with the horses. I'll see you later?" William drops his hand from mine. He shakes his hair out and runs to the barn, stepping in the puddles as he goes.

Mary grips my arm. "We have to get inside."

I nod, half-dazed.

We leave the fence and step onto the path, but there are too many puddles, so we shift to the grass. At the end of the street, a hunched figure in a hooded cloak darts in front of us.

"Hello, girls." Zeena lifts the edge of her hood. The old woman blinks and I swear her pupils are vertical slits before they round back out.

I swallow a yelp.

Mary and I retreat.

The woman follows. "You've invoked them, haven't you?"

"Invoked who?" I counter.

"The Gemini twins, Castor and Pollux," she hisses.

Thunder rattles my eardrums. The ground vibrates.

"You don't know what you've done." The old woman lunges and clamps her sinewy fingers around my wrist. Her grip is stronger than I expect. "Playing with such power is dangerous for an untrained witch. But I could teach you."

A tugging sensation draws me closer to her. It presses against my chest and squeezes my lungs. I struggle to suck in air. Pulling away, I cry, "Let me go!"

Mary swats Zeena's arm away. We dash toward the main path, fleeing the old woman's blood-curdling cackle. Lightning flashes like a strobe light.

"Let's get to Dad's smithy!" I wheeze, glancing over my shoulder to check if Zeena is following. I slip in the mud, landing on my knees and grinding more mud into Mom's dress. Mary catches me so I don't faceplant.

By the time we reach Dad's building, we're chilled through, covered in muck, and sobbing.

Dad rushes out of the back room. "What in the…Girls? What're you doing here? You're soaked! Mom's dresses."

I sit on the wood floor while Mary rests her hands on her knees. We're both panting. I'd say, "Thanks, Captain Obvious," but there's no way my mouth can manage words.

I paw around my coin purse and my fingers latch onto my inhaler. Dark spots crowd at the edge of my vision. My chest burns and body shakes. I need to stop this asthma attack.

Dad rushes over to me. "Anne, take slow, deep breaths, honey. Imagine the air going into your lungs. You can do it."

I nod, opening and closing my mouth like a guppy. My insides twist and tumble, rubbing raw from friction. It's hard to hear Mary and Dad over the pounding of my heart and the rain beating on the tin roof.

"Get her some warm water," Dad barks. He rubs my back as if that'll make my lungs more efficient.

Mary scurries to the other room. She reappears with a bottle of water in seconds. She holds it to my mouth, but her hands shake so badly that she spills water down my chin.

"I'm okay," I manage to squeak out the words.

"Freak storm, eh? Triggered an attack?" Dad leans back on his heels, still pressing a hand on my shoulder.

Mary caps the water bottle. "Um, we, uh…" She looks at me, eyes round.

My tongue feels like stone. I open my mouth to say, "An old lady attacked us," but my lips won't form the words. My voice box won't produce sound. And it's not because of asthma. I literally can't say anything.

Mary claps a hand over her mouth. Is she mute too? Holy crap.

Chapter
Twelve

"Your mom's dresses are ruined. She's going to be furious." Dad's patience disappears into the frown lines fracturing his face. Apparently, my inability to breathe doesn't worry him, but whatever we did to Mom's dresses does. Negotiating with a dragon is impossible, after all, and trying it will leave you a charred mess.

"Sorry, Dad. We...we got caught in the rain and Anne's asthma flared when we ran." Mary twists the water bottle in her hands. The plastic crinkles and pops.

Wait. She can talk?

Mary looks at me wide-eyed. I shake my head. What's going on?

Dad stands. "Good luck telling your mom that, though."

Oh sure, leave it to us to tell her. Thanks, Dad. I suck on my inhaler. "The s-storm came out of n-nowhere. It's not our fault. We were at the joust, handing out cards—doing our *job*. We can't control the weather, for cripes sakes."

Mary shakes her head.

Dad heads to the counter and I glare at her. "What?"

"The weather does weird things whenever you mention…" her eyes dart from left to right. "The *twins*," she whispers.

Outside, streaks of sun slip through the clouds, highlighting the rain so it shimmers like glass beads. Murky puddles dot the dirt path and slick the stairs.

I match her hushed tones. "It was just a storm. They're called pop-ups for a reason." I tug at the sleeves of my dress, suffocating from the humidity, the weight of the soaking fabric, and from the crazy idea that I have, in fact, caused this weirdness. It's becoming harder to ignore Zeena's accusations.

Mary huffs. "You either believe this stuff or not. You can't keep changing things to fit your argument."

"I'm not changing things."

"Yes, you are. One minute, you say it's real, and the next you back off and say it's just a storm."

"I don't know what you're talking about."

Her lips thin.

Dad picks up a yellow legal pad and scribbles something on the page. "Maybe there's a rainbow somewhere. That'd be a pretty picture, Mary. Your mom would like it."

Mary nods, but looks at me with a you've-got-to-be-kidding-me expression.

"Dad," I start.

"Feeling better, Anne?" He circles around the counter and lays out some pieces of metal.

"There's this old wo…wo…" Again, my tongue folds in on itself. I look to Mary for help. Why can't I tell him about Zeena?

She shakes her head as if to say, "don't bother trying."

Dad scratches his head and points his carpenter's pencil at each piece, counting. "Something's missing," he mutters.

I ease off the floor and stumble to the wall. Lack of oxygen always makes me dizzy. At least there's a handy shelf here to steady me.

Mary gloms onto me, but it's way too hot and sticky. I wave her away. She sighs, but gives me space.

"If you girls want to be helpful, you'll grab some tools I need from home." He reaches into a box on the counter, pulls out a notepad and pen, and scribbles a list of items. He hands it to Mary. "Don't take too long, okay?"

"Sure." Mary folds the paper and stuffs it in her coin purse. I hope to heck she knows what he wants, because I can't identify a wrench from a ratchet. Fine, so I'm exaggerating, but Mary's the detail person and has a ridiculous memory.

Dad heads into the back room where he keeps other tools and supplies, leaving us to carry out his mission.

"Something stopped me from telling Dad about the old crone. Not that he was listening anyway." Caught up in his own smoke-filled, smithy world, he's so freaking clueless that he has no idea what we're going through. I press my hands against my cheeks as if manipulating the muscles will free my mouth.

"Yeah, me too. Totally bizarre." Her eyes dart back and forth. "What happened?"

"I don't know." I fiddle with my inhaler. My body tingles, jonesing for a hit I don't need. Too much albuterol jacks me up like a kite with a jetpack. "Maybe Zeena jinxed us."

Mary's eyes narrow. "Or it could be our chant."

"How? Our chant had nothing to do with her and she doesn't have anything to do with our birthday party. We should be able to talk about her, unless she's done something."

"Listen to us, talking like this magick stuff is real." She fluffs her hair, spraying me with water.

"Hey, watch it." I wipe droplets from my face. "Magick *is* real, you know."

Mary smirks.

"Zeena's real. You can't deny that. Didn't you see her eyes? They were totally weird."

Thunder rumbles overhead at the mention of her name. I want to yell at the sky and tell it to just stop it already.

"She's old. All old people have strange eyes." She falls into practicality.

"*Vertical* slits for pupils are different from *old people eyes*," I counter.

She puts up a hand. "Just stop it, Anne. That woman was creepy, but it's the Renaissance Faire. She was in character. She probably wears contacts or something."

"Now who's changing her story?"

"Oh, none of this makes sense." Mary cups her palms on either side of her face and runs them over her hair. With Mary, it's all logic and reason, order and science. Magick is the opposite. It's more fluid, circular instead of linear, misty instead of solid, and volatile.

"Back to the question at hand. Why can't we talk about Zeena?" Another blast of thunder breaks.

Mary shivers. "Stop saying her name."

"Good thought." I nod. "Maybe we were misinterpreted. We asked for magick and for it to be kept secret…"

"We? This was *your* idea, remember?" She stomps her foot.

"But you said the spell with me. We couldn't have invoked the Gemini twins otherwise." I say it like I'm an expert on magick spells. Then again, there was that little chant with the stardust. But that was for William.

"So, she was right. We *have* invoked Castor and Pollux." Lighting flashes. She cringes.

Guess I need to accept the evidence as much as she does. No more explaining things away. No more flipping back and forth between rationalizations. I gulp down the cold, hard pill of truth. "There's your evidence for you."

"Lightning?"

"Yep." I drag my fingers through my matting hair. It's like I've superglued thick layers of felt to my head. Acceptance is the final stage. Maybe we can move forward from here.

She nods, wringing a hand around her wrist. Her lids droop shut. "Anne, what have we done? Chanting, invoking the twins, talking with Zee—" She catches herself before the whole name spills out. "Oh, what are we going to do? Especially since we can't talk to anyone about it."

This is such a crap way for her to believe in magick again. And it's all my fault. Had I listened to Gamma, we could've done this the right way. "We should tell Gamma. I already mentioned Z to her…"

What I should do is keep my mouth shut. I had wanted to get more information about her for Gamma, but how would she react to this news? An old witch giving me real stardust is one thing, but the witch coming after us because I invoked the Gemini twins is another.

"You did?" She sniffs and wipes her nose with a sleeve.

"Y-yeah, without any problems." I extend a hand, brain whirring. I need an alternate plan ASAP, but it's not like there's a ton of people around who'd listen to me prattle on about magick. "It'll be okay. She'll help us."

Mary ekes out a tentative smile. "Okay."

"Girls? What are you yapping about? Can't you talk on the way? Storm's over, you know." Dad calls to us from the back room.

"Sorry, Dad. We're leaving," I reply.

"Why don't we stop by the arena on the way? We could check on William." Mary tries—and fails—to twirl her hair back into ordered curls.

William. Her idea is an irresistible peace offering. I bet she's hoping to catch a glimpse of Evan again, but I can't blame her.

I pat my head and find a million lumps and bumps. My hard-earned straight hair is gone. Messy, freaky, glommed-up hair has taken over. Fantastic. "No, we don't have to."

Mary purses her lips. "You're worried about your hair? It looks…"

"Awful, I'm sure." I keep smoothing the frizzy curls with my fingers. As if that'll make it better.

"No, it's just wet, that's all. It'll dry."

"Yeah, and it'll look like Aunt Meredith's wig. The thing has more knots than a string of Christmas lights." I groan.

A knocking comes from the doorway. It's William.

"I figured you guys would come here." He runs his hand through his dark hair. A random strand breaks loose and flops in his face, blocking one of his turquoise eyes. His boots clomp on the wooden floor as he walks inside. He smells like rain, sweat, and mud. My knees wobble.

"Are the horses okay?" I want to simultaneously leap into his arms and dive under the counter. The self-conscious monster—SCM—crowds my brain, taunting me. I shouldn't listen. William and I have known each other for *so* long. He's seen me without makeup, he's seen me in my pajamas; heck, he's even seen me after three days of not showering during a camping trip. Why do I care if my hair is a level-three disaster?

"They're fine. Made for an exciting show, though, didn't it?" His smile would normally ease the raging battle between Operation Fuzzy Confusion and Mission Sharp Excitement, but his eyes keep darting to my hair and right now, OFC is winning.

Mary chimes in. "I didn't know Evan was a squire."

"He's trying it out." William adjusts his sword and rests his hand on the hilt.

"Yeah, and I didn't know Shequan was a ninja." I laugh like a hyena.

Mary raises her eyebrows.

Blushing now would turn the awkward moment into a mortifying one. The thought instantly brings heat to my face.

"I totally owe him one." William rolls back and forth on his heels. "You were talking about wigs?"

"Oh, no, not really." Mary clears her throat. "So what're you guys doing tonight?" She gracefully carries the conversation, which makes me blush even more. I'm a total doof. A doof with bad hair.

"The equipment will need cleaning now that it got soaked." He spins the silver Celtic knot ring on his right ring finger. I gave it to him for his birthday last October, to cheer him up because his parents had forgotten to get him a gift. Workaholics through and through, they couldn't be bothered with celebrating things like birthdays. I know the feeling. The fact that he's wearing it has to count for something, right? Mission Sharp Excitement takes the advantage and slips ahead of Operation Fuzzy Confusion.

"Sounds like a lot of work." I smile like a buffoon. Duh, of course it'll take a long time. Ugh. Oh, and the more he keeps glancing at my wonky hair, the more I want to run away. OFC retaliates by launching another assault.

"We all pitch in. Shouldn't take too long." He scratches his temple.

Mary clears her throat. "We have to get some tools for Dad. You want to come with us?" She nods at me, while tilting her head in his direction.

"Sure. I just need to tell Marcus on the way. I don't want him to think I ditched."

"Of course." I lead the way, forcing myself not to keep both hands firmly planted on top of my head.

Mary pulls me aside while William talks to Marcus. "What's the matter with you? It's like you can't act normal or something."

"I'm okay." I'm so *not* okay.

"William keeps giving you strange looks."

"Oh, thanks, that helps." I pull the elastic out of my hair and bend over to shake out my damp locks. Throwing my head back creates a pleasant head rush. "There. Better?"

Mary snickers. "You're still worried about your hair? Is that the problem?"

"I suppose you wouldn't do the same if you saw Evan?" I retort.

She smirks but glances around anyway. "I thought you said William was just a friend."

"He is." But he's more than that. He's my best friend. He's sweet, smart, cuter than cute, and always there for me, ready to help whenever I need something. He's my Knight, as corny as it sounds.

I blink, struck by the inspiration-tipped Arrow of Duh. If we tell him about Zeena, he can help us figure her out. Then we won't have to tell Gamma and she won't have to get mad at me all over again. Win-win. "Shhh. Here he comes. We need—"

"Your hair is fine." She fusses with a couple strands.

"I don't care about that."

Her expression—a mix of, "yeah, right" and "what are you plotting now?"—wallops me.

"Okay, I do care about that, but what I'm trying to say is we should try to find a way to tell him what happened without telling him what happened."

"Oh, Anne, come on. What will bringing William into this accomplish? He doesn't know anything about magick."

"He'll understand."

She spins on her heels and presses her back against the fence. "Is that so?"

"Okay, maybe he won't, but he's the least likely to think we're crazy."

"You said Grandmother—"

William jogs up to us. "Ready?"

Mary shoves off the fence. "Let's go. We're just getting tools, right, Anne?" She gives me a toothy grin.

"Sure."

"And that's all."

I give her a non-committal, "Um-hmm," and she groans, walking ahead of us with her hands fisted.

William falls into step next to me while Mary leads the way. "You guys fighting?"

"What's new?" I shrug.

"Your hair looks nice curly."

"Thanks." I tuck a strand behind my ear. Operation Fuzzy Confusion can suck it. "We met a new merchant today." I change the subject and ignore Mary, who circles back to walk with us. She immediately starts gnawing on a fingernail.

"Oh, yeah? Who?"

"Ze, Zee, Ze…" A *zuzzy* sound comes out of my mouth when I try to say Zeena's name.

William leans in as we walk. "Who?"

"Er, a…collector." I almost whoop, "Huzzah!" at the success.

"What do they collect?" He kicks a stone from his path. It splashes into a puddle.

"Z-z-z…z-o," I cough and stumble over my own feet.

"Zoo? I don't get it."

"No, she collects z-z-z." I point at Mary, then me.

"Twins?" He frowns.

I'm running out of ideas. "You know the symbols in astrology. There are twelve of them?"

"What is this, twenty questions?"

"Just guess," I snap.

He clears his throat. "You mean the zodiac?"

"Yes!"

William flinches. "Are you okay?"

"No, she isn't." Mary rolls her eyes.

William scratches his neck and sucks in his cheeks.

"Never mind." I drop the subject and we fall into silence. None of us speak until we finish gathering all the items on Dad's list. His workshop is so cluttered and full of spare wrought iron, broken metal pieces to be repaired, rusted tools, and works-in-progress that it takes us a long time to locate everything. Good thing William came with us because he identifies the things Mary and I don't know.

"Looks like we got everything. Finally." Mary folds the list and puts it in the toolbox we're using to carry Dad's tools.

"I'm not heading back until I get into some dry clothes," I groan. And maybe a hat, though at the rate my hair is expanding from frizz, I'd need a garbage bag to cover it all.

"First good idea you've had all day," Mary digs.

"I'll wait for you guys on the porch." William keeps his distance as Mary and I storm into the house.

Mom's waiting for us at the base of the stairs. Her arms are folded across her chest and her tongue is pushing out her cheek. She nods the nod of the all-knowing. "I knew I couldn't trust you two." She eclipses the distance between us in two strides and drops to her knees, clutching at our skirts. "Just look at these gowns! They're ruined!"

My insides go all fluttery, like every organ wants to liquefy and pool into my feet.

Mary whimpers.

"The storm…it came up so fast." I try to explain, but my voice barely makes it past my lips.

"How am I supposed to advertise now?" she wails.

"You could rent a shoppe at the faire instead of letting other vendors sell your dresses on consignment. That way, people can watch you work and you'd have all the advertising you could want."

Mom wipes her runny nose with her arm and does a backward crab-walk to the stairs. She stuffs her hand in her pocket, digging for her trusty cigarettes and lighter. Her hands shake as she dips the cigarette to the flame. After a long drag, she says, "Doesn't matter anyway. I don't want your help, if this is what your help is." She stands and exhales smoke in my face. My lungs instantly seize. "Get out of my sight."

Mary tugs me toward the stairs. Mom retreats to her workroom and slams the door.

I'm out of breath by the time we reach our room. I flop on the bed, sopping dress and all, and take yet another hit of my inhaler.

"She's heinous." Mary twists and yanks at the dress, peeling it off inch by inch. The dogs huddle around her feet, sniffing at the fabric.

"Beyond heinous." I close my eyes and force the smoke out of my lungs, repeating the mantra, "Good air in, bad air out," in my head.

Petal-soft fingers flitter over my forehead. "Come on. I'll help you get out of your dress."

I open my eyes. Mary's dressed in a puffy-sleeved pirate's shirt with black leggings. A wide belt cinches her tiny waist and her coin purse dangles from her hip. Instead of a parrot, a beaked creature with feathered wings, a raccoon tail, and dragon's claws adorns her shoulder. Its cerulean-blue wings pop against its black body and bright blue eyes shine with intelligence. She's strung the wire that controls his mechanics down her shirtsleeve and has the button palmed. "You're bringing Julius. Cute."

"You should wear your pirate costume. I'm sure Maximus would like to go for a walk."

I glance at the top of my bookshelf where Max hangs out most of the time. His cream-colored body matches his flexible wings. Lime-green eyes frame his white beak. A fluffy spray of pale gray hair frames his face, and the same color fur covers the rest of his body.

"Borrow my hat if you want to cover your hair, even though it looks *fine*."

Fifteen minutes later, Mary and I creep downstairs. We tug on our knee-high boots outside. Neither of us says anything to William about Mom's screaming and he doesn't ask. He doesn't have to.

"Thanks for waiting," I say.

"Sure thing. About that Zodiac stuff…" His eyes sparkle with curiosity. He takes the toolbox from me—after greeting Max and Julius; they are creatures that thrive on etiquette and refuse to be ignored—and swings it casually as we walk to the faire grounds.

I cringe, waiting for a clap of thunder, but nothing happens.

Mary looks at the sky and hugs herself.

"Do you know there are new vendors in the woods?" I ask, hoping a hybrid of charades and twenty questions will go better this time.

"Yeah. Why?"

"Let's find…the…shoppe." If we can talk to her, tell her we're not interested in doing magick anymore, maybe she'll leave us alone. Should've thought of that sooner.

Mary stops. We're only a few feet away from the main gate. "Are you crazy?"

William's gaze slides from Mary to me.

"We can't go back there."

"We need to find out what's going on." I dig my fists into my hips.

"Uh, no we don't. We need to stay as far away from… you know who as much as we can." Her eyes bulge. To bring the point home, she manipulates Julius's mechanics and turns his head side to side.

"That won't make her go away," I counter, pressing the button on Max's control so his head goes up and down.

"What are you guys talking about?" William asks.

"Nothing," we reply in unison.

"Right." He walks in front of us, shaking his head. The guard doesn't check our passes.

A dark cloud hovers over the smithy. Mary tugs on my sleeve and points. "Anne."

"I see it."

William looks at us out of the corner of his eyes. "I don't know what's going on, but you guys are acting weird."

"I'm sorry, William. I want to tell you, but I'm having trouble finding the right words." Understatement of the Sixteenth Century.

"Oh my God." Mary stops short again, this time on the smithy steps.

I follow her gaze.

Zeena. She's standing next to Dad. They're both leaning on the counter, chatting. Why isn't he freaking out? She has vertical pupils. No one else on the planet has vertical pupils. It's a strictly animal trait, which means Zeena is not entirely human.

Dad nods. He's grinning weirdly and his eyes have a vacant look, like he's not really seeing anything. My heart squirms in my chest. "Yeah, the whole family is into it. I'm the blacksmith, my wife makes costumes and gowns, and my daughters Anne and Mary—they're twins—they just love to dress up."

"Oh, how lovely." The woman's fake sing-song voice grates on my ears.

Dad nods. His gaze shifts to us. "Hello, girls. William."

"Hi, Mr. Devans." William waves, then flips his hair out of his face. I melt, but only for a sec. I can't let him distract me from Zeena.

I take the toolbox from William and stare the old woman down as I stalk across the room. She's not the only one who can play scary. "We got what you asked for, Dad."

Dad checks the toolbox. After a moment, he slaps the lid shut and says, "Excellent. Well, I'm going to get back to work. Nice talking to you." He smiles at Zeena, then nods to us. "I'll be late for dinner, girls. Make sure your mom eats something." He disappears into the back room, leaving us with the collector.

Mary and William flank me. We create a wall of solidarity and I feed off the vibes. "You shouldn't be here."

The woman smiles at me, exposing her crooked and yellowed teeth. I step back, and our line of strength snaps. Brittle pieces litter the floor at our feet. My power wanes.

Zeena crowds closer. Her bad breath is as deadly as her words. "Be careful, Anne. Castor and Pollux don't like to be toyed with. They are jealous, especially of friendships with outsiders. They will turn against you, quite unexpectedly and for little reason." Her reptilian stare slips to William. "What a handsome boy."

He clears his throat. "Um, hi."

That's it. I won't give her the chance to talk to William like she talked to Dad. I fold my arms, as if that'll stop my heart from pounding straight through my rib cage and out of my chest, the flipping coward that it is. "I don't know what you're talking about."

"That's right. You don't." She sidesteps me to approach William. She presses a bony hand to his face and whispers something in another language. His face contorts with confusion, then goes blank. "Libra. How nice. Very balanced."

"Are you done?" I slip back in between William and Zeena. Hopefully, my weak knees won't buckle.

"Anne," Mary warns.

The woman glances at her, then grins at me. "She's the steadier one, isn't she? And you're the fireball. Prone to anger like your mother."

"You don't know—"

"Oh, but I *do* know. The stars tell me everything. You're too bold to understand that I've already won, and it's only a matter of time."

"Won what?" My brow furrows.

"Exactly." She retreats on her own, but her laughter lingers, just like her musty smell.

Mary lets out a breath. I lean against the counter, gasping for air in the vacuum Zeena left behind.

William blinks several times, then looks around the room like he's seeing it for the first time. "What's going on? Why were you so rude to that old lady?"

"Rude? No, she…" I gurgle, stuck on the explanation. Zeena's muting spell is as potent as ever. "I can't do this. We have to change the…you know." I throw my hand out and wiggle my fingers.

Mary nods. "I know. Otherwise…"

"Wow, you guys are making no sense. I'm gonna go. When you figure out what you want to tell me, let me know." William rolls his eyes and leaves.

"Wait." What the heck? He rushes away so fast that I have to jog to catch up to him. "William."

He spins on me. A different version of William stands before me. The lines of his face are hard and his eyes stony. He's never looked at me this way before, not even when we're mad at each other. "What is it, Anne? You act like you can't talk, you keep doing sign language with Mary. If you don't want me around, why don't you just tell me?"

"What are you talking about? We want you around. *I* want you around. It's just we…can't tell you. We—"

"Never mind. It's a sister thing. I understand. The old woman said you'd keep secrets from me."

An avalanche of subzero shock smothers me. My heart shivers from the cold. "What? When did she say that?"

"Don't act like you don't know." He sprints away.

"William!" My chest tightens, but it's not from an asthma attack. It's from the jabs of pain from William's accusation.

That old witch must've enchanted him or something. I press a shaky hand to my lips. Zeena is more powerful than I could've imagined. All it took was a few seconds, a couple words, and my friendship with William is broken, tearing further apart with every step away he takes. Tears burn at my eyes, melting my soul and sparking a chain reaction of fury and hurt. I'm not losing my best friend because of some old woman. It's time to chat with Castor and Pollux— the twins, not the dogs.

Chapter Thirteen

Mary watches me set a candle in each of the four corners. She sits on her bed and eyes her closet like it's begging her to reorganize it again. "Can you at least put away all the stuff that might fly around? I don't want to get a pencil lodged in my forehead. And let Castor and Pollux out."

Thunder crashes from above.

"Really?" I glare at the ceiling, then pour some stardust on a small plate and set it in the middle of the room. Sitting on the floor, I flip through the pages of my spellbook and search for a modification spell. Not returning it is another promise to Gamma I'm breaking. This one is for a good reason, though. I want to fix all this stuff before Gamma finds out about it. Otherwise, I'll probably never have another chance to learn magicks from her.

"We might have to change the dogs' names." Mary bites her fingernail. "I don't know about this, Anne. What if we make it worse? Didn't Gamma say to bring the book back to her?"

"For goodness sake. An old witch is after us, our parents are lunatics, and William is mad at me. How much worse can it get?"

"Never ask that question." Mary collects the knickknacks from her bedside table and shoves them in a drawer. Then she carefully places Julius and Maximus in the trunk at the end of her bed. "Come on, pups, out." She ushers the dogs out of the room. They immediately start scratching at our door.

"Stop it, Cas and Pol!" I holler. No thunder. Guess the Gemini twins don't respond to nicknames. Good. The scratching stops but whining ensues. I pull out my notebook to jot down some verses.

"Why don't you apologize to him? You did act pretty weird." She stuffs loose papers into the desk.

"I think the old woman warped his mind somehow." I crumple the paper I scribbled on and start over.

"I wish Grandmother never gave you that book." She kneels on the floor, directly across from me.

"I know you hate this stuff. But you don't have to rub it in."

"I'm not rubbing it in. Gawd, you can be so sensitive sometimes." She pulls her hair into a ponytail.

"Whatever." I impale the page with my pen. My mind is a wasteland, frigid and stark like the Arctic Circle. Sheets of white ice cover my brain, suffocating the brave seedlings of ideas. A moan trickles across the barren landscape. I know nothing about magick and I really think I can go up against a master at it?

"So we're going to do a reversal spell, right? Make everything the way it was?"

"Something like that." Her idea jostles the glacier coating my neurons. I jot down anything and everything that seeps through the cracks, then review what I wrote. It's junk. I rip out the page and toss it.

"What're you doing?" She crawls around the room, picking up the trash and loose balls of paper.

I huff and open the spellbook again. "Reversal spells are complicated. Involve warping time and erasing peoples' memories."

She leans forward. "Wait. What?"

"At least, that's what I read in the book."

"We're not going to travel in time, are we?" She picks up a leftover shard of Castor's bone and pokes at the pad of her thumb.

"No." I can't get a simple secret spell to work, let alone pull off distorting the time-space continuum.

"Ouch!" She drops the bone fragment and squeezes her thumb. A drop of blood plunks on the stardust. "Jabbed myself."

"Better wash it."

Nodding, she paws through her drawer for hand sanitizer and a Band-Aid. The bottle is half-empty and she's only had it a week. She flips open the lid, drops a dollop the size of Texas into her palm, and sticks her thumb in the goop. Her face scrunches and she sucks air through her teeth. "Then how do we fix it?"

I run my fingers along the edge of the pages. "Forget the reversal spell. The best way to solve the problem is to ask the Gemini twins permission to speak freely and for protection from Z."

Wind howls outside and presses on the window. The house creaks and stutters in reply.

"Don't say her name." Her green eyes flicker with fear.

"There's one problem. If Z is doing her own chanting, we might be fighting to use the same power. She's the Zodiac Collector, after all. Why else would she be so mad at us for invoking the twins?"

"But we control our sign, right?" She pries open the Band-Aid. After wrapping the bandage around her bleeding finger, she drops to her butt.

"Yeah, but she's gathering all the signs' powers. We're blocking her from completing her collection." The words tumble out of my mouth, caught on their own cascade of interlocking chain links. As individual pieces, they were weak and brittle, but together, they wedge us in a predicament somewhere between dire and futile.

She moans and drops her face into her hands. "This isn't supposed to be happening. We're supposed to be studying for SAT, wandering the faire…"

"Flirting with Evan?"

She lifts her head. "You're one to talk. All you can do is make googly eyes with William these days."

I slump. "And he's mad at me right now. It's her fault. We should chant for her to disappear."

"Can we do that?"

"I don't know."

"Grandmother would. Why don't you want to tell her?"

Confession time. "Gamma wants me to return the book."

"Are you serious?" She's on her feet and pacing the room in a flash. Her hair bounces with every step, highlighting her agitation. "Why couldn't you listen to her? Why do you always have to go and do everything on your own?"

"I know. I'm sorry. This is all my fault."

She halts in front of me.

I stare up at her, twisting my eyebrows in a forgive-me pose.

She hooks her thumbs through the belt loops and kneels. "We're in this together. We'll figure it out. It's not our fault some old lady is totally crazy."

"I don't deserve a sister like you."

"I wish you'd remember that more often."

I stick out my pinky finger and she hooks hers with mine. "I need you."

"Ditto. Even if you are a witch."

"Gee, thanks."

We giggle. The lights flicker.

"All right. Let's do this." Striking a match, I light the candles as before, calling out the directions and the elements.

"What about the chant?" Mary asks.

"Just close your eyes and concentrate. Let me do the talking."

I hold out my hands, palms up, and Mary holds her palms down, hovering above mine. The same steadiness that linked us when we stood in a line confronting Zeena courses through me. My skin tingles like a million ants are scurrying along invisible tracks along my hands, arms, and up to my chest. I chant:

"Castor and Pollux,
Masters of Gemini,
Hear our plea.
Change the magick you've done,
Set our minds and mouths free.
Castor and Pollux,
Masters of Gemini,
Hear our plea,
Keep us strong and safe from our enemy.
Castor and Pollux,
Masters of Gemini,
Hear our plea,
Keep Zeena far from our friends and family!"

"There. All done." I let go of Mary's hands and blow out the candles.

Everything goes dark. Like locked in a coffin kind of dark. The only sounds are my whooshing pulse and my stringy breath. I gasp, sucking on an empty void. My throat burns, thirsting for the cool, blast of refreshing air that doesn't come.

"What is that?" Mary's scream rips into the anti-matter stuffing our room. The anti-matter explodes with a screech. The flutter of a thousand bat wings shudders above us. My hair whips around me, clamps over my face, and tries to suffocate me.

I dive for my bed and wiggle under the covers, scraping sticky strands from my mouth.

The dogs bark and scratch at the door. The hinges whine. A deep moan shifts the ceiling. Tiny beaks pick at me through the blankets.

"Anne, make it stop!" She yanks the covers up and dives under with me. We pant in each other's faces.

"I don't know how."

"Can't you tell the twins?"

"Maybe."

"Try it!" Her breath is hot and heavy with terror.

"Castor and Pollux, please stop!"

The magick pummels us with one last round of pecks and halts. Soft light glows through the blanket, and while breathing underneath it reminds me of sucking on a blow dryer, at least I'm getting air into my lungs.

"Anne. What did we do?"

"The chant. It must've worked." I hook an arm around her waist. "Castor and Pollux heard us."

Shrill laughter scrapes along the walls.

"Not again," Mary groans.

I toss off the covers. "Why are you trying to scare us?"

The laughter cuts off. A lightning strike flashes and fractures off in too many directions to count. Mini-bolts shoot into the room, through the window, and divide off into four lines, igniting the candles I'd blown out minutes ago. Orbs of yellow light hover over the wicks. It's not the yellow of ordinary fire. This is brighter. Purer.

I creep toward a candle like a member of the Scooby gang sneaking up on the masked villain, one agonizing step at a time. Mary tries to pull me away, but I slither from her grasp and reach out to touch the ball of light. My fingers graze the edge of it and it bursts into a firework. Sparks envelop my hand, but they don't burn. My skin absorbs the bits of light energy and begins to glow.

"So cool," I whisper and bring my hand closer to my face.

"So freaky," Mary replies.

I spin around her and touch the next candle with my other hand. The orb bursts like the one before. Now both hands are glowing yellow. I leap to the third candle. Light streaks up my arms, in a jagged pattern, like lightning is traveling along my flesh.

"What is it?" Mary stares at my transformed limbs, eyes wide.

"I don't know, but it's awesome. Wanna touch it?" I extend my hands.

"No way." She leaps on her bed and cowers at the headboard.

The only light in the room comes from my skin and the plate of stardust at our feet. I bend over to pick it up.

"I wonder..."

"W-wonder what?"

"Gamma told us two very important rules. We have to be united for the magick to work better." I extend one glowing finger. "And we have to give a worthy sacrifice. What is more precious to warriors than blood?" I extend another.

"Huh?"

"Cas—"

She glares at me.

"The twins were warriors, Mary. When your blood mixed with the stardust, it must have upped the ante. I bet the twins accepted it as a true sacrifice. That's why they blessed us with this energy." I fist my hands. A warm buzzing charges my nerve endings. My whole body is electrified. Powerful. "I bet the chant to get rid of Z will work if we try again."

"What are you betting on?"

I wiggle my fingers. "This."

She eyes me warily and glances outside. "Does this make you a superhero or something? And you get your power from the weather?"

I peer outside. It's so dark I can't even see the tree in our yard. There's no moon, no stars, no light anywhere. It's like the world is gone. "It's not the weather. It's our Zodiac sign."

She shakes her head and drags a pillow under her chin. "What does this have to do with stars? Aren't they condensed balls of fusion floating in space a gazillion miles away?"

"The signs aren't only connected to the stars. They also govern the elements, and planets, and other stuff."

"And other stuff." She repeats me, doubt seeping into her tone.

"Yeah."

"Why don't they just appear? Why can't we see them?"

"Maybe they're ethereal beings."

"That's a lot of maybes."

"And *maybe* they're everywhere, able to cross the entire universe in a blink. It *is* magick, after all."

She sighs in surrender. "So, what do we do now?"

"What do you mean? We find Z." I return the candles to their designated place on my side of the bookshelf. The glow is already fading, but the energy remains.

"Are you crazy? We can't confront her."

"Why not? I've got the twins' power. I can do anything." I set my spellbook next to the row of candles. It's too late to return it now. I figured out how to do the magick.

"You're not serious."

"I'm very serious." I slip my feet into my red and white polka-dot rain boots and stuff my hair into a baseball cap.

"You *can't*." Shards of anxiety pulse off her and bounce against my flesh in a high-pitched ping.

"I need you to be strong or we'll never beat her."

"That's not fair." Her face crumbles into despair. The energy fueling me pools around my feet and seeps toward her.

I retreat to the door. Tiny cracks splinter across the invisible armor surrounding me, and more energy leaks out. We have to go while I've still got Gemini power. Before I lose Mary's support. Before our bond breaks. Frustration burns in my stomach and I clench my fists. "Are you coming with me or not?"

"Anne, please."

"I'm going, with or without you. You don't want me to face Z alone, do you?" I affix my Gemini pin to my collar for good luck.

Her lips thin. She shoves her feet into her galoshes and grabs a flashlight.

We pass the faire gate in ten minutes. I'm soaring on the raw power that is encasing me in a force field of invincibility. Arcs of yellow lick at the grass, trees, even the dirt beneath my feet. Another field strobes around Mary in an Aurora Borealis of amber. Ribbons of light mingle with mine, tarnishing their brightness.

"I think I can see your aura."

She doesn't answer.

I walk ahead, determined to confront Zeena head-on and tell her to leave us alone once and for all. She'll see the power around me and back off. She has to.

"You're walking too fast." Mary scurries to keep up as I march on, slopping through puddles and sliding on wet grass. I'm unstoppable, and Zeena's going to get a taste of it.

"Anne, what's your problem?" Her cold fingers wrap around my wrist.

Her touch dims the light of my field.

"Nothing." I wiggle out of her grip and speed ahead. Sweat slicks my skin. I tug at my collar as if it'll release the steam pouring off me. Zeena's words zip through my mind. *You're the fireball. Prone to anger like your mother.*

Maybe it's the spell. Maybe it's the power. Maybe it's Mary's doubt. Maybe, maybe, maybe… I spin toward Mary. She skids to a halt and stares at me with wide eyes. It's the same look she gives Mom when she's ranting. And she thinks Mom is a lunatic.

"Why are you looking at me like that?"

Her gaze falls to the ground. "I…I'm not. I'm sorry."

I flinch at her apology. That's not what I wanted. I shake my head. "Why are you apologizing?"

"You seem angry. Is it the magick? Z said it's hard to control." Her voice is so soft I barely hear it.

I step closer, so our noses are inches apart. "Are you saying I can't handle it?"

Her gaze cuts to me. The amber strands fork out like snake tongues, cutting into my spinning rings of gold. "No, I'm worried. I don't want you to get hurt. Stop jumping to conclusions."

"You're draining my energy." I sprint away from her, heading toward the wooded path. "We have to hurry. There isn't much time. When we get home you can snark at me all you want."

"Wait up!"

Darkness embraces me with its long, decaying fingers as I continue deeper into the woods. Mary's calls fade. On my own, I give myself over to the magick. I become the Zodiac energy. A grin stretches across my face. In a few minutes, Zeena and I will face off, and I'll send that old harpy fleeing to the edge of the universe.

I trip over an exposed root and I fall, smacking my cheek against a rock. My shield of gold shatters and melts into the ground. The impact doesn't knock any teeth out of my head, but it sure does jostle the anger out of me. A mind-numbing ache throbs along the left side of my face. I choke on hot, salty, guilty, and bitter tears.

Zeena's voice fills my ears. Her rank breath fills my sinuses and sours my stomach. "Tsk, tsk, the Gemini twins left you, Anne. I told you the forces you played with are fickle. You can't contain the Zodiac power. Come with me and I'll relieve your burden, but I'll need both of you. Call to Mary."

I roll my gaze toward Zeena. She towers over me, an obelisk of evil. A wide grin distorts her already crusty features. "Castor...Pollux..." I wheeze. A breeze flutters through my hair, then dissipates. Alone, I can't expect them to share more power with me. I need Mary.

"So young and foolish to think you can control the twins. Relinquish the Gemini to me, dear Anne, and your pain will end." She croons.

I spit out blood-tinged saliva. I bit my tongue when I fell.

"Anne!" Mary's footsteps pound into the earth. Their vibration strums through my body.

"Call the brothers," I croak.

"Shush!" Zeena yanks my hair. My head snaps back and I yelp.

Mary kneels to my side. One hand presses into my back while the other strikes Zeena's arm. The old woman growls, but lets go of me.

"Castor and Pollux! Help us!" Mary yells.

Wind wails through the trees and stirs the loose underbrush and twigs littering the forest floor. Zeena stumbles away from us, carried by the gust.

"You cannot control the twins. You will need my help in the end!" Her howls graze my ears as she's lifted into the sky and carried away on an updraft.

The night stills. I cradle my cheek with a sore palm. Mary helps me stand and brushes me off. "Are you okay?"

A pathetic squeak pinches out of my throat. "I keep screwing up. I'm sorry."

"Never mind." She peers down the path. "There's no sign of Z. Did we really send her away?"

"*You* did."

"Wow."

Brittle silence invades the forest and fills the space between us. I'm disconnected from her. The solitude of it leaves me raw and shivering.

"Do you think she'll stay away?"

I wait until we emerge from the woods to answer. "No."

She slides her hand in mine and squeezes. "We'll figure something out. Grandmother can help us."

I'm not looking forward to that conversation. On the other hand, I have no other option.

We're in the eye of the storm, waiting for the back wall of the hurricane to slam us. And the hurricane is Zeena.

Chapter Fourteen

We find William in the barn cleaning tack. The joust is over for the day and he's in plain clothes. Since our green gowns are ruined, Mary and I are dressed in matching fairy costumes, complete with wispy, glittery wings. I tug the floppy tip of my fairy hat, hoping it'll hide the blue-purple bruise sprawling across my cheek.

Me, zero.

Rock, one.

William catches sight of us and waves a soapy brush. It splashes suds all around him. He drops the brush in a bucket and drapes the bridle he's working on over a hook. "No fancy dresses?"

"No. The rain ruined them yesterday." Mary gives him a haphazard grin. "Is Evan around?"

Go, Mary! At least someone's holding onto optimism. I dropped mine somewhere between yesterday and my stunning performance at the whiteboard during math class.

"Should be dividing the grain." He juts a thumb behind him. A door partitions off a little room where the grain and hay is stored. It's open, since Evan's in there, but it's closed at night to keep out one of the geldings—he's an escape artist and knows how to unlatch his stall. Good thing he doesn't know how to use a key or he'd hit a jackpot and eat himself to death.

"Thanks." Mary heads in the direction William just pointed. She pauses to glance at me.

I raise an eyebrow at her.

She twists her mouth to the side and tips her head toward William.

I glare at her.

She twirls and heads for the grain room. Man, when did she get so grab-life-by-the-proverbial-horns?

I, on the other hand, am the opposite of take-charginess. I hesitate. Last night really took the vinegar out of me.

"You okay?" William stands and steps around the bucket, bringing us inches apart.

I dip my head. "About yesterday…"

"What about it?"

"Are you mad at me?" My gaze drives into the ground and I wish I could stick my head in the dirt.

He replies by hooking a finger under my chin and lifting it. "Why would I be mad at you?"

His voice melts me. The only thing holding me upright is his fingertip. Without it, I might collapse in a pile of my own swoon. "Erm, for acting weird and stuff."

That same lock of unruly hair slips over his eye. He brushes it away before I have a chance to. Dangitall. "Oh, you mean when we were in character. Yeah, that flower was a nice touch, right?"

Crap. The rose was part of the act. My heart deflates like a runaway balloon fleeing the safety of the helium tank before it's tied off. "Sure."

He clears his throat. "I know you like lilacs better, but the rose was all I could find."

He knows my favorite flower! Strap me to a rocket so I can fly to the moon! I bite my lip and tell myself to calm down. Of course he knows I love lilacs. We've known each other since we could speak full sentences. "It's really pretty."

"You liked it?"

"Of course."

His dimples flash. The smell of horse dung and sweat surrounds him. It doesn't matter. I still want to throw my arms around his neck and kiss him. My hands ball into fists. I clamp them at my side in case they develop a mind of their own. Full, a little pouty, and surrounded by a bit of scruff, his mouth just calls to me. Yep, all I have to do is stand on tippy toes and slap my lips against his.

Focus, Anne. There's more important shizz going on right now.

"There was something I wanted to talk to you about." My throat catches at the very thought of mentioning Zeena, but I don't think it's because of the secret spell. It's because I've so horrendously screwed everything up and have done such a glorious job of it that I've included people I care about. I fiddle with the hem of my shirt. My cheeks blaze like the surface of the sun.

"Did we fight or something? 'Cause I missed it." He scrunches his nose.

He doesn't remember?

The chant did work! At least part of it had. "I don't remember either. Truce?" I stick out a hand.

"Truce." His hand is sticky from the tack soap.

I try not to say "ew." I also try not to feel disappointed when he lets go.

"Your cheek is bruised."

"It's nothing, really. I fell in the woods. Broke my fall with my face." I angle the left side of my face away, but it's too late. He steps closer, peering at me.

He sucks in a breath. "Bet it hurts."

"William, you remember that old lady who was in Dad's shop earlier?" I cringe at even bringing her up, but I have to know.

"Yeah. She smelled like cigars and cat pee."

I let out a nervous giggle. "Well, she…we have a problem with her."

"Why?" His face contorts.

"It's…you know, it might be better to show you. Hang on a sec." I step around him—reluctantly—and peek into the grain room. Mary's giggling. Evan's leaning over her really close and has a hand draped on her arm. Her fingers play at his collar. Wow, vixen city. Didn't know she had it in her.

I hate interrupting, but… "Mary?"

She slides her gaze to me. "Yeah?"

"Can I talk to you for a sec?"

She fluffs her ponytail and gives me a curt "Sure."

Evan sticks his tongue in his cheek and goes back to sorting buckets of grain. He doesn't strike me as the faire-going type—I've seen him a couple times at best over the years, wandering the shoppes with his little sister in tow. And yet here he is, giving his time, sweat, and energy to the stable, to being a squire, and to being William's super-awesome friend.

I lead Mary outside for some privacy. "I think we should tell William what we can do."

"Anne." Her tone mimics Dad's when he thinks we're being so loud it might provoke Mom.

"Really. He deserves to know."

"Why? Z's gone."

I pick at a loose splinter on the siding. "I don't think it's over."

"It will be when we tell Grandmother. Let's not drag anyone else into this."

"I owe it to him."

"To tell him some nonsense that a normal, sane person wouldn't believe?"

"I'm showing him." I turn on my heel and march back inside.

"Ugh, I wish you'd stop being so impulsive!" she barks.

Inside, William is wiping the bridle's reins with a cloth. "Ready?" I halt beside him.

He drops the reins. "For...?"

"Come with me." I clasp my hand around his wrist. He follows easily, but the look on his face is priceless—brow arched with confusion, mouth twisted with surprise, and eyes sparking with curiosity. He won't be disappointed.

Evan peeks out of the grain room. "What are you guys doing?"

Mary sidles next to him. "Nothing. I'll help you with the grain."

William gestures for him to come along. "Anne has something to show us."

Evan eagerly joins us. "What is it?"

Mary scowls, but reluctantly walks by his side.

We stand in a line, facing the arena. The sun is shining brightly and there's not a cloud in the sky.

"This isn't a good idea," Mary mutters to me.

"Too late now," I shoot back.

"What're we looking for?" William makes a show of craning his neck every which way.

I throw my head back and shout, "Castor and Pollux, show us your power!"

Immediately, dark, roiling clouds explode overhead, swirling in and around themselves, forming convoluted patterns and funnel-shaped masses. Sharp cracks of thunder precede dozens of lightning strikes. Gusts of wind assail us, whipping our clothes. My fairy hat flies off and is carried up into the sky.

"Oh!" I shout, mouth agape. I've done it now.

"Holy crap." William covers his head and ducks out of the way of a loose branch. It slams against the wall and scrapes its way to the ground.

"Stop, stop, *stop!*" Mary's voice tremors.

"Get under cover!" I push Mary toward the barn.

Evan swoops in to her rescue.

William does the same for me. His palms press against my back, pushing me along. A deluge of golfball-sized hail smashes the ground just as we cross the barn's threshold. We turn to face the storm, each of us panting and shaking. The funnel clouds swirl faster and stretch to the ground.

"You can conjure up *tornadoes?*" Mary screeches.

"Castor and Pollux, we get it. Please stop!" I beg.

The wind dies down enough for me to hear the satisfied cackle of an old woman. Zeena is nowhere to be seen, but her message is clear. She's far from gone, and she owns the elements just as much as we do.

William says, "Whoa."

"Anne, did you hear that?" Mary tugs at my sleeve.

"Yeah, I heard her."

"Oh, I wish we'd never done this." She drags her hat off her head and slaps it across her thigh.

"You keep saying that."

"I know, but we just keep making it worse." Her hands are fisted and her eyes are glossy with tears.

"Help me close the door!" William hollers over the chaos and dashes to the door. Evan is at his side in an instant. They slide the door shut on its track and William flips the latch in place, locking it.

Evan sits on an overturned bucket and William leans his back against the door. "What the *heck* was that?"

"Gamma gave me a Zodiac spellbook for my birthday. We—Mary and I—invoked the Gemini twins. And an evil sorceress is after us." Short and simple. Sums up a ridiculously complicated mess.

Wait. I didn't go mute! Goosebumps erupt all over my body. The spell *did* work. Cool.

"You're joking." William shakes his head.

I give a sheepish grin. "No?"

He pushes off the door and closes the distance between us, his gaze stabbing me. "You can control the weather?"

I can't tell if he's pissed or impressed. "Yes?"

"Because you evoked Gemini…like the stars?" His arm flies upward and swings in an arc.

"Invoked," Mary corrects.

William tilts his head in her direction. "*In*voked."

"I don't really know how it works, except Cas—" I catch myself. "The Gemini twins have power and Mary and I tapped into it."

He blinks.

"Each sign of the Zodiac has its own gifts. Like Libra is balanced and peaceful, Gemini is clever and open-minded, and…" I glance at Evan. "What's your sign?"

"Uh, I'm Aries," he says, his gaze cutting to Mary. He flips over a nearby bucket and slaps it.

She sits on it.

He laces his fingers with hers.

"Like Shequan." I say.

Everyone looks at me.

"Aries are brave and always ready for action," I finish.

Evan extends his legs and crosses them at the ankles. "Nice lesson, but what does it all mean? And what does it have to do with the weather?"

"Each sign affects a different element. Gemini and Libra are air signs. Air affects weather."

"And Aries?"

"Is a fire sign."

"So if I invoke my sign, I can start fires? Cool!" He grins and snaps his fingers.

"It's not cool." Mary pats his arm.

"And what does it have to do with this sorceress?" William crosses his arms. His muscles bulge.

"Zeena—" I gasp.

Mary glances at the rafters above. "You said her name and the sky isn't crashing down on us. Why?"

"What does she want?" William leans forward, buying into my story.

"She's a Zodiac Collector."

"And?" William rolls on his heels.

"I don't know." I glance at Mary.

She slowly rises. "You met her at Dad's smithy."

"Wait, that old lady is the sorceress?" William laughs and flops on a stack of empty pallets.

"She can change the weather. Like us." The hail bombarding the roof softens. Could be switching to rain.

He shakes his head. "This is unreal. If you hadn't made the sky explode, I'd have wondered if you'd gotten into your mother's medicine."

His words whack me in the chest harder than a semi colliding with a wall at a hundred miles per hour. Of anybody, he should know not to joke about that. Tears sting my eyes. I blink them back, fumbling for my inhaler, but the lack of air isn't from an asthma attack. "I can't believe you said that."

"What?"

"My mother's medicine? Really?" I prop a hand on my hip.

He leaps to his feet and leans over me. "It's just a joke."

"Funny." I brush past him and unlatch the door. A grunt escapes me as I yank it open. I leave the safety of the barn and slosh through puddles and mud to the main path. It's still raining pretty hard, but I don't care. Mary calls to me and I start to jog. I stumble over several stones and nearly slip twice before a strong hand grips my arm and whips me around.

William. He stares down at me, jaw clenched, brow furrowed. A storm—more volatile than the one we're standing in—tumbles in his eyes. Water pelts us, drips from our hair and noses, and soaks through our clothes. I'm getting so sick of all this rain.

"When did you get all sensitive? You're the one who dropped this wild magick stuff on me."

Sensitive? Is he for real? I slap his hand away and take a step back. "Forget it."

He jerks his head toward the barn. "Come back inside."

"No."

Mary jogs up to us. "Anne, you can't run off alone. Not with that witch out there somewhere."

She has a point. "Not until William takes back what he said."

"I didn't mean to make you mad." He fake-punches my shoulder. "We're best friends."

Friends. Exactly what I didn't want to hear. "Whatever." I hook arms with Mary and we head to the barn.

Inside, I shake out my hair and squeeze the excess water out of my shirt.

"What'd I say now?" William barges in.

"Nothing." I lean against a stall door. The bay gelding leaves his hay and comes over to me. He nuzzles my neck. It tickles and I giggle involuntarily.

"None of this makes sense." William takes off his shirt and wrings it out. His jaw clenches and unclenches some more, and his muscles flex under his tanned skin. My gaze drags over every bulge and dip, each hard line and angle. I clear my throat, willing myself not to blush. My anger promptly flakes out. I catch Mary's smirk. I arch an eyebrow at her and she grins.

"I'm the one who should apologize. All of this is my fault." I scratch the gelding's cheek. He nickers.

William shakes his shirt out before putting it back on. "How?"

"Z's here because of me."

"You don't know that," Mary says. She and Evan sit on their buckets again and hold hands. He's dependable, quiet, and strong. Exactly what she needs.

"We have to stop her. Then maybe things will go back to normal." My voice trembles more than I like.

"How do we stop her? She's using Zodiac power too." Mary leans into Evan.

The gelding gets bored of my scratching and returns to his hay.

"If we pool all our energies together, we might be able to beat her," I say.

"We just did a spell to keep us safe from Z, and now you want to go after her?" Mary digs her toe in the dirt. Evan wraps a protective arm around her.

I absently slide my fingers across my Gemini pin. I gasp. We may not be the only ones in danger. "Her trinkets."

"What about them?" Mary clasps her free hand on Evan's wrist.

"Gemini, Aries, and Libra were all missing."

"So?" she mumbles.

I finish the thought. "So it means she still needs to collect those."

"I'm a Libra," William says.

"And I'm Aries," Evan adds.

Mary rests her forehead on Evan's shoulder. "I don't get it. What do pins have to do with *people*?"

He dips his chin to her head.

My heart aches. I want William to hold me like that. But we're "friends." Nothing more. "I don't know."

Mary closes her eyes. "And why is she after us? Why doesn't she pick someone else?"

"I don't know."

She jolts upright. "See? We don't even know what she does or what she's capable of. I don't want to mess with her. Maybe if we leave her alone, she'll leave us alone and move on."

"I doubt it." I fold my arms.

William squints and twists his mouth like he's sucking on a lemon drop. I want to kiss him like they do on every primetime teen drama. Geez. He doesn't even like me that way and all I can think about is locking lips with him.

"We need to have a plan in case she comes back." I lift my chin and plant my feet shoulder-width apart.

"How?" Doubt seeps off Mary in waves.

William steps in my line of sight and sets his blue eyes on me. "We need information."

For the love of Castor and Pollux, where do we even start?

Chapter Fifteen

"Girls? Is dinner ready? I'm famished." Mom calls for us just as we put on our matching black hoodies. I scowl.

"It's ten o'clock. She wants dinner now?" Mary unzips her hoodie and has it half off before I grab the sleeve.

"She can eat leftovers. William's waiting for us."

"So we're going to sneak out of the house, just like that? She'll catch us on the porch or something."

I sigh. She's right.

"We can scramble some eggs. It'll only take a few minutes." She wraps her hoodie around her waist.

"All right."

We file into the kitchen.

Mom's butt sticks out of the refrigerator. She's half-dancing, half-scrounging, so her backside wiggles back and forth in an awkward rhythm. A strand of gold embroidery thread sticks to her pants. It snakes from her hip all the way down to her knee.

I glance at Mary. Her eyes are already affixed to the metallic strand. Her face is contorted in an "I really need to pick it off her pants" expression. We've been through this too many times before. Medicated Mom would be appreciative, but Manic Mom will just blow up at her for being too "particular."

I grab her wrist.

She bites her lip and tugs at her hair.

"Mom. Want some eggs?" I walk ahead, announcing our presence with as light a tone as possible. I pull a bowl out of the cupboard while Mary paws through the utensil drawer for a whisk.

"Hmmm?" Mom twists around to face us. A broad smile is plastered across her face. Her hair is kinky and her clothes are more wrinkled than Great-Aunt Edna's face.

I come within inches of her to pluck the carton of eggs from the fridge and immediately regret it. She reeks of stale smoke and body odor. "Um, why don't you hop in the shower? Mary and I'll make eggs and home fries."

She lights a cigarette and takes a long drag before answering. "What? You sayin' I stink? Nice way to treat your mother. I should make you drink dish soap."

Mary ducks her head into the pantry cabinet and returns with a large potato, keeping her back to Mom while she cuts it into even strips, sniffing every now and then.

What gives Mom the right to treat us this way? Turning into a Grendel because she doesn't want to take medicine? Totally unfair.

I gave up crying about Mom's mood swings a long time ago. Anger rears its scalded, pimple-covered face and urges me to smash her over the head with the frying pan. Then it whispers a plan. Drag her unconscious body to the backyard, douse her in dish soap, and set the sprinklers on her. Lost in the fantasy, I burn my finger on the side of the pan. That's what I get for imagining something so gruesome. I suck on the burned skin, but it only intensifies the scratchy pain.

"Have you been drinking the ale again?" Mom shoves my shoulder and laughs. It sounds like steel grating on concrete.

"No, I don't like the taste," I retort, scrambling the eggs as they cook.

She whacks the back of my head with her palm. "Hey, don't be smart."

"I wasn't." I rub my scalp.

She must not have heard me because she continues to rummage through the fridge. "Ah! Found it." She clicks open a can of beer and takes a long drink. The bitter scent wafts toward my nose. Gross. Why anyone likes the taste of the stuff is beyond me. "I'm celebrating. I finished the Queen's coronation gown. Just have some finishing touches on the ladies-in-waiting costumes."

I plate the eggs and dump the sliced potato into the pan. It protests in a chorus of sizzles. Mary puts the dish into the microwave to stay warm. Maybe if I turn up the heat, the home fries will cook faster. I draft a chant calling on Castor and Pollux to whisk Mom away like they had Zeena. I bite my tongue.

The clock ticks off the seconds. Frying potatoes crackle and spit in the pan. Mom likes them extra-crispy—of course. I hope William and Evan don't think we've ditched them. I hope they don't go poking around on their own looking for clues of what Zeena's up to.

"I'll take the eggs, Mary." Mom lights another cigarette.

Mary brings the plate to her and hands her the ketchup. It's like we're her little servants. My brain burns. I take a deep breath, careful not to blow it out on the stove.

"What's the matter, Mare? Forgot how to talk?" Mom snorts, then shoves a huge forkful of food into her mouth.

Screw it. The potatoes aren't done, but I don't care. I slide them onto a plate and slam the pan back on the stove burner. I spin the dial to *off* and storm out of the room.

Mary chases after me. "What's the matter? You want to get her going?"

"I don't care. This is ridiculous." I march out the front door, down the steps, and into the damp spring night.

"What if she follows us?"

"I wouldn't worry about it. She's stuffing her face." Wouldn't be long before she's downed a couple six-packs. Once she clicks open one can, she doesn't stop for several hours.

We cross the street and hop over the chain gating the faire grounds. The bright, nearly-full moon casts the night in slate blue and charcoal. Where do poets get the silvery glow nonsense? There's nothing silvery or glowy about it.

It's darker in the forest. We need to use both our flashlights to avoid large stones and exposed roots. I still manage to trip every other step.

"Where are William and Evan? They were supposed to be at the gate," Mary whispers.

"I don't know. They promised not to go into the woods."

"What if she got to them?"

My stomach flops. "She'll come after us first."

"How can you be so sure?"

"We made her angry."

"So?" Mary groans. "We shouldn't have agreed to meet here. We should've gone somewhere else. Like Grandmother's."

"Gotta get your digs in, eh?"

She huffs. "Give it a rest, Anne."

A tall figure hops out in front of us. I leap back and Mary yelps.

"Shhh, guys, it's just me." William flips on a flashlight, nearly blinding me. I can hear Evan hee-hawing in the bushes. Jerk.

"What the heck are you doing? Are you trying to kill us?" I growl, slapping the light away.

Evan stalks out of the underbrush and laughs harder. Double jerk. "Aww, don't be upset. We're just having fun."

"This isn't a joke." Mary shoves him. "I nearly peed my pants."

"You said you'd meet us by the gate." I punch William's chest, but my blow isn't hard enough to do any damage.

He raises his arm defensively. The light bounces around the trees and makes me dizzy. "Yeah, well, you guys are late. So we investigated ourselves."

"Find anything?"

"I think so. The old woman is in her shoppe. She's talking, but I can't make out what she's saying. And there are all these weird flashes of light in different colors. Come on, I'll show you." He strides away, confident with each step. He and Evan sound like a herd of stampeding rhinos.

"Will you guys try to be quiet?" I grumble.

Mary and I hurry after them. The forest isn't exactly thick and overgrown—we're in a park, for God's sake—but the moonlight fades the deeper we go. It gets colder too and soon our breath puffs out in plumes. I suppress a shiver. It shouldn't be *this* cold.

"What's going on?" Mary shivers.

"Could be Z's magick." I grab hold of William's sweatshirt and give it a tug. "Hey, wait a minute."

He turns and flashes the beam in my eyes.

"Oh. Sorry." He lowers his arm.

"You feel that?"

His eyes dart back and forth.

"It's cold."

"It's night."

"Duh, but it's way colder than it should be. We must be getting close. You should put out the flashlight."

Mary shook her head. "We won't be able to see anything."

"Yeah, but Z…she might be able to see us, especially with you waving the flashlight around everywhere."

A gust of wind silences our argument. The scent of decaying old woman lingers. I swat the flashlight out of William's hand and flick off the switch. Mary protests, but I clamp a hand over her mouth. Thankfully, William and Evan keep their mouths shut.

"Castor and Pollux, make our way visible," I pray. I hold my breath, waiting.

The leaves rustle in the breeze and a peal of thunder reverberates through the sky. I peer into the night and see a faint flickering glow after my eyes adjust. I take a tentative step. Mary clutches my sleeve, but follows. So do the boys.

A beam of moonlight highlights the path, guiding us to a small one-story shack hidden in a clutch of hemlock. Zeena's shoppe.

"This is it," I whisper.

We creep up to a window and peek inside. It's cracked open a couple of inches. Mary and I peer inside while Evan and William crowd behind us. Lit candles dot the room and the unnatural glow of a computer screen radiates from Zeena's favorite corner. What the heck would she need a laptop for? I squint to make sense of the white dots scattered across the black screen. Lines connect some of the dots. They form several Zodiac signs. Geez. Hadn't pegged her for a modern technology user.

Zeena's in the opposite corner, crouching over someone. Her scratchy voice carries on the air, but the individual words don't. The rhythmic cadence sounds like chanting. This can't be good. She shifts to the bookcase and selects a bottle.

Whoever's in the chair garbles out a muffled plea. Oh man, he's gagged! He wiggles and nearly tips the chair over.

Zeena steadies him. "Easy now. Don't want to get hurt."

He shakes his head and grumbles some more.

Zeena laughs and chants faster.

A red glow surrounds the kid. It illuminates his face. It's Shequan! The air itself shimmers and warps over him like an oasis on a hot summer day. His eyes roll up into his head. His body jerks around and his muffled scream comes out choppy. Then, with a burst of red sparks, he disappears.

Everything goes black.

I hold my breath while Mary dips her head. William's breath tickles my neck and his palm warms my back.

A speck of light appears where Shequan was. It wobbles and doubles in size. Then it triples, quadruples, and starts spinning. Zeena picks up her chanting. Wind howls and blows my hair in my face. The red vortex swirls, flaring the edges into the shape of a spiral galaxy.

Zeena raises her arms like a priest does when he prays over his flock. Only she's not praying. She shouts and claps her hands above her head.

The light condenses with bang louder than a gunshot. Half a beat later, it bursts again, this time in the shape of ram's horns. Aries!

The symbol fades and shrinks to the size of a half-dollar. It flashes in the candlelight and drops to the floor with a clatter.

Zeena cackles and picks up a silver trinket from the floor. That's how she collects the signs. She transforms *people*.

And all she needs to complete her collection are Libra and Gemini.

"I think it's time to leave," I whisper, retreating. A twig snaps under my heel.

Zeena's head whips toward us. Her hound-dog nose twitches, scenting us.

"Run."

We spin away and sprint toward the path like Olympic athletes. Leaves crunch beneath our feet, releasing their musty fragrance. The cold air burns my lungs. My airways constrict, making each breath harder and harder to pull. Soon, I'm lagging behind Mary, Evan, and William. I hear them smashing through the woods, yelping and panting.

"Where's Anne?" Mary calls.

"Keep going," I wheeze. I can barely hear myself.

"She was right behind us," William answers.

"Anne!" Evan shouts.

I lean against a tree and snake my inhaler out of my pocket. The pain seizing my chest eases some after I take a hit.

Zeena's cackle explodes to my left.

I suppress a yell and hobble in the other direction, going as fast as I can despite my handicap. Mary rushes to me and pulls me along.

"Faster, Anne, she's coming."

"I can't...you go ahead...without me." I do a limping jog, somewhat faster than a walk, but much less coordinated.

"I'm not leaving you."

"Me neither." William appears at my other side.

Together, they tug me along toward the field. The moonlit night shines bright beyond the trees. If only we can make it.

I pause to take another puff of albuterol. Mary frets at my sleeve. William keeps his hand on my shoulder. His body heat warms me from the unnatural cold.

"Let's go," I cough.

"And what makes you think I'll let you get away this time?" Zeena pops out of the bushes in front of us.

"Get Anne out of here." Mary shoves me into William's welcoming arms.

He latches his hands around his wrists, buckling me in his grasp, and drags me away.

"No, we can't leave her!" I struggle in William's grasp.

Zeena walks closer, an amused smile mangling her face.

"Wait. Mary!" I yell.

Mary steps toward Zeena, her fisted hands at her sides. "You can't use this kind of magick on people. It's not right."

Zeena throws her head back and laughs. A strong gust shakes the trees. Her cloak flutters and strands of white hair break free from her hood.

"Stop it! Stop laughing!" Mary's shoulders are shaking. "Castor and Pollux, stop this woman from hurting people. Make it as if she never came! Erase the memory of her, please."

Evan bursts through a mass of briar bushes and clings to her side. "Mary, let's go!"

"Don't chant. The wording has to be right," I wheeze.

Zeena sweeps her arm and chants something in a foreign language. Wild wind beats against us, whipping our clothes and hair, knocking us from side to side. I would have fallen if William hadn't been holding me.

"Quit fighting. We need to get out of here." He lifts me off my feet and whirls me around toward the path.

"Let me go. She doesn't know what she's doing. Mary, run!"

"Forget about me!" Mary yells over the storm and shoves Evan toward William and me.

"Silly girl, but you have given me a handy idea." Zeena raises her hands to the sky. "Gemini twins, by all means, clear the minds and hearts of those who've seen me since my arrival here. And erase the memory of those I've taken."

"Please, don't," I beg, clasping onto William's and Evan's arms. "Castor and Pollux, let us remember."

A lightning bolt is followed by a clap of thunder. The tree next to us snaps in half and falls to the ground with a groan. Evan dashes to the side and William throws us in the opposite direction. We land in a heap with him on top of me. His weight crushes me into the ground.

Another flash of lightning strobes over us as Mary screams.

Chapter Sixteen

Everything is quiet. I wonder if I've gone deaf, except I can hear myself panting.

William rolls off me, but stays close. "You okay?"

I don't care about myself. "Mary!" My voice is hoarse, like I took sandpaper to my vocal cords.

"Guys?" Evan thrashes in the woods to our left.

"Is Mary with you?" I get on my hands and knees.

"No." Evan replies. "She with you?"

"No, man, she's not," William replies.

"Mary!" Why isn't she answering? My heart thrums in my chest and my lungs tighten. I topple like a house of tarot cards and roll on my back. Air. I need air. She could be hurt and here I am gasping for oxygen like a weakling. "Where is she?" I sob. "Mary!"

"She has to be close." William leans over me and wraps an arm around my waist.

"She's gone. *Gone.*"

"Hey, shhh, it'll be all right. We'll find her." William brushes flyaway strands of hair from my face and cups my cheek with his palm. "Just breathe, Anne. Breathe."

I cough-gasp and concentrate on his face, his eyes, his mouth.

"Breathe. In and out." He's so calm. Strong. Solid.

Tears blur my vision and I rapidly blink them away.

He traces a thumb along the edge of my bottom lip. "Feel the air going into your lungs."

I close my eyes and listen to the sound of his voice, savor the sweetness of his breath against my skin, and allow the closeness of his body to envelop me in comfort.

"Better?"

"Yeah." And it is. I'm breathing normally again.

I sit up. William shifts behind me so I can rest against him. The adrenaline from struggling to breathe is leaving my system and I feel drained, almost flattened out like a used tube of toothpaste. Yet my heart continues to pound. It rivals any drum solo I've heard pouring out of Mom's workshop.

William rubs my arm. "Can you stand?"

"I don't know. Maybe?"

He does a crane impression and hoists me upright. I have to lean into his rock-hard abs for balance. Giving into the cocoon formed by his arms, I rest my forehead against his chest and inhale his woodsy, clean scent.

The moon, which had lit our path earlier, slips behind the clouds, and the night resembles fresh tar. My body trembles and tears burn at my eyes. "Why did Mary call on the twins?"

William fumbles with the flashlight and finally flicks it on. "Maybe she thought it would help."

This is all Z's fault. "Zeena! Show yourself." A low rumble of thunder travels overhead. I stomp along the path, grinding my heels into the loose pebbles as I go. My ankle twists and I teeter to the side.

"Whoa, easy." William catches me. I collapse into him, throwing my arms around his waist. It's that or drop to my knees. He pulls me closer. I settle against his shoulder, absorbing his warmth. I bite my lip. Mary's gone and I'm thinking about being close to William. Well, this is the first time a boy has put his arms around me, you know, in a white knight sort of way. Heat flares in my cheeks.

"I have to find Mary." I squeeze him tighter, then peel myself out of his grip reluctantly. Limping into the forest, I grimace at the sharp jabbing pain in my ankle. I call out Mary's name every couple of steps. The farther I go, the more the agony of losing Mary slithers through my guts.

Despite the darkness, I rush through the wild bushes, tripping over fallen branches and roots. Without William at my side, I slam to my knees, but launch up again in a flash, ignoring the burning ache of scrapes and bumps.

"Anne, wait up!" William crashes behind me.

I'm running with my hands held out in front of me. Sharp branches scrape my arms. I dip to the left and collide with something solid. Whatever it is collapses and I fall onto—

"Oof!" It's Evan. "Anne?"

"Evan? Where's Mary?" I push myself up off his chest and stand.

William catches up and locks the flashlight beam on us.

"I don't know. I can't find her." Evan pops to his feet and brushes loose dirt off his clothes.

"Sorry I smacked into you." I wince.

William reaches out and picks a leaf out of my hair. "The old woman's gone too, that's for sure. If she was still around, we'd have seen her."

I nod, my throat growing thick again. Calling on Castor and Pollux might bring Zeena to us for another tussle. Then again, if I find her, I might find Mary.

I spin in a circle, trying to right myself. "Which way to the path?"

William points behind us.

I stride past him.

He and Evan scramble to follow.

"Where are you going?" William lights the path with the flashlight.

"To Z's. She might be there."

"Is that a good idea?" Evan's voice sounds pinched and tight.

I halt and face him. "It's the only one I've got. You don't have to come, but I have to find Mary, and I bet that old witch knows where she's at."

His Adam's apple bobs up and down. He nods. "I'm coming with you."

"So am I." William clasps his fingers with mine and gives my hand a squeeze.

I stare up at him. His eyes are dark and serious. "Thanks."

"We're in this together."

Zeena's shop is dark when we get there. Not a good sign. I test the door—it's unlocked. The sorceress could be waiting to trap us, but I don't care. I blast inside.

"Mary, are you here?" My voice bounces back to me.

William jerks the flashlight beam around the small shack.

The shoppe is completely empty. No jars, no candles, no odds and ends. Everything is gone. Even Zeena's chair and laptop.

"How'd she pack up so fast?" Evan's mouth hangs open.

"Magick." I slump to my knees. If I hadn't opened my spellbook, if I hadn't been so mad at Mom for ruining our birthday every year, if I hadn't tried to call on Castor and Pollux, then maybe we'd never have met Zeena.

And I'd still have my sister.

"I'm so stupid." I barely get the words because I'm sobbing like a baby who's lost her pacifier.

William's warm hands cover my shoulders like a blanket. "It's not your fault."

"Of course it is. This whole spell thing was my idea. Z wouldn't have gotten her hands on her... None of this would have happened if I had just..." I snort in a breath. So not attractive.

"It's okay. Maybe Mary's just wandered deeper in the woods and can't hear us...or something." He rubs his hands up and down my arms. When did he get so perfect?

"Really?" I sound like a kid who lost her balloon and her dad just told her she could get a new one.

"Yeah. Let's retrace our steps. We'll find her." He hands his flashlight to Evan. With more confidence than a chivalrous knight, he extends his hands and helps me up. Again, I catch myself staring into his perfect eyes. He smiles, but it's not a happy one. It's a gee-I-hope-I'm-right-or-things-really-are-that-bad kind of smile. Not reassuring at all.

"M-m-maybe the Gemini twins will help us find her." I wipe fresh tears away.

"We can try that. What do I need to do to help?" William doesn't let go of my hands.

"We need to invoke your sign in order to call on your power." My mind whirls with words and chants, guilt and pain, and I crumple all over again.

William presses a hand to my lower back. "Then that's what we'll do." He glances at Evan. "You in?"

Evan rubs his jaw. Then his gaze locks onto mine. "Tell me what I have to do."

"I need supplies."

"Like what?" William asks.

"My spellbook, candles, stardust...everything. It's all at home."

"Your parents will be up." William shakes that unruly lock of hair from his eyes.

I check my watch. It's midnight. "I can sneak in. If Mom's working..." I leave out drunk as a possibility. "She won't notice, and Dad will be asleep."

"Are you sure?"

"We have to try. I have to do whatever I can to get my sister back."

"Let's go," Evan leads the way.

William walks next to me. His confident, calm energy is an ointment for my wounds. His soft, but firm, grip on my body when he held me up, the way he talked me through my asthma attack, and his unquestioning commitment to helping me find Mary... It could all be in my head, but he's acting more than best-friendish.

On the main path, I catch a glint of something shiny at the trail's edge. It could be anything—a bit of tin foil, a tab from a soda can, or a discarded faire coin. I halt. An invisible wall blocks me from taking another step while a persistent tug jerks the base of my spine. I lift my foot and extend my leg forward. The sensation rockets up to settle in my neck. It drags me back. I have to look again.

I latch onto Evan's arm and swing the flashlight toward the way we came. A trinket lies on the ground, nestled in decaying leaves. I pick it up and examine it in the light. Its silver metal is shiny, not dull. One side is smooth, but the other is jagged and sharp, like part of it was broken off. I run my finger on the rough edge and nearly puncture my skin. "Strange."

"Looks like the letter I." William peers over my shoulder. His breath warms my neck.

I take in a shaky breath and close my eyes for a moment to compose myself. I flip the thing over. It doesn't have a pin glued on the back and doesn't have a loop or anything to attach it to a necklace, so it's probably not jewelry.

"Any Zodiac symbols look like this?" Evan jabs at the thing with his index finger. Each tap reverberates in my soul like an electric shock. Weird.

I close my fingers around the symbol. The jolts stop. Double weird. "It could be half of the Gemini symbol."

"What does that mean?" Evan stuffs a fist in his pocket.

"Z chanted a spell that turned Shequan into the Aries symbol. What if...?"

"What?" William turns his flashlight into my face.

I swat him away. "What's the first rule of using a flashlight? Don't shove it in someone's face."

He snickers. "Sorry. I keep forgetting."

I hold the symbol between my thumb and forefinger. It buzzes with some unnatural force. "What if this is Mary?"

Evan stiffens.

The vibrations can't be in my head. I hand it to William. "Take this. Tell me what you feel."

His brow furrows, but he accepts it and cradles it in his palm. After staring at it for a full minute, he shakes his head. "Nothing. Why?"

I pluck it from his hand. The quaking resumes. "Castor and Pollux, what have you done?"

Lightning flashes and a tearing crack of thunder shatters the night.

"Whoa." Evan sounds just like that dude in *The Matrix*.

"Is this my sister?" I hold up the symbol, as if showing it to the Gemini twins, like they can see it from the sky. Their constellation isn't even visible from our position on the planet, but whatever.

Thunder sweeps overhead. It sounds like an old man grumbling.

Or twins arguing.

Chapter
Seventeen

Sure enough, the bay window of Mom's workroom is open and the whine of an angsty singer streams out. She says music keeps her moving, but really the mania keeps her moving. She doesn't need any help.

At least the noise provides some cover so we don't have to creep up the stairs. I usher William and Evan to the far side of the porch. My gaze falls on the spot I'd first used stardust and made a candle disappear.

I tug on a loose strand of hair, yanking on stringy thoughts frizzing in my brain. "The stardust worked better when Mary's blood was mixed in with it."

William dips his chin. "Are you serious?"

"It's an offering, a sacrifice. If we each add a drop of blood to the dust, we can—"

"Blood. You need my blood." Evan collapses on the bench and tightens his hands into fists.

"Just a drop to mix with the stardust. It works better than everything else I've tried." I tell them about the yellow orbs and how they absorbed into my skin, gifting me with Zodiac power.

"You said Z gave you the dust. Can you trust it?" William leans his butt against the railing and grips a nearby column. His head taps against a hanging basket of geraniums. He ducks and slides to the side, rubbing his scalp.

I shrug. "The stardust itself isn't bad because Mary and I did a good spell with it. Besides, it works, and what other choice do we have?"

"You promise, just a drop?" Evan chews on his bottom lip.

I glare at him. "This is for Mary. I thought you cared about her?"

He shoots to his feet. "I do. Mary's awesome. She's smart, pretty, and she laughs at my stupid jokes." He rubs his spiky hair and licks his lips, as if priming himself for a big reveal. "I've never met anyone like her. I only decided to join William on the jousting team so I could see her more at the faire. Pretty lame, huh?"

My rage flees like a cockroach running from a can of Raid. "It's not lame at all. In fact, that's one of the sweetest things I've ever heard."

He scuffs his foot along a worn floorboard and nods. "Thanks."

William clears his throat. The perfect opportunity to jump track and hop onto a new rail of conversation so Evan doesn't have to stay all exposed and vulnerable under our dissecting stares.

"So what's your problem with blood?" I ask.

He grinds the toe of one shoe to the other. "I…" He gulps.

"What?"

"I faint." He tucks his chin to his chest, then sneaks a peek at me through his eyelashes.

"Oh." I've heard of blood phobia before. Guess I over-judged. "Well, you can keep your eyes closed."

He puffs his cheeks like he might spew. "Uh-huh."

William's eyes are wide. "Dude, I didn't know you were scared of blood."

"Well, it's not something I like to share." Evan drops down on the bench.

It's time to pull this train into the station, so I carry on. "Once I sneak in and get what I need, we can mix our blood with the stardust, invoke your Zodiac signs, and pool all our powers together to help bring Mary back. It might overwhelm Z. She'll never see it coming."

Evan nods and rubs his stomach.

"You're not going to puke, are you?" I retreat a couple steps.

"No." He gulps so hard I can hear it.

"You think calling Libra and Aries will bring Mary back? What about Shequan?" William shifts so his back is against the column and crosses his ankles.

"I don't know what else to do...for either one of them." I chew on a fingernail and pace the length of the porch. Dad paced like this when Mom slashed her wrists last winter. She hadn't showered in days, so I figured it was weird that she suddenly went into the bathroom. When she didn't come out after an hour, I checked on her and found her passed out in a tub of bloody water. The straight razor and several empty pill bottles lay scattered across the floor. Mary called 911 while I pressed washcloths against Mom's cuts. All Dad did was pace. Right now, without Mary, I feel as useless as he was.

"What if the symbol isn't Mary?" William gestures to my hand.

"How can it not be?" I squeeze the thing and almost cut my skin on the jagged edge. It barely weighs anything, but the buzzing is so intense that I struggle to keep my hand steady.

"Why would Z disappear and leave without Mary?" William asks.

"Maybe she doesn't realize she lost the symbol." I pause. This is my sister I'm talking about. Sweet, level-headed, not the slightest bit interested in magick, Mary. Forced into chanting with me because of my incessant nagging, Mary. Morphed into a one-inch half-Gemini symbol, Mary. I flop on the iron bench next to Evan.

He slides over a bit to give me space. "Maybe we should call the police?"

"Yeah, and tell them what? My sister and friend have been turned into Zodiac symbols by a witch?" I tuck my hair behind my ears and bite my lip.

"Well, she's been kidnapped. We're not sure this *is* her. I mean, how could she be turned into…" Evan points to the little "I." "This?"

"We saw what happened to Shequan." My shoulders slump. He's starting to flake. After everything he's done to help William out at the stables, to chum up to Mary, to treat her like a treasure, and he's drawing a line at sharing a teeny-tiny drop of blood?

William stands. "You have to tell your parents, Anne."

I shoot to my feet and square off with him. "How can you say that? Even if I could get Mom to listen, she'd totally freak out."

"What about your dad?"

I shake my head. "He'd never understand. He barely pays attention to us anyway, and there's *no* way he'd believe in magick."

The porch light flips on and the front door swings open. Dad peeks his head outside. He's wearing a blue and gray plaid robe and flip-flops. His hair—what remains of it—is sticking up in several places and his eyelids are droopy. "I thought I heard voices. Hi, William. It's a little late for you to be here, isn't it?" His gaze lands on Evan.

"Uh, yes sir, we were just leaving." Evan jumps up. He stands so straight he looks like a soldier waiting for inspection.

William clicks the switch on his flashlight and tucks it into his back pocket. "We were talking about our SAT. Lots to strategize."

The lines in Dad's face deepen with sarcasm. "Is that so?"

I build up William's story. "Dad, we were studying, and William and Evan walked me home."

"Get in the house, Anne." He juts his chin in that I'm-the-parent-do-as-I-say gesture. It's about the only time he tries to do anything remotely adult-ish. Otherwise, he spends his time playing with iron and torches.

"But we were just—"

"Inside. *Now.*"

I roll my eyes and head inside.

"G'night, Anne." William calls.

"Bye," Evan adds.

"See you tomorrow, guys," I reply.

Dad shuts the door and locks it. He shuts off the front light, regardless of if William and Evan made it down the stairs or not. I try to peek outside, but he blocks me.

"What're you doing out at this hour, with a boy—*two* boys—on a school night?" Dad folds his arms. He's got Band-Aids on three fingers and a puffy blister on the back of his right hand. Must've gotten burned from smelting.

"Dad." I sidestep to the stairs and rub the newel post. If my palm was sandpaper, I'd be rubbing off the varnish and digging into the wood fibers. My throat chokes on the words I want to say. There's no easy way to bring up magick.

He leans against the door. "I know you and William have been friends for a long time, but you're getting older now.

I don't think it's a good idea for you and him to be hanging out all the time anymore. And that other boy; he's been at the faire, right? You shouldn't invite him to the house until we've been properly introduced."

Stifling confusion washes me in a pyroclastic flow of "what the...?" and "did he really just say that?"

He scratches his beard. "It's natural for teenage girls and boys to *experiment* with things, but I don't want you to get into something without knowing what you're doing and then regret it later. Maybe it's best if you and William only see each other on weekends and at the mall with a group of friends. Not alone. And certainly not in the middle of the night."

The current of puzzlement—a scorching combination of hot ash and volatile gases—threatens to obliterate me, but I glom onto a key word and fire off a question to extinguish the eruption. "Experimentation? Dad, what are you talking about? William's my best friend."

He shakes his head. "I know it's awkward to discuss..." He waves his hand around in some floppy, Egyptian-esque poses as if it will help him find the right words. "Sex. But your body is going through a lot of changes, and girls your age can be taken advantage of and—"

I fold my arms across my chest and sit on the stairs. Embarrassment broadcasts itself across my cheeks: Level Two Major Disaster commencing in 3...2... "Dad, we're not having sex."

"It's after midnight and you were alone with two boys."

"And you think I'm having sex with them? With my clothes on? What, do you think we take turns or do it at the same time?"

His face turns a ruddy tomato-red and the disaster level upgrades to One: Catastrophic Disaster. There's no way I can get out of this conversation intact. "Anne Devans. Don't be so crude."

"You're the one who brought it up."

He closes the distance between us and leans over me. His breath smells like beer. "Then tell me the truth. What were you doing with those boys?" His voice is level, but the heat from his eyes is enough to vaporize me.

I can handle Mom's screaming and throwing things, but Dad's anger is more lethal in a lot of ways. I can't play it off as crazy.

"If you don't start talking, I'll have to draw my own conclusions."

Hazard sirens bleat in a mind-stripping chorus. I have to tell him something, but there's no way he'd believe the whole story. "Something awful happened."

Alarm creeps into his gaze, sharpening his pupils to laser points. "Did they hurt you?"

"No, of course not!"

"Then what?" His head shakes a bit, like a volcano trembles before it blows.

Mary's gone. Two words. Impossible to say. Thick bitterness rises in my throat and squeezes my windpipe. The slithery tentacles of fear and agony wrap around me and threaten to pull me down through the stairs, basement, and into the earth's bedrock. I fight the urge to fling my arms around him and sob against his round belly. It worked when I was a kid, but it'd be totally weird now. Particularly since he looks like he wants to go all Vesuvius on me.

He straightens. "Anne?"

I clamp my fingers around the railing—grabbing something solid *might* prevent me from exploding. "Mary was…kidnapped."

Dad blinks furiously. His face squashes into a frown. "Mary who?"

My heart drops to my stomach like a rock plunging into a muddy pond.

"Does she go to your school?" Dad's eye twitches. It does that sometimes, especially if he and Mom are fighting. Or when he's drunk. He drinks when she's manic.

"Mary, my sister." I hold back from saying, *Duh*. But just barely.

"What, like BFF or something?" He air-quotes BFF.

"No, like *sister*, sister. Flesh and blood. Twin. Genetic replicant."

He sighs again. "Aren't you too old for an imaginary friend? Is this some kind of spiritual mumbo-jumbo you picked up at the faire?"

Imaginary friend? Mumbo-jumbo? My brain implodes. I open my mouth to say something, but nothing comes out. After a Level One disaster, the state governor calls on help from the government. In this case, I have no one to call.

"Okay. Go to bed. I'm too tired to discuss this right now. We'll talk about William and Evan and your total disregard of any kind of curfew tomorrow." Disappointment is plastered across his face, from the vertical line creasing the middle of his forehead to the thin line of his lips.

"But…"

"Now." He snaps his fingers and waits for me to get up and start climbing.

Inside my room, I lock the door and press my forehead against the frame. He couldn't have been serious about Mary being a figment of my imagination. I take a deep breath. He hadn't asked if she'd been out with us either. Maybe he thinks she's in bed, sleeping. She's the good twin, after all, and I'm the troublemaker.

I reach out to flip the light switch and turn around.

Mary's bed is gone. So are her bedside table, polka-dotted lamp, pictures, books, *everything*. Instead of a row of hangers holding her rainbow-sorted clothes, dozens of fabric swatches fill a compartmented shelving unit.

She's not only gone, but her life has been erased. All of it. That's why Dad didn't know who she was.

My chin trembles. "No," I sob.

Outside, rain pelts the world, slicking away the memory of the day.

I stumble to my bed and collapse on the mattress, glaring at the trinket. "What have you done?"

My lungs go all wheezy again. At this rate, I'll run out of medicine in a week rather than a month. I take a hit of albuterol anyway and curl into a shuddering ball of panic.

Castor wiggles in his bed and whines. Pollux rolls on his back and wags his tail. At least both dogs are here. I take it as a good sign.

"Poor pups. Here. See Mary?" I kneel next to them, my knees resting on the hardwood floor, and show them the trinket.

They hop up in unison and sniff at it. Pollux barks and practically leaps into my hand. I close my fingers over the half-Gemini symbol and clutch it to my heart. Fresh tears slide down my cheeks. Castor and Pollux plant their front paws on my arms, bodies wagging as much as their tails.

"It *is* her, isn't it?" I pat their heads and stand. I search my dresser drawer for a scarf. I wrap the trinket in it and slide it into my pocket. "I promise, I'll get you back."

Dad's heavy footsteps stomp up the stairs. He belches in the hallway. A moment later, the door to his room slams.

I watch the clock for a full half an hour before creeping downstairs, sticking to the wall—it's my best Spider-Man impression yet—to avoid the creaky spots. The living-room door is open and Mom's music isn't blaring. I duck my head in to see if she's there. Nope. I bite my lip. She could be anywhere in the house.

In the foyer, I stay perfectly still, focusing on any tick or hitch in the house. The thrumming of my pulse drowns out anything I might catch. I can stand here forever or I can move.

I choose to move, but I hold my breath until I reach the front door. The hinges creak and I scan the foyer, expecting Mom or Dad to hop out of the shadows to tackle me.

Halfway down the driveway Dad's mega-angry voice stops me from the porch. "Anne Devans. Get inside the house. Now."

Was he at the window waiting for me to sneak out? Since when did he turn into a night watchman? I want to scream. A lot. Instead, I swallow my frustration and scuff my way back to the porch as a bolt of lightning streaks across the sky. Crackling thunder erupts. It's like the weather knows my mood.

Dad grabs me by the arm and jerks me inside. "Get up there. I told you repeatedly to go to bed. I have no choice but to ground you."

"Dad, no, you don't understand." I lace my fingers and slap them to the top of my head. "Castor and Pollux," I mutter.

Another boom of thunder shakes the earth.

"I do understand. William is a nice boy, but you don't have permission to hang out with him all night. Or sneak out of the house. I don't understand why you're doing this. Is it because of your birthday?"

"No, Mary's—"

"Enough! I'll call his parents in the morning. You're grounded." He holds out his hand. "Come inside."

I stare at him, immobile. He's never grounded me before. Heck, he's never been so nosy before either.

"Anne." His green eyes flash with fury.

I can't refuse.

He grabs hold of my arm and shoves me toward the stairs. "I hope your attitude improves by morning."

I hope I have a plan to save Mary by morning.

Chapter
Eighteen

No one asks me about Mary all day. The teachers don't say her name, or Shequan's, during roll call. The other students don't ask if she's sick and no one mentions Shequan at all. During a study break I draft chants to invoke Libra and Aries instead of studying for the SAT. William, Evan, and I cross paths during lunch—so many students are preparing for the exam that we're in different review groups—and agree to meet at the faire after the joust.

I don't bother going home after the final bell at two-thirty. The joust is at four, so I have some time to kill. Maybe I can catch the guys before they need to perform.

The barn is full of activity. Horses are lined up along the main walkway, dressed in their tack and attached to the cross ties. Shequan's dad races up and down the line, barking orders and checking to see if everything is in place. He's focused, sharp as a ninja sword, and way too steady, considering his son is missing.

If Zeena's chant really did erase the evidence of her work, why do Evan and William and I remember? My lungs tighten. Maybe my counterchant protected our memories. Guess I have to be thankful to Castor and Pollux for that small gift. In a normal world, the police would be canvasing the area, missing child reports would be blowing up the news, and parents would be distraught at the loss of their son or daughter. In my world—a quirky, magickal world— no one even notices things have changed.

I swallow a lump of terror. What a horrible thing, to be forgotten.

"Anne!" William jogs up to me in his squire costume.

I jump, startled into reality. William would remember me and so would Evan. "You're already dressed."

"Yeah, I left early. Wanted to talk to Marcus before everything got really busy." He tugs on his shirt and straightens his belt.

"How'd it go?"

"Awful." The skittish mare at the front of the line knickers and paws into the dirt with her hoof. William pets her nose and she settles.

"Tell me." I drag my fingers through her white mane.

He leans close and whispers in my ear, "He doesn't remember Shequan."

My finger gets caught in a snag. I shake it out and try to unravel the twisted strands. "I figured."

"How?"

"Z erased everyone's minds," I reason.

"How come we can remember?" He slides his palm along the cross tie as he edges to a nearby stall.

I join him. "I asked the Gemini twins to let us."

"Scary."

"Totally."

"Did anyone ask you about them at school?"

"No. You?"

"No." He digs his booted toe into the dirt. "I don't want to be forgotten."

"You stole the words right out of my mouth. We have to figure out how to beat Z."

"And how do we do that?"

I chew my cheek, eating the anxiety of what I'm about to say. "I have to talk with Gamma. She can help...after she kills me."

"Huh?" William squints with confusion.

"I... Well, she's mad at me for doing magick."

He gives a low whistle. "Things are pretty messed up."

I groan and flop against a stall door, propping my elbows on the edge and smacking my forehead on my arms. "And it's all my fault."

William's warm hand caresses my hair. He brushes it to the side and leans close to my ear. "You didn't do anything wrong. That old witch did. And the way you stood up to her... Well, I've never seen anyone so brave."

I lift my forehead and glance sideways at him. "Yeah?"

"Yeah. Listen, I wanted to run and hide like Jimmy Banks did after he tripped off the bus and landed with his pants around his ankles."

I giggle.

He tugs on a strand of my hair. "It's good to hear you laugh."

Marcus calls for the knights and squires to get ready.

William walks backwards to his position. "We'll go to your Gamma's after the joust."

Evan rushes by. "Hey, guys."

William gives him a bro punch to the arm. "We'll catch up after the joust. I have some news."

"Cool," he calls, sliding to a stop next to his knight's horse.

Marcus strides up to me. "You're not supposed to be here."

"Sorry." I duck my head and skedaddle to the benches.

Dad's standing at the edge of the crowd. Odd—he doesn't usually watch the joust. Unless he's on the lookout for me. I use three maidens walking along the fence line as a human shield and slip behind a large oak tree on the opposite end of the hill. No need to run into him right now, considering I'm supposed to be home, thinking over how wrong it was to be with William so late at night.

A smart person would've developed some kind of disguise, but I'm not a smart person.

The crowd cheers after the King and Queen are introduced. Next up are the knights. The guys really feed off it, yelling, "Huzzah!" and tasking their horses with tricks such as bowing, spinning on their hindquarters, or rearing. Usually, I'd get caught up in it too, but today I can't. Instead of excitement, there's a gaping dry socket of agony where Mary should be.

During the ring joust, I leave my hiding spot and loop around the back side of the faire. Mary and I like this area the best. It has tarot and palm-reader tents tucked in among hemlock groves, near the woodcarvers, painters, and jewelry makers. Incense dances on the air, but not enough to make my asthma flare up. I enter a costume shoppe at the corner and head directly for the wall of masks. Some are frilly with feathers and sequins, in girly colors like pastel pink and sky blue. Others are grotesque with blood splotches sprayed across the surface or large hooked noses protruding out several inches. A few have horns, and a couple come with black or red contacts.

I select a green mask with gold sequins bordering the edges. It's large enough to cover my forehead and cheeks and has bands to fit around my head. At the end of the line of masks is a row of veils. I pick a black one. It comes with a strip of adhesive so I can attach it to the mask and either cover my entire face or let it drape down my back. Since I'm wearing a black peasant shirt, black jeans, and boots, the outfit looks complete and I can pass as any suited-up faire patron.

The cashier is dressed in simple wench's clothing—a chocolate bodice and brown skirt with a white shift underneath. Her hair is pulled into a braided knot and a flower crown adorns her head. She greets me with a friendly grin. "Good even, Anne. How fares thee?"

"Well, thank you." I plop the goods and twenty bucks on the counter.

"Perchance thy Mathair will stop by?"

"Mom's working on the coronation gown." I drop the faire speak.

"Prithee, is it as comely as last year's?"

The freaking thing is ugly, but I can't say that. "Aye."

She hands me some change. "Wouldst thou like a bag for thy wares?"

"No, thank you." I collect the mask and veil and exit the shoppe. Between two buildings, I edge the mask with adhesive and press the veil to the sticky side. It holds fast. I gather my hair in a low ponytail, stretch the elastic bands over my head, and spread the veil around me. The mask blocks my peripheral vision, closing me inside a molded restraint. Thieving claustrophobia sticks his spike-covered fingers down my throat and scratches at my lungs. I close my eyes and picture valiant air fending him away with her blade of oxygen and shield of calm.

When the battle ends, I step into the path and wind my way to the jousting area. At a fork in the road, three of Mom's biggest customers huddle together. They're gabbing about the coronation ceremony.

I dawdle by pretending to window-shop the wood carver's wares. An elephant's foot stands by the shoppe's entrance. It has a wooden cover with several holes drilled into it. A cane is lodged in each hole. Each one depicts a different animal or creature—a lion, bear, alligator, and something that reminds me of Man-Bear-Pig from *South Park*.

The one dressed in a crimson velvet Elizabethan gown has the loudest voice. "That woman is crazier than a loon. I'm scared to call her half the time. I never know if I'm getting wild Liz or mellow, medicated Liz."

I flinch.

The woman dressed as a pirate chimes in. Her black, pointy hat is so wide her friends have to stand at least two feet away from her. "She is insane, but she makes some fine dresses."

I bite my lip against the pain of their razorblade tongues and wander closer, keeping my body at an angle to them.

"And a drunk for a husband?" The lady in waiting fans herself with a painted silk fan.

"He probably drinks because of her," Victorian Lady snarks.

"I feel bad for their daughter. All alone in that house with those two for parents." Madame Pirate clucks her tongue.

Daughter. Should be daughters, plural. Crows of misery land on my shoulders and cackle in my ears. Their talons dig into my flesh and their beaks snip at my eyes. I wipe the wetness of bitter tears from my cheeks and slink away, carrying the taunting black birds with me.

The women glance at me as I walk by. None of them recognize me. The costume is perfect. I don't have to worry about running into my drunk father and having him blow up.

"Life is so hard, isn't it, Anne?"

The gravel in her voice scatters the crows of misery. Bats of fear flutter around my head in their place.

To my right, a cloaked figure sits at a mosaic-inlaid table, her hood nearly covering her entire face. All that's visible is her wide, wrinkly mouth, which is twisted in a satisfied, but cruel, smile.

"Zeena," I croak.

A brisk wind blows my veil.

"That's right, child." She lifts an arthritic hand to her hood and draws it back, exposing her cold eyes.

My body quakes and my muscles tighten. A steady buzzing hums in my pocket. It's the trinket. It's Mary.

The old woman closes her eyes and sniffs. "Your sister is near. Have you found her?" She opens her eyes. Her gaze impales me. "You don't know how to get her out, do you?"

"Tell me how to release her."

She cackles. "Why would I do that? Especially when I'm so close to completing my collection. All I need is you and Libra. How is your friend, William? He seems a wealth of untapped power. I sensed it swirling in his aura." She extends her arm and makes a circle motion with her index finger. Her lips move rhythmically and a steady murmur rises from her.

The wind picks up again and the sun goes under, slipping the world in shadow.

A bolt of light erupts from her finger and lances me in the chest. She closes her hand into a fist and yanks her arm in. I jerk forward, tethered to her.

"Come here, little Gemini."

The light rope between us is taut. Another tug brings me a step closer. I grab hold of it, scream at the instant blistering burn, and lean away. The rope expands around me in a net of crackling energy. Invisible hooks pierce me from the top of my skull to the bottom of my feet. They tear at my flesh, dragging me forward.

I'm trapped. My head twists from side to side, my teeth gnashing from pain. No one pays us any attention. Don't they see me struggling? Don't they see the wire of light connecting us?

"Relax, Anne. Let it happen. This pain will end if you give in to me."

I whimper.

"No one will miss you. Come to me."

The buzzing in my pocket from the half-Gemini symbol grows into a scorching heat, as if I'm carrying a red-hot piece of coal. It and the tether anchor me, with the light rope and netting drawing me to Zeena, and the coal pulling me away.

Both forces duel and I'm caught in the middle. Deep inside, my organs stretch and joints pop, separating and ripping apart. Every cell in my body is torn in half by a magickal buzz saw. I drop to my knees. "C-C-Castor...P-Polll-ux...help."

A bolt of white lightning zaps the tether, breaking it in half. Zeena's end drops to the ground while the bit attached to me flutters away like ash. I fly backward, arms and legs flailing, and land in a heap across the footpath.

The sorceress launches out of her chair. "No!"

A roll of thunder cuts off her cry.

Patrons gasp and yelp in surprise. A dude dressed as Peter Pan stoops down and clamps a hand around my upper arm. He hauls me to my feet. "Better watch where you're going."

"Y-yeah." I'm panting and shaking, sweating from pain and terror. "M-mask b-blocks my v-vision."

"Do you need to sit down?" He smacks the dirt off my back.

"No." I twist away from him, sights locked onto Zeena.

Folks have already moved on from my impromptu break-dancing and crowd the path between us. The old witch stares at me, teeth bared in a sneer. She lifts her hands toward me and a white glow expands from her fingertips.

I take my cue to run.

♐ ♈ ♊ ♏ ♓

On the way to Gamma's house, I quickly update William and Evan. "She's still here. Almost got me, too." I rub my arms as if it'll erase the ache from my body. Red dots speckle every square inch of exposed skin.

"Maybe you should put something on that. It looks painful." William tucks the Zodiac spellbook under one arm and pushes my veil out of the way with his free hand.

"Not sure if aloe trumps magick." I take a quick peek down my shirt. A dark purple splotch marks where the tether smacked me. It itches worse than a raging case of hives.

William cranes his neck to take a peek.

I press the fabric tight against my collarbones. "*Hey.*"

"Sorry." His ears flush. "I wasn't trying to get a glance at the goods, I just wanted to make sure you're okay."

I trace my fingers along my collar. "Right, like I'm going to buy that."

His mouth twists into a smile and his dimples go live.

Evan squeezes between us. "Why don't you guys kiss and get it over with?"

We stop short and gape at him.

He shrugs. "What? William, you can't stop talking about Anne, and Mary says Anne can't stop talking about you, so make like Nike and Just Do It."

Gamma's in the backyard, sitting on a wicker loveseat in her gazebo. Two chairs and a table with a glass top complete the set. "Girl, where have you been?"

"I meant to drop the book off sooner, but I've been busy with the faire and studying." Nothing like starting the conversation with two plump lies. I take the spellbook from William and set it on the table.

"Been an awful lot of weather happening." She props her feet on the table and stares me down.

I ease into a chair. William grips my shoulder and Evan sits in the only free seat.

"Know anything about it?" Gamma's gaze slips to the book.

I ball my hands into fists. "Gamma, I've really messed up."

"Tell me everything."

I do. Slowly and with a shaky voice, I repeat it all, day by day, moment by moment.

By the end, Gamma's perched on the edge of the love seat. "You...have a twin?"

"You don't remember her?" My insides wither.

"Not one bit."

Evan chimes in. "If someone's been erased, can they be brought back?"

I grip William's hand. He winces, but doesn't break free.

"This sorceress is powerful indeed if she's wiped all our memories clean of a twin." She picks up the spellbook and rests it on her lap, tracing her finger along the Zodiac wheel. "Let me think."

"Don't forget about Shequan," Evan whispers.

I guide William's squished hand to my opposite shoulder. He slides into my chair and tightens his hold around me.

Gamma flips open the book. "You boys invoked your signs too?"

Evan shakes his head.

William says, "No."

"I thought about having them do that, but I wanted to talk to you first." I rest my head on William's chest.

He tangles his fingers in my hair.

Gamma's eyes twinkle. "You two have gotten close." She flips the pages of the spellbook and settles on one. "Libra and Aries are cardinal signs. We should be able to lump them both together into one chant. Did you take that stardust off the table?"

"Yes." I draw the bottle from my pocket and palm it.

She purses her lips at me, then says, "Go fetch some candles, matches, and pins from my den. And grab some rubbing alcohol and tissues from the bathroom."

Evan visibly pales. "What're the pins for?"

"A drop of blood is the quickest way to invoke a sign," Gamma says. "Off you go now, time's a'wastin'."

I pop up and lay the stardust on the table. "Okay."

William helps me gather the items Gamma listed off. When we return, Gamma has the stardust spread on the table. Evan kneels across from her. His eyes are closed and his breathing is slow.

"What did we miss?" I place candles at the four corners and light them.

Gamma adjusts her glasses. "Your friend is afraid of blood, so he's meditating to stay calm. He could teach you a thing or two."

I take the lick and kneel next to Evan. William settles in next to me.

Gamma douses the pins in alcohol and pours some on William's and Evan's index fingers. William pricks his finger with a pin and squeezes a drop onto the stardust. Evan does the same. His hand shakes and he keeps his head turned away as he adds his own offering. I'm the last one to prick my finger and shake a drop of blood in.

"What do we chant?" I press a tissue to my finger. It throbs in time with my pulse.

"I'll do that, dear. Just concentrate." Gamma holds her arms out, palms up, like a priestess preparing to pray over her flock.

"Four elements of life,
Earth, fire, water, air,
We invoke thee.
Four corners of the earth,

North, South, East, West,
We invoke thee.
Four elements of the Zodiac,
Earth, fire, water, air,
We invoke thee.
Four bodies of the cosmos,
Planets, stars, moons, comets,
We invoke thee.
The Twins of Gemini,
We invoke thee.
The Scales of Libra,
We invoke thee.
The Ram of Aries,
We invoke thee.
The Goat of Capricorn,
We invoke thee!"

As I've come to expect, a blitz of lightning and thunder rounds out the chant's finale. At least one sign has given an answer. I have no idea how the others will respond. A goat's bleat? The smack of rams' horns echoing? The balancing of scales? Because that sounds like...*nothing*.

"Look!" Gamma slowly scans the four corners where the candles sit.

Following her lead, I take in the yellow orbs of Gemini and Libra, the green orb of Capricorn, and the red orb of Aries. Each takes over a candle flame.

"Wow." I blink, and the orbs leave their fiery posts. They float toward the stardust and hover above it. Gamma and I lock gazes.

"We invoke thee," she whispers.

The orbs respond by rotating in a circle. Faster and faster they spin, until they blur. Their combined motion creates a whirring louder than a room full of four-prop planes and just as much wind. All the colors blend into one, creating a burning white light brighter than the sun.

I squint and hold a hand in front of my face.

"What's happening?" Evan calls. He ducks, covering his head with his arms.

William drags me to him and uses his body as a shield. For me.

Peeking over his shoulder, I watch the light expand. It envelops us in a flash. The glass rattles and shatters. I stuff my face into William's chest. His chin pushes against my skull. A frail scream rips through the air.

"Gamma!" My yell is muffled.

"I'm okay. Stay covered, Anne!" Her voice wobbles.

Evan screams.

I twist to face him.

Or at least where he was.

"Where'd he go?" William shouts.

"Evan!" I crawl to the spot where he huddled seconds ago, scanning for signs. Signs of what, I don't know. Maybe an Aries symbol or something.

There's nothing.

Gamma sits up and brushes her fingers through her hair. Her glasses sit cockeyed on her face. The left lens is cracked. "Who's Evan?"

William and I glance at one another.

"He's a friend. He helped with the invocation chant." I get to my feet and help Gamma sit in the love seat.

A delighted cackle blows in on the breeze.

Gamma rubs her temple. "Eneaz?"

She must be delirious from the intense chant. "No Gamma, it's Anne."

She squints up at me. "Oh."

We're way too exposed out here. "Let's get to the house."

William and I help Gamma stand. We walk alongside her, William on her left and me on her right. Raindrops pelt us, soft and questioning. They become stronger and more forceful with every passing second.

We climb the front steps and usher Gamma inside.

Hail covers our tracks, erasing our steps, cleansing the memory of our chanting.

"Where we headed?" William has an arm hooked around Gamma's waist and I have one looped above his.

"The kitchen."

We guide her to her favorite seat. William plunks in Mary's seat and I put a kettle on the stove to boil.

"What just happened? Why would Evan disappear? Did Z take her? Doesn't she already have Aries?" William fires his trebuchet of question bombs while we wait for the water to boil. He plucks a single hydrangea blossom off a cluster and spins the tiny stem between his finger and thumb.

"How is it that, every chant I do, Z's always there, swooping in to ruin it?" I buzz around the tiny space, gathering tea, spoons, mugs, sugar, lemon juice, and milk, slamming cupboards and refrigerator doors as I go.

William catches my wrist after my last delivery. He draws me into his lap and rubs my back. "Hey, relax. We'll figure something out."

I stare into his serene eyes. They're cool, collected, and envelop me in a pool of calm. "I wish I could believe you."

His fingers trace the line of my jaw while his gaze affixes to my lips. Then they slide in Gamma's direction and I'm on my feet again, moment broken. I cross the cracking linoleum tiles to save the whistling kettle from the fire.

When I pour steaming water into Gamma's cup, she blurts, "I have something to tell you, Anne."

My hand wobbles and I spill some on the table. I set the kettle on a potholder while William dashes for a towel. "What is it?"

"I may have led you astray by helping invoke Libra and Aries." She twirls her long string of beads around a finger.

I drop into William's chair before he has a chance to. She can't think this is a mistake. It may be our only way to get Mary, Shequan, and Evan back.

William sops up the spilled water and wrings the towel out in the sink. "I don't think what we did was a mistake. This is pretty cool. It's like I'm hyped on five Red Bulls without the jittery after effects."

Gamma shakes her head and releases her necklace. "I didn't realize how truly terrible things had gotten."

"Gamma?" I drag my chair to her and clasp my fingers over her hand.

"Magick doesn't solve everything." She slips her hand away. "I should've prepared you better."

"No, Gamma. I'm the one who messed up. I couldn't wait to start chanting and I screwed everything up because I didn't listen to you."

Gamma cups my cheek with a shaky hand. "My sister loved magick too. She thought she could solve every problem, fix every mistake, and right every wrong with it. But it doesn't work that way. Magick can't solve everything."

"Can it bring Mary, Evan and Shequan back?"

Gamma's eyes drown in tears.

She doesn't answer.

Chapter Nineteen

I rock back and forth for hours on my bed, bedsprings creaking with the motion. I half-expect Dad to come in and tell me to knock it off, but he doesn't. Castor and Pollux avoid me, preferring their own beds as opposed to my shaking one. My eyes burn from watching the clock measure the passing minutes, each second ticking by in a regular rhythm.

Dad leaves before dawn, giving me the opportunity I want. With darkness as a cloak, I make my way down the stairs, out the front door, and to the road. The brooks brim and bubble from too much rain, washing out the bridge I'd generally cross to get to William's house. I have to wind my way through muddy fields and ankle-deep ponds that have formed overnight. My purple zebra-striped galoshes come in super handy.

The sun crests over the surrounding hills by the time I circle around to a different route. A police barricade of two cruisers with lights flashing blocks the road to William's.

Three officers dressed in highlighter-yellow raincoats mill about. My cousin Tommy, a rookie cop, is one of them.

"Anne, what're you doing here? It's six o'clock in the morning. Go home." He frowns until his dimples create Grand Canyon-sized craters in his cheeks. I stare at his plastic-covered hat. A couple of summers ago, he was thrown out of the family reunion for being drunk. To think he represents the law now.

"I'm heading to William's house. We…we're working on stuff for the faire before school."

"The road is closed." He waves his flashlight at the pavement beyond the cruisers.

"Why?"

"Rain washed it out."

I click my tongue against the back of my teeth. "How am I supposed to get to William's?"

"You're not. You should go home. The faire won't be open with this weather. Whatever you're working on can wait." He jerks his head toward the way I came.

"I can't go home." I wonder if I should tell him about Mary and see how far the spell goes…even though I can guess the answer.

"Why not?"

"It's important."

"*Go home*, Anne. I can't do my job with you hanging around." He's so endearing when he whines.

"Someone took Mary." I blurt.

His face contorts. "Who's Mary? You got a stuffed teddy bear or something?"

My jaw drops. A teddy bear? "My twin sister, that's who."

He laughs. "Is this some pretend faire thing?"

"I hate Z!" I stomp my foot, splashing mud right onto Tommy's uniform pants.

"Hey!" He grabs my jacket at the shoulder. "Enough. I don't have time to play around with your silly games. Get home before I call your parents."

"But—"

"No buts, just go." He waves his hand.

"Fine." I pretend to head back home, but veer off into the woods after rounding a corner. Carefully, I step along the path, making sure one foot is securely planted before lifting the other.

Finally, I reach a two-story blue house—William's house. I sneak to the back, where his bedroom is on the second floor. His parents are usually off on business trips, so there's a good chance they aren't home. I pick up a couple of loose stones and toss them at his window. They ping off the glass.

Moments later, he appears and throws opens the window. "What're you doing here?"

"Can you get out?"

He frowns. "I'm not in prison." He shuts the window and disappears.

I pace around the backyard until he joins me. He's wearing sweats and a red hoodie.

He stretches and I catch a glimpse of his flat belly. "This whole thing is out of control, Anne."

"I know." I play with an oversized button on my Kelly-green trench coat.

"What should we do about Z? You think she'll come after us?" He tugs on the strings of his hoodie.

"We have to prepare in case she does. And we still have to figure out how to rescue Mary, Evan, and Shequan."

"We'll find a way."

"How? None of the magick I've done has helped."

"Your grandma said magick doesn't solve everything. Maybe there's another way." He grabs my hand, moving closer.

"Like what?" I duck my head.

"Dunno yet."

"I wish I could rewind time to the day I first chanted to the twins." I bury my head in his chest.

"What, and miss out on spooking horses, flying tree limbs, freak storms, running in the woods at night, scraping your knees, and hanging out with a witch who has bad breath?" He wraps his arms around me.

I turn my head to the side and laugh. "There are other things, too."

"Like what?" His voice rumbles through his ribcage.

"Spending more time with you." I pull back, sniffing and wiping my nose with my sleeve. "I'm glad you're with me. I couldn't do this without you."

"Glad to be of service, m'lady." He takes a bow.

I giggle and slug him in the arm. "Why are you always so calm?"

He rubs his arm, laughing. "Dunno. I'm freaked out about everything that's happened too."

"You don't look freaked out," I complain.

He shrugs. "Things changed since we invoked Libra. I think it helped somehow."

"I wish I had your sign."

The edge of his mouth creeps up.

I sigh and use my fingers to shake out my hair. "We have to go back."

His head tips to the side. "Go back where?"

"To the faire grounds. Maybe we'll find some clue or something about where Z went." I pick at a fading red dot on my arm.

"Like what? She took everything."

"We have to do something."

"Come inside. We'll eat some breakfast and think about this logically." He tugs on my belt.

A flash of Zeena's light rope crashes into my mind. I jitter and retreat from his hold. "I can't sit around and do nothing."

"Whoa, take it easy."

"I can't." I storm away from him, too jacked on adrenaline to care if I slop in mud. My toe catches on a rock and I crash to the ground. I can't even get walking right.

William grabs my elbow and tries to haul me up.

I shove him off. "Stop it. I can do it myself."

He doesn't really let go until I'm fully upright. "So stubborn."

I scrape the muck and mud off my jeans and coat and end up smearing it all over. "Yeah, I know."

William's blue eyes spark. "I know you blame yourself for all this, but you shouldn't. And you don't have to solve this alone."

"I *am* alone."

"Weren't you just saying a couple minutes ago how glad you were to have me around? What am I supposed to do? Hang on the bench until I'm called into play?"

"Huh?"

His mouth twists. "Sports reference."

"Oh."

He leans close, until the space between us fizzes with possibilities. His mouth is so close to mine I can feel the warmth of his skin.

"William?" My brow arches.

"Yeah?"

"What're you doing?"

He smiles. "Something else happened when we invoked Libra. I got this *clarity* about things. About how I should trust my instincts and stop putting off things I know are right."

"Like what?" So unfair. I didn't get anything like that from invoking Gemini.

"Way to ruin the moment, Anne. I'm kissing you. If you shut up, that is."

I suck in a breath.

His lips brush against mine, light as a whisper. I fall into him. He pulls me closer and sucks on my bottom lip. I run my hands through his thick hair and give a solid yank. A laugh barks from his throat and his hands move lower. While our mouths duel, our auras meld. The wild energy from Gemini leaches out of me in golden streams, and the calming force of Libra soaks in through my pores, immobilizing my worries and fears as it goes. Inside, a flux of power sloshes around, turning my brain to mush and my heart to a hard jewel of flame.

The war within pours out of me and splits us apart.

William pants. "Wow."

"Yeah."

"I'm not sure what just happened."

"Me neither."

"It was pretty cool. We should try again."

I don't disagree. Mud is caked on his sweatshirt. Impulsively, I brush it off. "If I don't at least try to look for some clue or something, then I'll never be able to stand it. No one remembers Mary, Shequan, or Evan exist, so who else will look for them?"

"So, no more kissing?"

I stare at his mouth. For a long time. "Come with me to the faire?"

"I'll go wherever you go."

The faire is shut down due to the weather, like cousin Tommy said. It's the first time that has happened in my lifetime. The paths are just as washed out and muddy as the main roads. William has a harder time walking in his grubby three-million-year-old sneakers. We shift to the grass, which is slightly more solid, but way more slippery. It's like walking on gelatin instead of sponges.

"My feet are soaked." *Squish, squish, squish.*

"I doubt those were ever waterproof. Why didn't you put on boots?"

"Didn't think I'd be sloshing through mud lakes." His eyebrows waggle.

"At least you're not covered in mud." I turn toward the woods. This part of the faire grounds is on a hill, so we don't have to worry about puddles, but we do have to be careful about not slipping and sliding on saturated leaves and mulch. Finally, we get to the old witch's shoppe. While the sun bathes it in rich yellows, there's a hollow quality to it, as if I'm wearing 3D glasses. I swipe my hand, testing it for solidity. My palm smacks the siding with a *whack.*

William taps the wood himself and peers at me. "What're we doing?"

I drop my hand. "Nothing."

Inside, I spy a white pillar candle perched on a windowsill toward the back of the shack. A matchbook sits next to it. I snatch both up and carry them to the center of the room. "These weren't here before."

William kneels across from me. "You think we should mess with them?"

"Maybe the twins are helping us."

"Maybe Z is baiting us."

"It's a risk I have to take."

"But there's nothing else here."

"Not everything can be seen with the naked eye. I'm going to ask our signs to reveal a clue." I call the four directions and elements. "*North, south, east, west. Earth, fire, wind, and water.*"

A tentative smile crosses his mouth. After everything that's happened, I'm surprised he's excited. Must be his Libra confidence.

"This anchors the chant. Say it with me."

"Okay."

I extend my hands to him.

He doesn't hesitate to tangle our fingers together. The same chemical reaction that happened when we kissed bubbles inside me. The Zodiac power is our reagent. Physical contact is the catalyst.

Ages tick by and nothing inspires me. I drop his hands. So much for finishing the experiment.

He plants his hands on his knees. "Something wrong?"

My shoulders slump. "I'm afraid to say the wrong thing."

He leans forward. "I believe in you. You can do this."

"I wish I could just tell them to bring Mary, Evan, and Shequan back."

"Then say that." He shrugs.

I think about it. "It's too easy."

"Maybe you're making it harder than it has to be. Try following the path of least resistance."

I take a deep breath. Okay. Right. Path of least resistance. Easy peasy.

"I'm here, Anne. You're not alone. Remember that."

I lick my lips, close my eyes, and chant:

> "Castor and Pollux,
> Hear my plea,
> Bring my sister, Mary, back to me.
> Castor and Pollux,
> Make us whole,
> Give me back my other soul.
> Castor and Pollux, let it be,
> That Shequan and Evan return to me.
> Castor and Pollux,
> Hear my plea,
> Keep Zeena far away!"

I open my eyes. We're surrounded by a gigantic soap bubble of swirling blue and yellow. The ripples reflect off our skin, casting fluctuating shadows.

William grins. "This is amazing."

"Where's the lightning and thunder and hail and wind?" I purse my lips at him and blow out the candle. The bubble bursts and the room goes black-hole dark.

"Crap, Anne, what's going on?" William's voice sounds distant, even though he's sitting inches away from me.

The familiar wind I was waiting for batters the shoppe. It protests with pops and creaks. A battering ram of energy slams into my back. I collapse onto the candle. Wax splashes my cheek, sticking to my skin with its brutal heat.

I yelp and swipe at the hot wax as my body stretches from the inside. An itchy tingle settles in my spine and gut. The invader's icy claws slash as they go, shifting muscle and sinew to burrow into a cavity by my pelvis.

"Anne!" William shouts. He scrambles somewhere off to my right. The doorknob rattles and light slashes into the room as the door opens. "Anne?"

"I'm okay." I rise up on my elbows and flop over on my back like an unsteady turtle. My intestines and liver are shoved higher than they're supposed to be and compress my lungs. I snake my inhaler from my pocket, but my fingers shake too much. It slips from my fingers and clatters to the floor. William retrieves it and holds it steady at my mouth. I hold up two fingers for two puffs. The rush of medicine seizes my lungs even more. I wheeze and cough, unable to eject the bitter tang from my airways. If the inhaler doesn't work, I'm going to need an ambulance. "What's...hap...penning?"

"We should get out of here." William half-drags, half-carries me outside. "Focus on slow breaths, Anne. Your lungs will open up. Don't panic, that'll make it worse." He talks me through it better than any coach giving tips to his star player. I lay helplessly in his lap, with his sturdy arms around me, tenuously grasping to his life, his force, his tender gaze.

I relax a bit. Fresh air flows in and I release the tears that beg for freedom. Every time my breath is stolen, I fear it'll be my last episode, the final one that will take my life. When the albuterol doesn't work, the terror goes from hypothetical to very real.

William wipes my face. Bits of cooled wax stick under his fingernails.

"Am I burned?"

"It's a little red, but I think you're okay. I still see freckles." He grins, even if it's only to make me feel better.

"Thanks."

William helps me stand. "Let's get you home."

I don't argue. We walk slowly, in silence, hand in hand. Together.

Chapter Twenty

I reassure William I can make it home on my own, but he keeps walking with me anyway. Coming up with a cover story will be hard; if Dad catches me with William, he'll probably send me to an all-girls' school or, worse, a convent. On impulse, I fling my arms around William and give him a hug.

He squeezes back. "What's this for? Not that I'm complaining."

"I'll call you later, okay?" I let go and rush off.

"Bye," he calls.

I skirt around the hedge marking our property line, using the greenery as camouflage. Mom's car is in the driveway, but Dad's truck is gone. Good. With any luck, Dad hadn't told Mom about grounding me.

I approach the house with SWAT-team stealth. Regardless of Mom's knowledge (or lack thereof), the situation inside could be critical and I don't want to trigger random open fire. My boots clomp on the porch so I shimmy out of them to deaden my footsteps. I shrug out of my jacket, pull it inside out, and tie it around my waist to hide as much mud as possible. Fewer visuals indicating my participation in mudcapades means less evidence for any potential interrogation.

The house is silent, like a funeral home at night. You know bodies are around, but you don't want to run into one. Shutting the front door without alerting the maternal guard is a miracle. When she's quiet, she expects the rest of us to be too. Even a whisper will irritate her.

I wince at every creak and pop of the stairs. It's not a crime to leave my room, but I don't want her to guess my whereabouts on the rare chance she is listening. Not until after I've changed into clean clothes.

The dogs greet me with happy yips and wet licks and ticking puppy paws. Poor things haven't had enough attention lately. I fight them off me to change, wary of the amount of dried dirt flaking off my jeans. Firing up a vacuum cleaner to suck up the evidence is *not* an option.

"Guys, really?" I palm the kerchief with Mary tucked inside. Then I undress, ball my muddy clothes, stuff them into a spare pillowcase, and rush downstairs. Mom's workroom door is open and she's not inside. She's not in the basement either, thank goodness. I load the wash and dump in extra detergent.

Once the washing machine hums to life, I slip back to the porch and grab my boots. The garden hose is on the other side of the garage. After a quick rinse in cold water, my hands are frigid, but the boots are clean. I dry them off with a spare rag and take them to my room, putting them away in their designated spot.

First time for everything, I guess.

I feed the dogs, take them for a walk, and take a shower. Daily rituals. Routine. Should be calming. But I'm not satisfied. My stomach twists on itself. I have to organize something, anything. *Now.*

The pile of school stuff on my desk could use tidying. Binders from the past school year belch loose papers, crinkled handouts, and torn folders. I carry the lot to my bed and dig in for a solid straightening-up session. When I finish, each page is filed neatly under the proper tab.

Unsatisfied, I scan the room and spy my bottom bookshelf. More binders are squished between the Eiffel Tower bookends. Soon, a layer of sweat covers me, and a rainbow of binders replaces the random chaos.

I stand and run my fingers through my hair. Instead of sighing with frustration at the curls, I luxuriate in the springy pop each lock gives when I let go.

Wait. I hate my curly hair. Mary is the one who—

"Oh. My. God." I whirl to the mirror next to the closet, legs weakening by the millisecond. My mouth drops open. Without thinking about it—because I was in such a hurry to get out of my muddy clothes—I've changed into Hello Kitty sweatpants and a matching pink T-shirt. Except I never wear matchy-matchy clothes.

Mary does.

The subzero intruder that had been slumbering during my cleaning fest shivers awake. It uncurls and stretches, climbing along my vertebrae to the base of my neck.

I pinch my eyes shut and open them again.

My curly hair fits. So does the pink outfit. I smile.

I close my eyes again and shake my head, jostling loose any funky thought. When I open my eyes and take in the curls sprouting from my scalp, I cringe.

"What the heck?" I ask myself.

The intruder taps my spinal cord.

"Ohmigod." I lean closer to the mirror. "Mary?"

Fireworks go off in my brain. I drop to my knees and clutch my skull.

Ohmigod, Ohmigod, Ohmigod, she's inside me, she's inside me, she's inside me!

My chant returns to me, riding a boomerang of, "oh, you've done it now." *Castor and Pollux, make us whole, give me back my other soul.*

They'd sent Mary's soul into my body. It has to be.

I dash to the kerchief and unravel it. It's empty. The symbol is gone.

I scream. And scream and scream.

I scream until Mom clambers up the stairs and bursts into my room.

"What is going on?" she screeches, wide-eyed and wild-haired.

I point to the mirror as if it explains everything.

"Is it a spider or something?" She clutches her hands to her chest and steps back, slumping her shoulders and perching on tiptoes like a humpbacked ballerina. She's terrified of spiders. The hellion who mimics Medusa with her craziness is afraid of arachnids.

"M-Mom, it's…M-Mary." I squeak. My hand trembles as it flicks toward my reflection. No, Mary's reflection. No, mine. No… Oh, I can't tell anymore.

Mom's face contorts. "Who's Mary?"

My hand falls and so does my heart, right through the floor and into the basement where it settles on the concrete and oozes blood.

She slams back on her heels. Fear is replaced by fury. Just like that. "I asked you a question. Who. Is. Mary?"

Panting, I frantically search my mind for a viable explanation. Thoughts ricochet around my skull, random and way too fast for me to grab hold of. *The spell didn't work. Mom is about to explode all over my room. I'm possessed by my sister. Castor and Pollux have a sick sense of humor. I wish William were here.*

Her face goes slack. "Are you feeling all right?" Her eyes narrow with suspicion.

My throat is too tight to speak and it burns from screaming so much. I tremble as I nod.

"Why were you yelling?" She tucks a strand of frizzy hair behind her ear.

I open my mouth. A gurgling sound comes out. My fingers scrape my neck to release whatever's blocking my voice box.

"Oh, Lord, not my baby, please, not my baby," she cries, tears already racing down her cheeks. Her whole body shakes with the prayer and she reaches out for me, like a grieving fallen angel unable to save herself. "Have you used your inhaler?"

I shake my head. This isn't an asthma attack.

She rushes to my nightstand and yanks an inhaler out of the drawer. Holding the thing to my mouth, she says, "Take two puffs."

I cry too. Of all the weirdness that's happened over the past few days, this is by far the strangest. Mom all maternal and caring? No way. The bitterness inside me swells while the desire to run into her arms twists itself in my guts. A sob escapes my mouth. I'd long ago given up the hope that Mom would show me some love. But Mary, she hangs onto it like a lion suffocating its kill. So are the tears hers…or mine?

It's too much to fight myself, her, and decide what to do. I shake my head and shift my weight back and forth from one foot to the other while clenching and unclenching my fists.

"Come on, do it!"

I push her hand away. "I don't need it."

Her eyes widen. Then her jaw clenches. "Did you just hit me?"

"No."

Mom pins me with her dragon's eyes. Her face ripples with the constipated wince of confusion, the hard angles of anger, and the blind openness of fear. "Are you using drugs?"

"*What?*" She's got to be kidding, but her eyebrows suggest otherwise. They're completely flat, like two cultured caterpillars resting above her intense eyes. Her lips are thin and pale. She's in total serious mode.

"Well? Why aren't you answering me, Anne? Are you tweaked?"

"No."

"No you're not tweaked, or no you're not answering me?" Her gaze scours over me, acidic and rough.

"I'm not on drugs." I bite my tongue to stop myself from saying, "You should be." I fight the urge to reorganize my closet. No, it's Mary's urge. I squeeze my eyes shut and whisper, "Stop it. Just relax. I can handle this."

"Who're you talking to? You better not be talking to me like that." Mom's totally over her sob fest now. Any hint of insult, whether imagined or not, whether directed toward her or not, will trigger the rage simmering beneath her thin crust of humanness.

The urge to organize intensifies. "Mary, please," I say under my breath. "No, Mom, I'm not talking to you." I put up my hands in surrender, hoping to calm the beast blocking my exit.

"Well, who else is here, Anne? No one. Which means you're hearing voices and talking to the devil or something." She folds her arms like she knows all. Her head tilts down, confirming the fact.

"No, I'm not hearing voices!" I stomp my foot. "You're the one who's crazy, and everyone knows it. Your customers are talking about you, you know. So why don't you just go to your workroom and pretend to create something!" I cover my mouth the instant the words gush out, but it's too late. The dam broke, and I can't collect the words hitting her in a flood of daggers.

Her face reddens. In the fraction of a second that time stops, I see the next series of events, a flash-forward of the scene to come. She covers the distance between us in an instant and has her fingers tangled in my hair and digging into my scalp so deeply a neurosurgeon would have to extract them.

Mom drags me behind her down the stairs so fast I almost slide down a few of them in my socked feet. She has the number to the hospital on speed dial, so she is able to call them and shove me in the passenger seat of her car at the same time. She's already barking out her intentions before she even turns over the engine. It doesn't matter that I have no shoes and she's still wearing her robe.

"My daughter, she's gone ballistic. I think she's hearing voices. She attacked me." Mom throws the car in reverse and squeals the tires, not bothering to check if any cars are coming. Luckily, we don't crash into anybody. She swings the steering wheel and off we go. "My name is Elizabeth Devans, my daughter is Anne." She recites our address and phone number. "I have her in the car now. No, I don't need the police or the ambulance. I can handle my own kid."

I find my voice again, thankful of its return. "M-Mom, please, don't—"

She shoves a finger in my face, letting go of the steering wheel to do so. "Don't talk to me, you're psychotic."

"No, I'm not. Please don't take me to the hospital." I pick at my nails, unsure if it's Mary or me. I can't go to the psych ward. They can't admit me for this, can they? If they believe Mom, they can. Doesn't matter that she's the crazy one.

I grip the armrest on the car door as she hangs a right turn without pausing for the stop sign. I hear a particularly angry car horn and I cringe, waiting for the crunch of tangling metal, but it doesn't happen. A green sedan takes up most of the side mirror. The driver is waving his fist at us.

Mom extends her middle finger at him. "I got a sick kid here, okay?" she growls, pressing the gas pedal. The car surges ahead and I'm pressed into my seat from the force of it.

I click my seatbelt in place.

The next two miles are taken up with her complaining about detours around the local bridges. I keep waiting for her to bark at some cop like the floods are their fault, but she's all too pleasant when one asks her to roll down her window at a blockade.

"The bridge is closed ma'am. Oh, Mrs. Devans, hey." Johnny Wilks smiles his charming smile and tips his hat to her. He knows Tommy and therefore he knows us. Fantastic.

"Hello, Johnny. I'm in a hurry, my daughter needs to get to the hospital." Mom speaks in her I'm-a-concerned-parent-looking-out-for-the-health-of-my-child voice.

"Oh, wow, Anne, are you okay?" He ducks down to look at me through the driver's-side window.

I lean against the seat belt. "I'm fine, I don't need to—"

Mom clamps a hand over my mouth. "She's…sick… you know," she rolls her eyes and clicks the button for her window to go up while easing her foot off the brake.

"Oh," Johnny frowns, probably confused, but not stupid enough to ask for clarification. No one ever does. It's like they think bad things don't exist if they don't see them firsthand.

I can't stay in the car with her. She'll have me locked away forever. I release the belt, unlock my door, and launch myself out of the seat, stumbling as my feet hit the pavement. I'm off in a flash, running back the way we came, not really with any destination in mind. Then it hits me. William's. I'll go to William's.

The car's engine roars. It's followed by the churning of gravel under rubber. Glancing over my shoulder, I catch Mom bringing the car around in stunt-driver fashion. Her tires spin and the car lurches toward me. I run faster, half-panicking that she'll run me over and half-freaking out that my lungs won't manage this pace for much longer.

And I don't have my inhaler.

My feet hurt from the loose stones littering the road, left behind by the rushing floods, but I don't stop. Pain streaks across my chest and my pulse pounds in my ears, but I push myself. I veer off the road into the nearby woods just as Mom whooshes past me. Her tires squeal.

I don't look back. My primary concern is not impaling my feet on the branches littering the ground.

"Johnny, help!" Mom's cry slices through the trees.

Soon, I hear two sets of footsteps crashing behind me. And they get louder. Tears sluice down my face, blur my vision, and burn my nose. A stitch in my side slows me before the pain in my feet does. "No, no, no," I cry. They'll catch me if I stop, but I can't go any farther. My freaking tightened asthmatic lungs throw up a roadblock the size of the Great Wall of China. My head pounds as I bash my skull against its ancient stones. Darkness swirls at the edges of my vision.

I trip on a tree root and slam into the ground chest first. It knocks the remaining air out of my lungs and no matter how much I open my mouth, nothing goes in.

A pair of hands slap onto my back.

First abandoned by air, then abandoned by freedom.

Chapter
Twenty-One

I wake to whispers and screams, shuffling feet and banging...and the worst headache of my life. Opening my eyes sharpens the pain.

The room is dark. The curtains are pulled and the door is closed most of the way, letting a sliver of artificial light smack against the painting on the wall next to me. I blink a few times and a pastel-colored still life comes into focus. Its theoretically calming colors are so boring that my brain waves flatline. I shift my gaze to the left. Another bed parallels mine, its far side pressed against the wall. The sheets are taut across the mattress.

Dry disinfectant and starchy bleach clog my sinuses and settle in the back of my throat.

The last thing I remember is...Mom chasing me in the woods. Me falling. Gasping for air. Passing out.

I gotta be in a hospital.

Another scream pierces my ears. It's coming from outside my room. Someone farther along down the hallway orders,

"Stop screaming or you'll get an injection to help you calm down."

The cry dies down to a steady moan.

Holy Mary. I know where I am.

A psycho ward.

I don't belong here. I shift to my side. Every muscle screams from stiffness. The universal protest tosses me onto the mattress.

My breath quickens and a squeaky wheeze shoots out with every exhale. I reach for my inhaler, then realize I'm not wearing jeans, but am dressed in a tent-ish gown. I follow the trail of non-fashion, hoping my legs are covered, but they're not. No pajama bottoms, ugh.

My feet are wrapped in bandages.

I jerk my eyes away. My inhaler's on the bedside stand. Reaching to pick it up, I wince at the stiffness of my ribcage.

A hit of the inhaler relaxes me.

The door swings open and the lights flick on. I squint at the brightness and duck my head. "Hey, ouch, light," I stutter.

"Anne Devans?" A woman in Mickey Mouse scrubs walks in holding a clipboard. Her name badge reads "Monika Drumme, RN." Beneath her name reads "Kings Hospital Department of Child and Adolescent Psychiatry."

"Sorry to wake you. How are you feeling?" Her mouth widens into a smile—the same glitzy white smile as the picture on her ID. Her brown eyes crinkle with her grin. They match the tone of her skin.

"Tired. Who was screaming?" My gaze darts to the door and the hallway beyond.

"Do you know where you are, honey?" She scribbles something on her paper.

I tuck my legs toward my chest. I know where I am. And I know why I'm here. Mom thinks I'm crazy. She's the one who's nutso. My insides go cold—Mary's pain is the same as mine. We're trapped here together. If only she could talk to me. But then I really would be hearing voices.

I shiver.

"Tell me all about it, dear. Let it out." Monika sits next to me and wraps an arm around me. Her hand is warm and slicks the goosebumps off my skin as she rubs her palm over my shoulder.

"I...I'm not crazy," I trip over every syllable. She's probably heard that line before at least a million times. It's the same one Mom uses whenever she's in the loony bin. In my case, it's the truth.

"No one said you were crazy." The frankness of her voice sobers me.

"Then why am I here?"

"Why do you think you're here?"

Sly. I've heard my mom's doctors do the same thing. Whenever you ask a question, they respond with another one. I figured that out during one of our numerous "family sessions" with a therapist. What a joke family therapy is when the crazy one doesn't admit she's crazy and spends the entire time blaming everyone else for "not understanding."

"Well?"

"My mom says I was hearing voices. I wasn't. I just...got scared, that's all."

"What scared you, honey?" Monika removes her arm from my shoulder and folds her hands on her lap.

Yeah, right, like I'm going to tell her. But I have no idea what Mom told them, other than she said I'd attacked her. I fiddle with a wrinkle in my gown. Mary hates wrinkles.

"Anne?"

I straighten my spine and square my shoulders. Enough of this "poor me" crap. No one will believe me anyway. If I say Mom's the one who went loopy, they'll tell her and then she'll never take me home. "So, you have some medicine to give me?"

The nurse jerks as if I'd just shocked her with crash-cart paddles or something. "Is that what you think you need?"

"You tell me." I scrunch back so I touch the wall. The sheets are crumpled beneath me. I fight the urge to smooth them out. Mary will just have to tolerate it. I'm in charge here, darn it.

Monika's mouth twists again and she clucks her tongue against her teeth. "All right, I thought we'd talk a bit first, but I see you get right down to business. Your medicine isn't due until bedtime. You hungry? We saved a tray for you." She stands and points down the hall.

"What time is it?" The curtains have blocked out all light and there isn't a clock in the room.

"Seven in the evening."

I've been unconscious all day. That's assuming it's the same day.

"If you don't want meatloaf and green beans, there's turkey and cheese sandwiches."

"I'm not hungry." Which is the truth. I couldn't shove anything down my throat right now, not even water.

"All right. Well, if you change your mind, we have snacks later on." She leaves, keeping the door open a sliver like before.

I have to figure out how to make people think I'm sane. Dad always begs Mom to take her meds. Says that'll get her out of the hospital sooner. She never goes along with it. Cheeks her meds instead. If she can manage it during her deranged psychotic episodes, then so can I. The difference is I'm sane and can fake better than her. They'll see. They'll take pity on me. I should be out of here in no time.

I hope.

♐ ♈ ♊ ♏ ♓

I yank the curtain open and huddle on my bed, staring at the moon as it tracks across the ebony sky. A silent watchman, cold and indifferent to our suffering. I wonder if Castor and Pollux are looking down at me. I wonder what they think. Are they laughing at this mess? Disappointed in me? Or are they simply Zeena's slaves? Hard to imagine such powerful warriors being slaves.

Monika comes in around nine o'clock. Apparently I'm not getting a roommate tonight, because no one has shown up to take the empty bed. I haven't left my room, so I have little idea who else is on the unit. Not that I care. I'm not like them anyway.

She hands me a paper cup. Inside are two pills, both small, round, and white.

"What are these?" I stare at them, head swirling from the quick jitter of my heart. I shouldn't be afraid of them. I'm not crazy, so they can't do anything to me. Right?

"They'll help you sleep, hon," Monika holds out a mini cup of water to make swallowing the meds easier.

"I don't need these." I hold the cup out to her.

She frowns, placing her free hand on her hip. "The psychiatrist ordered these for you and your mother agreed."

"I never met the *psychiatrist*. How does he or she know what I need?" I retort.

"You met him, honey, you just don't remember." Her eyes soften, like she pities me, but her posture does not ease.

"While I was unconscious? That's fair."

"You were awake a while ago. A little loopy, but you talked to him. Said you have another person inside you."

Everything goes cold. "No, I didn't. I wouldn't."

"This must be scary for you. Take the medicine. You'll feel better."

"Getting out of here will make me feel better. I have the SAT and...and..." A missing sister, two missing friends, and a deadly witch after me. All because I wanted to play with magick and do things my way. But I can't say those things or they'll never let me out of here. My hands shake and I nearly tip over the cup.

Monika peers at me over her glasses. The corner of her mouth draws down.

I square my jaw. My arm is starting to ache from holding it up for so long.

The moments of silence that pass during our who-can-hold-a-paper-cup-longer-and-stare-without-blinking contest ends with me lowering my arm and tipping the cup to my mouth.

Balancing the pills on my tongue, I suck down a swig of water and swallow. One gets stuck in my throat so I finish off the rest of the lukewarm drink.

"That's a girl," Monika praises me.

I try not to cry. The sting of suppressed tears brings a rush of heat to my face.

"Get some rest. Your mom will visit in the morning. She's worried about you."

"That's not true. She's the crazy one." I flop on the bed and tug the covers over my head.

"You'll feel better in the morning. And don't worry about your test. Once you're better, they can be rescheduled. Everything will be okay." She leaves the room, shutting off the light before closing the door behind her.

I push back the blanket. I'm immersed in darkness, save for the pale moonlight meandering in through the window. If I twist my head just so, I can see the white disc smudged with gray. I watch it crawl across the sky until I can't keep my eyelids open anymore.

♐ ♈ ♊ ♏ ♓

I sleep through breakfast and almost through lunch. Monika's not here. She must work second shift. My nurse today is Ingrid. She's the opposite of Monika. Stiff, strict, and a woman of few words. Whatever. She leaves me alone after walking me to the cafeteria.

Six tables crowd the plain space. Each table has five plastic chairs. Up to thirty kids can be here at any time. Seems like a lot, but I'm not an expert on psych wards. The patients—kids ranging from middle school to high school—line up along the wall. A gate trundles up on its tracks, revealing a counter filled with hot dish trays. Plates, napkins, and plasticware are at one end. Each kid picks up a tray while the staff dishes out breaded chicken patties, mashed potatoes, and broccoli. Bottled water and juice finish off the standardized buffet.

I catch a whiff of the food and my stomach growls.

At the front of the line, one kid yells, "Hurry up!" and whacks the back of another kid's head. The whacker is dressed in blue scrubs. His greasy hair covers his face. Bandages bind both wrists. The whackee is at least a foot shorter and wider. He rubs his skull and runs out of the room wailing. The other kids erupt in cheers and jabs. "Chase him!" "Way to go, nutso!" "You should've bashed his face into the wall!"

Staff let the victim go and focus on Greasy Boy. Ingrid leads the charge. "Charlie, calm down. It's not nice to hit people."

Charlie backs against the wall, both hands up and fisted.

The kids in front of me retreat, pushing me back. I slip out of the line and dart to the opposite corner, farthest away from the mess. This place is where Mom thought I needed to be?

Someone from the end of the line wanders toward me like a zombie. A towel is draped over his head. His arms don't move as he walks. I drag a chair from under the nearest table and position it between us. The boy halts, reaches up to the towel, and pulls it back, exposing his face.

My jaw drops. "*Shequan.* What're you doing here?"

His eyes are glazed over and his lips are cracked. He blinks so slowly I wonder if he'll open them again. "Who's Shequan?"

"You're Shequan." I grip the chair's back.

"I'm nobody." He turns and walks away.

I watch him sit in a chair at the next table and rest his hands on the laminated surface. He's staring at the chaos of people yelling and staff pinning Charlie to the floor, but he doesn't seem to notice. It's like he's empty, hollow…a non-person. His body is here, but his brain isn't. He can't possibly have forgotten who he is.

That's it. I'm not taking meds again, not if they do this.

Unless this is Zeena's work. When she chanted, I was certain she'd transformed Shequan into the Aries symbol. It wasn't like his mind got sucked out and his body was left behind.

I ease into a seat on his left. He doesn't move or act like he notices. "When did you get here?"

He blinks. Breathes. Blinks again. "I don't know."

"I saw you at the faire a few days ago, so it can't be long. A couple days at the most." I dig a fingernail into the waxy plastic coating ringing the table's edge.

"Fair. Dare. Bare."

"Why don't you remember who you are?"

"U, R, Y, I…"

This is going nowhere fast. "How did you get here? Where were you before this? Do you remember the witch chanting over you?"

His fingers spread out on the table. "Red light…pain…darkness…"

I lean closer. "You remember!"

"Blank…nothingness…silence…alone…" He starts rocking and cuts his gaze to me. His stare shoots through me like I'm not here. "I'm no one."

"What're you talking about? You were by yourself? Where?"

"Nowhere. Nothing. No one."

A chill skitters down my spine. She'd sent him somewhere, but nowhere. Traveling to another dimension might explain it. The disappearances, the wiping of everyone's memory. Not existing on the planet but on another plane makes sense.

"I can help you, Shequan. Tell you about yourself. You and I go to the same school. Your dad is a knight at the faire. He runs the joust. You're a squire. Remember?"

He bolts from his chair toward me and screams, "No one!" His hands clap on either side of my head and his fingers dig into my scalp, pulling at my hair. Spittle flies from his mouth and sprays my cheek.

"Shequan, let me go!" I pry at his hands and kick his shins.

"No one!" He keeps yelling and squeezing my skull.

At least three aides swarm around us. They take turns barking at him, "Let her go. Relax. Stop yelling."

Finally, his hands are torn from my head. Clumps of hair go with it.

Ingrid swoops me up and guides me to my room. Her nails dig into my arm. "What happened?"

"N-nothing." I collapse on my bed and curl into a ball.

My body quakes with terror. Zeena's stolen Shequan's mind, his soul, whatever makes him *him*, and left an insane shell. Mary's with me, but her body's gone. Is it wandering out there, somewhere, a puppet without a puppet master, or is her body caught in the other dimension? And Evan. Where's he? When—if—we find them and bring them back, they may be just as lost.

William and I are next.

I don't want to be hollow.

Chapter Twenty-Two

We're allowed one phone call a day—after dinner, so we don't have an excuse to miss groups. As the phone rings, I swallow down the anxiety clawing its way up my chest. *Please pick up, please pick up.*

"Talk." James. William's obnoxious older brother. He's more interested in partying and gaming than life. Music blares in the background.

"Get William."

"What?"

I cover the mouthpiece and my mouth with my hand. "Get. William."

"Who's this?"

"Anne."

Thunk. He dropped the receiver. Idiot. "Will!"

The song ends and another is half-done before more muffled sounds come out of the phone. I turn my back on the dozen or so kids waiting around to use the phone after me. They'll wait their turn. I had to. At least Charlie isn't around—he'd clock me on the back of the head. He had his privilege revoked.

"Hello?"

I sigh with relief. "William."

"Anne?"

It's so good to hear his voice. Soothing. I miss him like peanut butter misses jelly. My lip trembles. "Um-hmmm."

"Where are you?" Hinges creak and a door slams. The music fades to a dull roar. He must be outside.

"You're not going to believe this." I slump against the wall and hang onto the phone casing. It's bolted to the wall, reinforced so it can't be torn down. "I'm in a psych ward."

He doesn't say anything.

"Are you there?"

"How'd that happen?"

I turn to the wall. "I freaked out and Mom thought I'd lost it."

"What freaked you out?"

"Mary is inside me."

"Huh?"

"The chant we did in Z's shoppe. It was Mary who slammed into me."

"There's, like, *two* of you in there?"

Saying it out loud makes it sound weird. "I…think so."

"You think or you know?"

What's the best way to say this? "I organized my bookshelves into a rainbow and wore pink."

He sighs heavily. "Whoa."

"Exactly."

"How do we get her out?"

"I don't know."

"How do we get *you* out?"

"I don't know."

Another sigh.

"Shequan's here too. Only he…" I gingerly touch my sore scalp.

"What?"

"He doesn't remember who he is. I tried talking with him, to jog his memory, but he went wild and attacked me."

"Are you okay?" Tension tightens his voice.

I press the receiver to my ear. "Yeah, I'm fine. The sooner I get out of here, the better."

Someone taps my shoulder.

I whirl, expecting it to be a crazed, medicated kid ready to pound me.

It's Monika. "Phone time's over, Anne. You have a visitor."

"I just got on the phone. I don't want to see anyone."

"Hang up and give someone else a turn." She crosses her arms across her ample bosom, squishing the Hello Kitty pattern of her scrubs in the process.

Mom's standing behind her, a few feet away, eyes darting. She shakes her hair out and purses her mouth. Her bright-red lipstick bleeds into the tiny lines surrounding her lips. "I bring my daughter to the psych ward for treatment and she's hanging out on the phone?"

Monika glances over her shoulder. "They're allowed one call a day."

"She doesn't have anyone to call." Mom gives a smug half-smile.

"Why are you here?" I twist my hands around the phone.

I hear a muffled "Anne?" from the receiver. Poor William.

She runs her tongue over her front teeth. "I can tell the meds haven't kicked in yet. Tell the doctor to increase the dose."

"I can pass a message on to the doctor, but he and Anne are going to work out a regimen between them." Monika edges toward me, physically putting herself between Mom and me.

"She's my daughter and what I say goes." She's getting louder. Not good.

"Mom. It's okay. I'm taking the medicine, I swear." I hang up the phone. It kills me to cut off William, but it's better than Mom ripping the phone from my hand and screaming into the receiver. She's done that before.

She stabs a finger in my direction. "You better not be lying."

"I'm not."

"Are the voices gone yet?" She rakes a hand through her hair. "She's on an anti-psychotic, right? That's what the doctor said."

Several gazes are drawn to us, like magnets attracting iron shavings. Other staff members slowly wander closer. Kids pop out of their rooms and the rec room to watch.

"Ma'am, I'll ask you to lower your voice. If you'd like to talk, we can go to a more private area." Monika makes eye contact with the aides, who continue to surround us.

"I will *not* lower my voice." Mom rushes to me and clamps a bony hand around my upper arm. "I'm taking you out of here. You're all worthless!"

I wince. "Ow."

She yanks me down the hallway, her free arm outstretched as if to ram through the wall of aides and nurses blocking our advance. The staff huddles around us to keep the freak show contained, but they let us work our way to the locked unit door.

"Mrs. Devans. Please release your daughter. She's safe with us. We'll escort you off the ward now." Monika keeps her voice level, but her eyes are wide with determination.

Mom sneers at her like a rabid jackal. "You can't tell me what to do!"

Four aides close in, two on my side, two on Mom's.

Monika wedges herself in the middle of everybody. "Let her go, Mrs. Devans."

"This is unacceptable. I'll have all your licenses taken away." Mom gives me a shove before dropping her hold. She pins me under her stare and allows the aides to flank her on the way out.

I keep eye contact until she's on the other side and the unit door is locked. "Do you believe me now?" I rub my arm. It'll probably bruise.

Monika nods. "We'll call the doctor in the morning. He might want to inform CPS."

I grab her hand. "Wait. No. Don't call them."

"Honey, you can't stay in an abusive home." Her brown eyes soften. She really cares. Too bad she has no idea how serious things are. Or how the truth is impossible to believe unless you've seen it yourself. Or that magick is real and as devastating as any mental illness.

"It's not abusive." My voice cracks.

"With what I just saw, it certainly seems to be. Come on, why don't you take a break in your room?"

I fall in line behind her. In reality, it makes no difference where I am. Mary is with me. Zeena will find me. Then it'll all be over.

♐ ♈ ♊ ♏ ♓

A*nne.* Someone calls my name. My brain is fuzzy so it takes a few minutes before I start caring about it.

Anne. A whisper, nothing more. I'm not even sure it's real.

Anne.

"Who is it?" I groan, my throat dry.

Anne.

My eyes pop open. Without moving, I scan the room, squinting into the deeper shadows, waiting for movement. The light switch is across the room. The distance pins me to the mattress as my mind wheels with possibilities. Could be a dream. Could be someone hiding in the inky corner.

Anne.

I roll over. "Go away."

Anne!

The shout is inside my head. I gasp and sit upright, invisible monsters looming in the shadows forgotten.

Please don't freak out, Anne. I'm sorry. I didn't mean to let her get me.

I swallow. Hallucinations don't apologize. But my sister would. "Mary, is that you?"

We have to get out of here. Z…I can feel her. She's getting close. I don't really hear Mary's voice, but it's her thoughts, for sure. They stir in my brain and make my heart vibrate in my chest like a pulsing subwoofer.

"Where is she?" I scan the room, seeing everything and nothing at once.

Her spirit. I can feel it pulling at me. I'm scared, Anne.

"Don't go near it."

I don't want to, but she's making me.

"If you go, we'll go together and then she'll have both of us," I warn, rising to my knees. The sheets tangle around my legs and pull me down.

Something near my spine twists and flutters, like a thousand butterfly wings have taken flight in my body. They ramble toward my neck and make my skin crawl.

"Don't go to her, Mary, please."

It's hard to resist. Do something!

"Stay with me." I tear at the blanket holding me down and leap out of bed.

What are you going to do?

I pad to the door and peek into the hallway. It's empty. The aides do rounds every fifteen minutes, so I don't have a lot of time to figure something out.

Anne?

"Magick doesn't solve everything." I slip out of the room and scurry along the wall toward the nursing station.

The aide's sneakers squeak. He's coming closer.

My head bonks against a red fire alarm.

White letters spell out the instructions—Pull in case of fire.

Squeak, squeak, squeak.

I extend my hand, curl my fingers around the handle, and pull.

A high-pitched wail sounds the alarm and white lights dotting the hallway flicker like flash bulbs.

I dash to my room, pulling the door shut behind me, then push it back open a crack and peek through.

Overhead lights—dimmed for nighttime—pulse and go out. A second later, a series of pops relay across the ceiling. Pipes groan and hiss.

"What the…"

The sprinklers click to life and douse everything in teeth-chatteringly cold water.

Screams—from other kids, and probably some of the staff too—spring around like bouncy balls in a wind tunnel.

Emergency lights spring to life.

What's going on? Mary scurries toward my lower spine.

"Dunno. Didn't expect the power to go out."

What if it's her?

"We have to get out of here." I rush to the window and check for latches. There's a hole where a handle should go, and several screws impale the window's inner casing. It's locked shut. Doesn't matter. We're on the third story without a ladder or fire escape to climb down.

Monika barges into my room, sliding on the puddles of water slicking the floor. Her hair is matted to her head and her uniform is soaked. "Anne, let's go. We have to evacuate."

I whirl and rush after her while Mary squeals with delight. *A way out!*

With Monika taking the lead, we slide between flailing kids and the overwhelmed staff trying to console them. Patients outnumber nurses five to one, so I'm lucky to have Monika on my side.

Apparently convinced the fire (that doesn't exist) has been extinguished, the sprinklers slow to a drippy trickle and the emergency lights blink out. A wave of screams swells in the darkness.

Monika and I reach the door. I jiggle the handle with both hands.

"It's still locked. I have to swipe my badge."

"But it's an emergency! Shouldn't it just open?" I hop on my toes.

"We're going to get out, but you have to stay calm." She shifts me to the side and uses her penlight to illuminate the keypad. She swipes her ID, keys in her passcode, and the door unlocks with a *clink*.

We launch into an equally dark corridor.

"Is the whole hospital fritzed?" Monika asks.

Nurses, aides, and the other kids press their hands against my back, shoving me along. Monika separates from me to wrangle the herd. We nosedive into another group of adult patients from the neighboring ward. I almost get trampled in the intersection between crowds. I push at them, but their combined strength squashes me in the corner. Soon, I'm immersed in bodies, lost in the mass.

It's the perfect cover.

While Monika ushers the kids downstairs, I swim in the opposite direction, crawling along the wall like I'm on a cliff walk. Kids, adults, and staff stream past me until I'm the only one in the hallway.

They've forgotten us. We won't find our way out. Mary's worry tingles through my spine and stiffens my legs.

"No, it's good they've left us behind. We can find our own exit." I blink, hard, half to make sure my eyes aren't closed—it's that dark—and half to break Mary's tantrum. Waving my hands in an arc in front of me, all I catch is air.

"Castor and Pollux, I could really use some light. Maybe an orb or something?" I mutter. A flicker of amber sprouts from thin air and courses down the hallway. It disappears for a millisecond, only to be replaced with a much larger, paler spike. The line swings from outlet to outlet, scalloping the wall in flame.

This is no orb. It's electrical. And it's coming straight at me.

"That's not helpful!" I should have never invoked the Gemini twins. All they've brought me is trouble, trouble, and more trouble. I slam all my weight into the door, compressing the handle and diving into the stairwell. An arc slices past me, in the exact spot I just stood.

At least this stairwell has windows. Streetlights and flashes of lightning highlight the steps so I can rush down them without worrying about tripping. When I finally get outside, the pouring rain soaks my hospital gown and plasters my hair to my forehead and neck.

While the rest of the patients huddle in front of the building, I slide around the corner and head toward the woods. I'm miles from home.

But I'm not going there.

Chapter Twenty-Three

I ring the doorbell and pray James doesn't answer the door. With any luck, he's lost in an alternate reality forged by the combination of video games, tobacco, and booze.

The lock disengages and William swings the door open. Rap music blares from deeper inside the house.

"Anne. What're you doing here? How'd you get out?" He slips out onto the front porch, barefoot and wearing only pajama bottoms. Incense and cigarette smoke sneak around him, and so does my resolve. I should've brought my inhaler. And my ability to resist touching a hot, shirtless guy.

"I escaped." I huddle in his shadow, arms wrapped around my chest, shivering. Rain-soaked and freezing isn't my favorite look, especially since I'm wearing a thin hospital gown and bandages on my feet.

His mouth drops, but he says nothing.

"Can I come in? I feel like a dork out here." My teeth chatter.

"Uh, yeah, sorry." He ushers me inside, closing the door quietly. The lock clicks with a flick of his wrist. "Mom and Dad are…working late."

"And James?"

"Basement." He looks me up and down. "You're soaked."

"It's raining."

He darts into the living room and snatches a lap blanket from the recliner. Wrapping it around me, he says, "I was worried when you hung up on me."

"Mom visited." I stare up at him.

William leads me upstairs. We've played in his room from time to time (as little kids). It's as familiar to me as s'mores and hot chocolate. I stand in the doorway, dripping on the sock-laden, gray carpet.

He slides open the closet door and pulls a shirt and sweatpants from the top shelf. "These'll be baggy, but they're dry." He offers them to me, his gaze flitting here and there.

Our fingers brush as I take the clothes from him. His hand is much warmer than mine.

Keep it PG, Anne.

I startle. She's been quiet for so long I almost forgot she was there, hearing what I hear, seeing what I see, feeling what I…never mind. "Sorry."

It's okay. William's sweet. He'll help us.

"Huh?" William tips his head closer.

"I mean, thanks."

William clears his throat and cracks his knuckles. "No problem."

I drape the sweats over my arm, unsure of who I'm thanking—Mary or William.

The silence between us settles in my heart.

Mary stirs. *Say something*, she nudges.

I jerk at the echo-y sound inside my head. "This is weird."

William smiles and his dimples make a cameo appearance. "Yeah. I mean, you're wearing a hospital gown. A sopping wet, thin, white hospital gown with nothing but a pair of panties underneath."

I dig a toe into the carpet and rejoice to Castor and Pollux that I've got a blanket around me. "You saw…" Oh god, what did he see?

He leaps up. "I didn't see anything, I swear."

"Except my underwear." I press a palm to my forehead. Melting into the floor would be an improvement to standing here, pinned under his watchful stare. I tuck strings of wet hair behind my ears instead and study his room. The faded baseball-theme border peels in places like it always has. His plaid bedspread lies rumpled across navy-blue sheets—no surprise there. The hunting knife Dad gave him last year during the faire's final week sits on his bed stand. I haven't seen that in months. He usually keeps it hidden away from his parents and five-finger-discount brother. And the things that used to line his bookshelves—stuffed toys, action heroes, puzzles, board games—are all gone, replaced by books, PS3 games, and…and a picture of him and me grinning like fools eating steak on a stick. Traditional faire food. That's new. I mean, I remember Mary taking the picture, but I didn't know William had a copy of it, let alone a framed copy on his bookshelf.

Guess it's been a while since I've seen his room.

"I'm gonna change." I tuck my head and leave. It takes every ounce of control not to run into the bathroom. I have no reason to be embarrassed. William's my best friend. He's the only other person who knows what's going on. He's seen me sweaty, puke-y, asthma-y, and brain freeze-y. We've swum together in our underwear, for heaven's sake. Okay, so we were preschoolers and it was in a kiddy pool in the backyard, but still, him seeing my undies isn't new. I have no reason to be embarrassed.

I'm confronted with my timid, blushing reflection. Dark circles stain the area between my eyes and cheekbones. There's an angry red scratch above my right eye. My lips are blue. A drowned Chihuahua would look better than me. I rest William's clothes on the vanity and drop the blanket.

First things first—getting rid of these muddy, yucky bandages wrapped around my feet. I run the hot water and fill the tub. My aching body needs a good soak.

I sprinkle some bath salts into the steaming water, drop the gown and take off my panties. I ease into the tub, wincing at the heat, then relaxing into it.

It's an hour later when I return to William's room.

"Hey." He's sitting on the bed, has a shirt on, and is folding the socks that had littered his floor. He stands and extends an arm to his chair. "Make yourself comfortable."

I can't help but smile at his properness. "Thanks."

His eyes linger on my feet. "Are you hurt?"

"Just sore. A soak in the tub helped."

"Oh. I wondered what took you so long. Figured you needed some time to yourself, though." He grabs some socks from his dresser drawer. "Here."

I slip my feet into them.

"Tell me how you figured out Mary was inside you."

"I…" I hesitate, riddled with hissing doubt. For a millisecond, I actually consider Mary's voice to be just that, a voice. A hallucination. Something my mind made up. And William and I spend so much time together, maybe we both believe the same delusion. It's called *folie a deux*. I came across it when researching mental illness. It was after Mom's suicide attempt, when I thought knowledge could keep me safe and help me save Mom.

William's brow furrows. "Anne?"

You know I'm real. Please, Anne.

My voice stalls and I clear my throat to restart it. William listens to my story without interrupting me. Mom's flipping out, her crazy driving, me leaping out of the car, falling in the woods and ending up in the psych ward, running into Shequan (who doesn't remember he's Shequan), his blow-up, Mom's visit, and my escape—I tell him all of it.

When I finish talking he's mute and completely still.

"So, that's it." I shrug.

He blinks. "Wow. That's…awesome!" He smiles and runs his hands through his hair.

"What?"

"You're like an action hero or something. Like, like Lara Croft."

"Who?"

He shakes his head, "One of my brother's games. Anyway, how come you didn't get caught?"

Oh, crap. That's right. The hospital staff will have figured out I'm missing by now. I lean forward and put my face into my palms, groaning.

"Anne?" William kneels before me. His hands alight on my knees, soft as moths.

"I can't stay here. They'll come looking for me sooner or later." I stand and pace the room. William retreats to his desk chair. "I need to figure out how to put everything right. Mary, Evan, Shequan… I'm not sure what happened to Shequan after Z took him, or why she dumped him, but he's a mess right now. He must not have had whatever it is she wants."

William's brows knot tighter with every step I take. "Do you think her spell went wrong?"

I shrug. "Could happen, though she's so powerful it's hard to imagine. Then again, maybe that's why she took Evan instead. Plus, he'd invoked his sign. That could be an important step."

"Would it help to know how she does the spells?"

"Of course it would. The words she used, which signs she invoked, the sacrifices she used, all of it. But I need Z to figure all that out. She's the one who's created all this chaos. It has to end with her."

"And how do we find her?"

"We'll have to search the faire. I'll need a disguise."

His head drops. "Haven't we done that enough already? Besides, the faire's been closed early from rain damage. Most of the vendors are heading to the next site early."

I drop onto the bed. "How far away is that?"

He shrugs. "Dunno."

I shoot to my feet again. *Step, step, step, turn. Step, step, step, turn.* "She won't go too far. Maybe she's heading to the next location with the other vendors."

"She doesn't have to stay with the faire, circuiting the country."

"She *is* the faire. Think about it. An old woman, dressed in a black cloak, selling potions, jewelry, and doing tarot readings—where else could she be?"

"If she can do magick long distance, it doesn't really matter where she goes."

He has a point. Then again... "Gamma said not everything is solved with magick. I didn't use magick to get out of the psych ward."

"But you said she was close."

I snap my fingers. "That's right. Mary felt her. Mary, you got any ideas?"

No, except she's not as close as she was.

"Mary says she's not close anymore. More evidence that she's traveling."

"You can hear her?"

"I told you that already."

"Yeah, but it's so wild." He snort-laughs.

"What if she's leaping across dimensions or the time-space continuum or something?" William twists in his chair and the gears squeak.

"Well I don't know how to do that, so I'm gonna have to track her the old-fashioned way, with Google."

"Google?"

I pause in front of him. "Is your computer on?"

He spins to face his desk and flips open his laptop. "Yeah."

"Good. Look up the next stop on the faire circuit, will you? I need a map."

He opens a search engine. "All right, then. Let's Google her." He searches for the "New York State Ye Olde Renaissance Faire" circuit calendar and within minutes has a map to the next location, Alabaster, New York, printed.

William traces a finger along the route. "This city is over four hours away. How are we going to get there?"

Can't ask Mom or Dad to drive us. And if I'm considered a fugitive of a psych ward, I can't take a bus or train. To come this far only to be beaten. "Crap."

The rap music rumbling through the house ceases. Of course! "James can take us!"

"I don't think—"

I'm out of his bedroom and down the stairs before William can finish his sentence. He rushes after me, slamming against each step so hard he might fall through.

"Anne, this isn't a good idea!"

I fling open the basement door and collide with James. He looks up at me, a startled expression on his face. His mouth gapes open. "Hey, Anne." He grins and shifts to walk past me.

I trail behind him as he winds his way to the kitchen. The click of a soda can opening precedes a long belch by mere seconds. "James, I—"

William rushes to my side. "Let me talk to him."

He approaches his brother much like a lion tamer approaches a lion. "Hey, man. Um, Anne was wondering if you knew how to get here." He points to the next faire location on the map.

James finishes off his cola and crinkles the can before chucking it into the sink. High class right there. He glances at the paper. "What does it matter?"

"I need a ride."

James laughs and scratches his bare belly. Both nipples are pierced with rods, and an eagle tattoo marks his left chest. And that's in addition to the gauges in both ears, eyebrow ring, lip ring, and bull ring in his nose. I dread to think where else he has piercings. His jeans hang low on his waist and the red plaid of his boxers is visible. "I could do that."

"Really?" I flutter my lashes—something I *never* do—and abruptly stop. Something knocks around my skull. Mary. I wonder if she has a secret crush on the grubby guy. Man, being in the same body really takes this twin thing to a new level.

Shh! Focus, she yells.

She does like him, ew! "What about Evan?" I counter in a whisper.

She replies, *I do not have a crush on Jimmy. He melts when girls flirt with him, Anne. I've seen it.*

I swallow my pride and lean into him, placing a hand on his. William stiffens—I catch it out of the corner of my eye.

It's okay. You'll explain everything to him later. Go on.

I wish there's a way to smack her, but I'd have to hit myself. I smile. "Actually, we both need the ride. We're meeting someone, and it'd be really awesome of you to help us out."

He slides his hand out from under mine and stuffs in his pocket to pull out a crumpled cigarette pack. He taps a cigarette on the pack and lights it up. After a long drag—it takes forever, I swear—he smiles at me and says, "Sure. Why not?" Smoke billows out of his nose like he's a dragon.

"Thanks." I sigh with relief and give him plenty of space. I'm done flirting, especially since staying in a five-foot radius of him puts me in danger of an asthma attack.

He fetches a bag of chocolate-chip cookies from the cupboard. "What're you going to give me?"

A hope-crushing sledgehammer descends, effectively squelching any plan I had of getting to Zeena. My heart gets mashed with it.

"I don't work for free, sweetheart. William should've told you that."

Hadn't thought of that.

"Well? What do I get for driving you to another state to *meet someone?*" He mashes the remains of a cigarette into an ashtray and tears open the cookie bag, jamming three of them in his mouth at once.

I twist my mouth to the side. He wouldn't be interested in my collection of scented candles and Tarot cards. I could go at him with a staple gun. As many piercings as you want for free!

Mary chuckles, and the vibrations shudder through my entire body. She can hear my thoughts?

Yep. I have all along, I just couldn't figure out a way to talk back until a few hours ago.

This'll make communication easier.

Yeah, you don't have to look like a raving lunatic.

Shut up.

She giggles and it vibrates in my lungs.

William glances at me and tips his head, motioning for me to follow him toward the stairs.

I mouth, "What?"

His eyes roll in the same direction.

"Aw, you guys are so cute when you make googly eyes at each other." James scratches himself, erm, *below decks.* "Let me know when you've got something to offer, then we'll talk about that little road trip. I take fifties and hundreds." He brushes past me and thumps his way to the basement.

William gives up his body-language signs and joins me in the kitchen. "There's no way he'll do anything for us unless we give him money, or beer, or weed."

"I don't have any of those things!"

He's such a jerk, Mary says.

"Sorry. I was hoping…" I trail off. Hopping on the counter to sit, I roll my eyes and huff. "One more stupid move for Anne."

William anchors his hands on either side of my legs. "Stop being so hard on yourself. You're not stupid."

"How are we going to get to the next faire site?"

William's mouth curls up in a smile. "What if we convince him with magick?"

"You can't change people. Besides, I'm close to my fill of magick."

"I'm not talking about changing him."

"Then what do you mean?"

His thumbs rub along my thighs. "It's totally weird, but these past couple of nights since we invoked Libra, well, I've been hearing things."

Great, more voices.

Listen to what he has to say, Mary tugs at my ears.

"It sounds crazy, but it isn't. I think it's the scales talking to me. They've been telling me about balance and how every person on the planet is governed by it. My brother is a taker. Maybe if I chant, I can pull on the giver side of him and he might agree to drive us."

"Might."

"Let me do this to help you." His lips pucker.

My ability to think clearly dissolves. He could tell me the sky is orange with pink triangle clouds and I'd believe it. "Okay. We'll try it. What're you going to chant?"

He takes a step back and holds out his hand.

I latch onto him and hop off the counter.

In the basement, James yells at the screen, thumbs jabbing at his controller like a pair of tiny jackhammers.

William walks right up to him. "Stop playing for a minute."

James grunts. "I'm busy. What do you want?"

"We need a ride." I fold my arms over my chest.

His grin widens. "I need five hundred bucks."

"Five hundred!" I screech.

He toggles his lip ring with his tongue. "Yeah."

"You're ridiculous." I slam my shoulder against the doorframe and pout.

Mary huffs.

James rolls his eyes and starts up the game.

William grabs my hand and drags me to him. "Concentrate."

"Wait. I might mess it up." I try to wiggle out of his grip, but he won't let me go.

"This will work, Anne. Trust me."

I fall into his blue eyes and drown, but I don't care. I trust him.

He chants, and every word echoes in my body, my mind, and my heart. They ring truer than any chant I've heard. It's pure, raw power. More potent than my chants.

> "Four elements of the earth.
> Cardinal signs unite.
> Scales of Libra.
> Influence my brother.
> Give him the balancing sight."

This chant feels different. What's happening? Mary asks.

William's powerful. I think it's because he's a Cardinal sign, I reply.

There's something else, Anne. A reason why our chants didn't work.

I'm afraid to ask.

It's because we fight too much. We're divided, and that makes our power weaker.

We're not divided anymore, I snark.

Mary stiffens inside me. *Maybe that's why the twins merged us.*

The proverbial light bulb goes on, only instead of it being one bulb, it's a rack of blinding stadium lights in the midst of a power surge.

James *woots!* again. The action halts and displays his stats. All-time high score. Good for him.

"James." William waves a hand in front of his brother's face.

He blinks and turns his gaze to William. "*What?*"

"About that ride."

"What about it?" James raises a pierced eyebrow.

Mary deflates and hides behind my lower spine. The chant didn't work. I shake my head. I can't be mad at William. He's new to magick. At least we gave it a try.

"You're such an ass. Have you ever considered helping someone without expecting something in return? Karma, man." William knocks the game controller out of James's hand.

"Karma? Pfft. Like that's a thing." He wipes his nose with the back of his hand. "Get me a soda."

"No."

James's tongue darts out of his mouth to play with his lip ring for the millionth time.

"I've done enough for you and I'm not doing one more thing until you do something for me to balance it out."

James whistles. "Oooh, little brother, the hero."

"Do this for us." The muscles in William's jaw ripple. There's a sharp edge in his eyes that I haven't seen before.

James rubs his shoulder. He stands up, shoves past us, and heads upstairs. A moment later, I hear his keys jingle. "You coming, or not?" he calls.

I gape at William.

He smiles. "Told you it'd work."

I follow him to the front door where he pauses and bends over to pick up a pair of sneakers. "These are my mom's. They might fit you."

They're three sizes too big, but they're better than socks. "Thanks."

Outside, James is waiting in the car with the engine idling. Its steady rumble mimics the thunder I've gotten so used to hearing.

"Incredible." I hop in the backseat while William holds the door open. He slides in beside me and reads out the address for James's GPS.

We take off. James plays rap music so loud that I can barely keep my teeth from chattering. He keeps yapping at me about what he wants to do with the sound system, but I can't really hear anything other than "woofer" and "sound."

Since William's on such a roll with magick, I should have him chant a muting spell on Jimmy's speakers. If I chant, I'd probably end up blowing out all our eardrums and quite frankly, I'm sick of making things worse.

Though, it seems to be my best skill lately.

Chapter Twenty-Four

James slams on the brakes so hard I crash into the back of his seat. And I have my seatbelt *on*. Dirt wafts around the car as the engine idles.

Four police cruisers, two facing north and two facing south, bracket the road's shoulders. Seizure-inducing blue and red lights flash on their roofs. A pair of floodlights washes out the double yellow lines and blacktop while orange cones siphon cars to single file. One officer directs traffic on our side, and I suppose another is on the other side doing the same thing.

"What a night for sobriety checks. Good thing I'm not drunk," James laughs.

Sobriety checks my non-badonkadonk booty. I'm a fugitive from a psych ward. I wouldn't be surprised if the FBI was looking for me.

Mary scrambles around in my abdomen like the alien from, well, *Alien. Run!* she screams.

I mumble, "I can't. They'll see and come after me. I can't go running through the woods in the dark."

William leans over to me. "Huh?"

"Mary wants me to run, but that's how I ended up in the hospital."

He presses his lips to my ear. "You think they're looking for you?"

"I don't know."

An officer taps on James's window with the butt end of his flashlight and I jump, bonking my skull on the low ceiling. William laces his fingers with mine. "Roll 'em down."

I drag the hood of William's borrowed hoodie over my head and scrunch down in the seat.

James does as the cop says. "Evening, officer. How can I help you?"

"You kids are out late." He points his flashlight at James, snapping his gum with every chew. *Chew, snap, chew, snap, chew, snap.* "Where you headed?" He sweeps the rest of the car, pausing on William and then me.

"Road trip," James coughs.

The cop zeroes in on James again. "How old are you, son?"

"Nineteen, sir."

"I'm going to need a clearer answer than 'road trip.'" *Chew, snap.*

"My kid brother's having a sleepover at his friend's house and I'm dropping them off." James jerks his thumb toward us.

"Grab your license and registration and get out of the car, please."

James releases his seat belt and paws around his glove box. He slides out a small piece of paper and opens the door. The cop escorts James to the front of the car and examines his paperwork.

"What're we going to do?" I whisper to William.

"They'll let him go and we'll be on our way." He gives me a reassuring nod.

The cop says, "Registration expires next month."

"Yep, I already sent the money." James leans on the hood.

"Who's in the backseat?"

"My brother William, and his little girlfriend, Anne."

A wave of heat fans across my face. I've never heard anyone use "girlfriend" to describe my connection to William.

The cop wanders to the driver's side and peers in at us again. "What's your last name, Anne?" *Chew, snap.*

Crap! Mary yelps.

"Yeah," I reply.

"Speak up, miss." The cop dips his head inside.

"Cripper." I blurt out Gamma's last name.

He pops his gum and wanders back to James. "Her name Anne Cripper?"

James twists his upper body. He's playing with his freaking lip ring again. "Nah. It's Devans."

Chew, snap, chew, pop. He saunters to us and sticks the flashlight into my face again. "Wanna try that again?"

"I'm Anne D-Devans."

"Anne Devans. Your parents are worried sick about you. Get out of the car." The cop waves over a couple more officers and puts cuffs on James.

"Hey, what's this for?" James protests.

"Did you know Ms. Devans escaped from a psychiatric ward earlier tonight?" *Chew, pop.*

James groans. "Will, I'm gonna rip you a new one for this."

"Best keep quiet, son, unless we ask you a question." The cop gestures for him to stay at the car hood. "Don't move."

A woman cop opens William's door and swings her arm. "Get out, please."

"William!" I claw at his sleeve.

"Chant, Anne. Anything. Just get us out of here." He caresses my cheek and slides out of the seat. "Remember, I got your back."

A third cop opens my door. "Come here, Anne." His hand cinches around my arm. He drags me to James and William. "What're you doing with these boys?"

"I'm not crazy. My mother is. The nurse threatened to call CPS. I didn't belong there." I blubber, the exact wrong thing to do when you're trying to convince people you're sane.

William reaches out to me, but the woman cop blocks him and says, "Sit tight, sir."

"Chant," he says. One word. A simple command.

An impossible feat.

"I need your help, Mary." I close my eyes and focus inward. The sounds of cops milling about, radio signals, and car engines dim. Exhaust fumes, stale cigarette smoke, and the cleansing scent of rain fades.

I take a slow breath.

A tingling, at first faint, then stronger, builds in my mind.

"What is she doing?" James asks.

I tune him out. "Mary. Help."

In the blackness of my closed eyes, a speck of light is born. It wiggles, sends off a flash, and grows. A web of gold flows out from the pin of energy.

Touch William! Mary barks.

I open my eyes and tear away from the cop restraining me. William yelps as I throw my arms around him. On contact, the light explodes around us and consumes us.

The rest of the world disappears.

Wind, thunder, and lightning imprison us in a cell of crackling currents and shearing drafts. The leaden tongue of gravity lashes out while the puffy arms of air buoy me. There's nothing beneath my feet. The only thing to hold onto is William.

I scream.

William hugs me tighter. His chin digs into my scalp and my cheek is pasted against his chest.

"Mary!" What has she done?

Hang on!

We smack into something hard. The air gets knocked out of my lungs. William's weight squishes me into whatever I'm lying on.

I open my eyes. We're in a field. Blades of grass seem to touch the sky, but it's only my perspective. "Can't...breathe."

William lifts his head. "Oh! Sorry." He rolls his upper body off me. Our legs are still tangled. I don't mind. His hand lingers on my face. That doesn't bother me either.

"You okay?"

He nods, panting. His breath is warm and fresh. "You?"

"Yeah."

"Where are we?"

Streetlights dot the background. They backlight one-story shacks and Tudor-style shoppes. It's like the faire, but in a different layout. We couldn't possibly have been transported to the next site.

Yes! We made it! Mary claps. Sounds like canon fire in my head.

"The next faire. Help me up," I say.

We hook arms and rise to our feet.

"How do you know?" William brushes off his pants and shirt.

I do the same. "Mary says so."

He taps my forehead. "Thanks, Mary."

I swat him away, but smile. "Get out of here."

He grins. "Couldn't resist."

Mary whimpers. *She's close, Anne.*

My heart flutters against my ribcage like a canary trying to escape its cage. I spin, searching the shadows for an old woman dressed in a cloak. "Can she sense our arrival?"

Maybe.

Dad always says the best defense is a good offense. I swallow the rising terror and stride ahead of William. He's got longer legs than me, though, and he catches up easily.

"So, where exactly are you headed?" he asks, still breathing hard.

"We need to find Zeena." A flash of lightning highlights my exasperation.

She's closer, Mary says.

I freeze. Did I call her by saying her name? "Where?"

Not sure.

"I'll walk around. Let me know if we're getting hotter or colder."

Okay. Hold onto William's hand. It makes us stronger.

I latch onto William's hand and tug him along. He doesn't resist. In fact, he laces his fingers tight with mine.

We walk toward the center of the faire grounds—I assume it's the center anyway, because more permanent-looking structures line a wider path. We follow the treeline until we find a thin, winding trail leading into the carefully cultivated forest. A sign marks the entry. It reads, "Mystic Wood."

Zeena likes the cover of trees and the mystery of wooded areas. Like any good Renaissance Faire, woods are a magickal place, full of darkness and the unknown. The ideal playground for an evil sorceress.

"What will we do when we actually find her?" William whispers into my ear. His breath tickles my neck.

I shudder and fight the urge to touch my skin where his breath lingers. "I don't know."

Maybe you should call Castor and Pollux and Libra, you know, before we come across Z, Mary offers.

As if the twins hear her, more lightning streaks across the sky and deep rolls of thunder rumble over our heads.

"Every time I call them, things get worse. Besides, I thought you hated magick," I mumble.

William frowns at me.

"I'm talking to Mary."

"I thought so, but sometimes it's hard to tell," he says.

I don't like it, but we have no other option and now that we're working together, we have a better chance of success. Mary points out.

"Are you suggesting we fight fire with fire?"

No, I'm suggesting we fight fire with air and water.

"Touché. But what do I say?"

"To who?" William answers.

I wave a hand at him.

"What should I do?" He kicks a few pebbles out of his way.

"Stay with me." I squeeze his hand.

"Always." William squeezes back.

A smile tickles my lips.

Mary laughs. *So romantic.*

"Shut up," I say.

His brow furrows.

I purse my lips. "Mary's making fun of us."

No I'm not!

"Now she says she's not."

William bites his bottom lip. "This is weird, having the both of you in there. Like we're alone, but not really."

I don't like being in here either. Imagine how weird it is for me.

"Mary says she doesn't like being inside me either."

He frames my face with both hands and presses his lips to my forehead, using it as a microphone. "This message is for Mary: We'll figure out how to get you out of there."

She snorts.

I bat him away. "Very funny."

We lace fingers again and carry on. Fueled by William's Libra power and Mary's half of the Gemini power, a chant takes shape in my mind. I mumble the words at first, gaining focus with every step.

> "Castor and Pollux,
> Hear our plea,
> Show Zeena to me
> Before she flees.
> Castor and Pollux,
> I beseech thee,
> Restore the signs
> And my sister to me!"

William swings my arm. "Will it help if I chant with you?"

I nod. "Yes."

Mary joins us. Her voice buzzes in my skull as William's and mine echo into the night. Our combined efforts drive the wind from a stiff breeze to a body-slamming gust that pushes and pulls at us at the same time. Air is forced up my nose, and down my throat, and debris from the ground flies at us from all around. Dirt gets into my mouth. Grit coats my tongue and sticks to my teeth. William ducks and tries to rub his eyes. I drag him ahead, refusing to give up.

His weight is against me. Our bodies touch from stem to stern. We're glued together. My toes curl. A guillotine of air slices the molecules between us and we fall apart.

"William!" I scream, flailing my arms. I catch the hem of his shirt.

Our gazes lock.

Another gust rips my hand away from him and we're carried in opposite directions. I'm twirled, spun, twisted, and beaten like pretzel dough. After about a dozen somersaults, I topple onto the ground square on my back. Streaks of pain wrap around my torso.

Mary pats my back—on the inside. *She's here.*

"William! Where are you?" I bleat.

Oh, miracle of miracles, he's at my side pulling me up. "Are you okay?"

"I'm alright. You?"

"A little windswept."

I smirk.

A thick bolt of lightning snaps nearby. It flashes again and a hunched figure emerges from the trees. The blustering wind attacks her robe, whipping the fabric around her legs. Her gray hair flies loose from her hood. She shoves it out of her face and trains her eyes on me. They glow an angry red, raging with a fire all their own.

"How dare you call upon the twins, you little witch! And Libra? Silly boy, the Scales are no match for my power," she roars. "All the signs belong to me. Just like you. Just like your sister. And just like your friends."

"Reverse the spell, Zeena!" I call back, fingers digging into William's waist as I strain to hold on.

"Castor and Pollux, what do you think of this little girl telling me what to do?" She throws her head back, arms raised to the sky.

The twins answer her by dumping rain. A deluge of water hits me like a million simultaneous rubber-band snaps. I nestle into William's shoulder and he ducks his head.

"Come to me, children. And you can all be together forever." She cackles, lowering her arms until they are stretched toward us. Though I can't see her legs move, she approaches like a leaf pushed along by the wind. Guided by unnatural speed, she's within inches of us before I can blink. She buries her fingers in my hair and pulls me from William's arms.

"William, don't let go!" I cry.

Zeena tosses me to the ground like a discarded rag. She points her index finger at him and chants:

"Castor and Pollux,
I order thee to do my bidding!
Bring me Libra and Gemini.
Scales of Libra,
I order thee to do my bidding.
Let these children come into my being!"

A light wire shoots out her index finger and impales him in the chest. He grimaces and drops to his knees.

"William!" I cry.

He yells, and then he is gone.

Lightning strikes a transformer nearby, sending sparks across the sky in arcs of orange. My eyes and nose run from the sting of melted metal. Despite the rain, flames trickle along the electric pole and slice along the wires, cocooned in a shroud of billowing smoke.

Without Zeena to provoke it, the rain trickles to a stop, the wind settles, and the lightning and thunder cease.

My breath rattles in my chest and oozes out of my mouth. I cover my mouth with a shaky hand to strangle a yell. The memory of Zeena's touch makes my skin crawl.

Mary cries. Tears slide down my cheeks, matching hers.

I close my eyes and peer inward. "Mary, can you tell where Z is?"

She sniffs. *No.*

"You're scared. It's okay, but I need you to try to find her. Please."

I can't. Mary shakes her head. My brain sloshes with it. I open my eyes and find something to focus on to stop the swirling.

"Yes. You. Can. Do this for William. For me. For yourself. If Z catches me, we're all goners."

Mary tightens and my spine tingles with fury. *Okay, I'll do it.*

She stretches out like tendrils from a spider web swaying in a midnight breeze. My own spirit tries to follow, but it's trapped in my body. I'm thankful that we have an anchor, but also worried what will happen if I let go. Will I die? Will she die if she lets go? Will we be trapped in the spirit world with our bodies wandering around zombified like Shequan's?

Wiry arms wrap around me. The scent of death and rot fills my sinuses. "I've got you now."

I scream.

I'm sorry! Mary cries.

Zeena chants, the sound is distant, even though she's holding onto me with an unforgiving grip. I struggle and buck against her. She's an old woman. I should be able to peel myself from her claws.

"Castor—" I yelp.

She cuts me off by clamping a cold hand over my mouth. "Hush."

A paralyzing chill spreads down my throat, over my arms and legs, and ties me to the ground. I tighten my muscles, but my body doesn't respond.

Mary! I scream inside my head. *Chant something like last time. You got us away from the cops, you can get us away from Zeena.*

She's deadly silent, unmoving, sitting like a marble statue on my vertebrae.

Zeena waves a small object in front of my eyes. It's the symbol for Libra, the scales. *William.*

"I have to thank you, Anne. Without you, I would not have completed my collection so easily. You see, I couldn't just take anyone. They had to show proficiency with contacting the stars. Poor Shequan discovered that the hard way, and Evan, thank you for bringing him to the Zodiac. Brave William proved himself so valiant by helping you. A mighty Cardinal sign and a wonderful addition to my collection."

I squirm, hot tears slithering down my cheeks.

"Don't move." She chants again.

My feet root into the earth, my heart slows, and a heavy tiredness draws my eyelids shut. Next, my thoughts creak to a halt. The world slips further away—there's no sound, no smells, nothing.

Zeena plants both hands against my back and gives me a shove.

I'm falling and condensing all at once. Spinning uncontrollably, my body contorts and writhes, free from the bonds of nature but tethered to an even more powerful force—Zeena.

Her voice echoes in the void. It cuts through the whooshing vortex. I open my eyes. Yellow smoke spirals around me, forming a funnel that pulls me down, down, down toward a gleaming metallic object forming into a symbol. I've seen it before.

♊

The Gemini symbol.

My arms coil tightly around my body. Clenching my abdominal muscles to twist counterclockwise away from the spin, I slow my progression, but only slightly. The wind howls louder, compressing my ears, stuffing into my nose and lungs. I squeeze my eyes shut and slide my arms up but they seem glued to my sides. I grunt with the effort—one finger, two, now my hands are loose.

My feet touch the trinket. A *crack!* grabs my attention and I look down. The symbol has split open, emitting a light so bright it blinds me. I pull my knees up, but it's too late. I'm caught in the tractor beam.

I clench my eyes shut and scream as my bones crunch together, shrinking, shrinking more, and then I disappear into the cocoon of light.

My first thought—this should totally hurt more.

My second thought—where the heck am I?

Have I become some puff of smoke spirit trapped in a trinket the size of a quarter? I suck in a shaky breath. I can hear it! If my senses are intact, then I must be made of something solid. Right?

But I'm not touching anything. Is my body gone? Wandering somewhere out there without me, a psychotic zombie mumbling incoherently?

"Oh God, oh God, oh God!" I rant.

Someone giggles.

My eyes fly open. In front of me, Mary's kneeling at my head. A big grin splits her face.

We're surrounded by a gray haze, shimmering here and there with streaks of yellow. The smoke shifts, and between the swirls two tall pillars emerge on either side of us.

"What is this place?" I ask.

She shrugs. "Dunno. But it doesn't matter. We're together!" She dives for me and wraps me in a hug. Her lavender-scented curly hair slaps me in the face while her delicate arms squeeze my ribcage.

My sister. She's here. We're together. And we're touching. I stiffen and pull back. "Are these our real bodies?"

Mary's smile fades. Fear settles behind her eyes. "I don't know. I think so."

"Have you been here before?"

She looks around, takes in the pillars, and watches the smoke spiral around. "I remember the fog, but...not the pillars. I didn't really explore much before you called me."

I slump. We're stuck, alone, with no idea where we are or how to get out. Zeena has won. Questions zing at me. Are we going to die here? Starve to death? Wait around for Zeena to call us out and do her bidding? How does all of this work?

"Anne?"

I shake my head, pressing the heels of my palms to my eyes. "What do I do? What do I do? What do I do?" I roar louder than a lion screaming through a megaphone.

Mary squeaks. "Um…Anne? Are you okay?"

I drop my hands and pound my thighs with both fists. "No I'm not okay. That old witch has won. We're trapped who knows where, William's gone, Evan and Shequan are gone, and we're all alone with a bunch of freaking smoke! What if we're stuck here forever, like this is some form of purgatory?" I swing my arms.

"Have you gone bonkers?" She slides away.

"Mom thinks I'm crazy. She committed me. So why not act crazy?" I rotate a finger in the air at my temple.

"We need to figure out how to get out of here." She folds her arms across her chest.

I bend my knees and wrap my arms around my legs. "I'm sick of figuring things out. I only make it worse. You decide what to do."

Mary kneels in front of me. "I'm not deciding anything by myself. If you've been paying attention at all, then you should know we have to work together. It's the only way our power will work."

I purse my lips at her.

Her right eyebrow arches and her cheeks hollow. "Drop the attitude and suck it up."

My jaw drops. "You've changed."

She leans toward me on all fours. "That's right. You're not the only one who can be stubborn and bossy. Now give me your hand and get to your feet. And don't think you'll get away with saying no 'cause I won't let you."

Sobered, I reply, "Gotta say, I like the new you."

"Shut up."

The instant our palms make contact, a gust of wind whistles through the hazy void. Smoke closes in, encasing us in a moist, warm cushion. The fog solidifies and hauls us to our feet.

"This is weird." I cling to her waist and she clings to mine. "Is it Z?"

"I don't think so." Mary shakes her head. She lifts her gaze to the sky…erm, or where the sky should be. "Castor and Pollux, is that you?"

On either side of us, two pairs of arms and legs, two torsos, and two heads take form. Lefty nods. His surface shimmers and morphs to gold with the movement. His twin, Righty, nods next and turns to a rich amber.

"Oh. My. Gosh," I whisper.

"Which one of you is Castor?" Mary asks.

Gold guy nods.

I address Righty. "And you're Pollux?"

He nods.

"Wow," Mary whispers.

"Nice to finally meet you," I add.

Benign smiles emanate from the Gemini twins. In unison, they point toward an archway connecting two pillars. More yellow streaks form in the gray mist, tracing a path through the arch and curving away.

Mary glances at the archway and then back to them. "You want us to go there?"

Castor and Pollux nod.

"Why?"

Their smiles fade as they dissipate into the fog.

I paw at the air where they'd stood. *Swish, swish.* "Did we really see that?"

"Yes." She takes my hand. "Come on, let's go."

The yellow streaks remain, showing us the way.

"We don't know where that leads," I say.

"True. But we can't stay here, can we?"

As soon as we pass through the arch, thunder booms.

Mary snorts. "Do you think they're happy we're gone?"

Chapter Twenty-Five

It's hard to tell time when you're in another reality. It seems like Mary and I walk for hours. Without the yellow streaks, we have no direction. We could be going in circles anyway. Our silent partner, the ever-enduring smoke, undulates in an irregular pattern of circles, arcs, and lazy swirls. We're not met by any more pillars.

Maybe this is Zeena's way of keeping us occupied until she needs us. Maybe Castor and Pollux are playing with us. Or worse, maybe they are punishing us for calling on them in the first place.

I rub my throat and pine for a hot soak in the tub. A cool glass of water and a cheeseburger sound good too.

"Anne, I hear voices." Mary crouches, mimicking our neighbor's cat zeroing in on an unsuspecting chickadee. She tugs at my shirt and I slip down with her.

"Sounds like arguing." I strain to make sense of the pattern of short yelps and hollers. "Yeah, but who?" She bites her bottom lip. "Let's go another way."

The yellow streaks appear out of nothing and wind ahead of us. They grow in intensity, silently beckoning us.

"Maybe we should follow them," I say.

"Maybe we should avoid the noise. We don't know what or who is there. Come on." Mary pulls me along with her, away from the commotion.

Our inanimate guides twirl around us and push us back to our original path. The more we stray from them, the more agitated and darker the smoke gets. Soon, it's buffeting us, slapping us away from our new trail. Mary whips her arms at the stuff, but it slips through her fingers, unharmed.

"We have to go back!" I yell over the din.

As soon as we turn around, the prodding stops.

Someone screeches and I speed up, drawn by an instinctive need to help. It could be William, or Evan, or Shequan.

"Anne, wait!"

"They could be hurt."

The streaks brighten the faster we go, agreeing with my desire to help. I jog. Somehow, my lungs are freer in here and I don't have the tightness asthma ordinarily gives me. Mary keeps up with me, even though I can tell it's the last thing she wants to do but that it's better than being left alone. We cross under another archway. It's much larger and wider than the one we left. A bright yellow Gemini symbol marks the keystone.

Inside, the mist thins and ultimately disappears. Finally, our new world introduces itself. Under our feet is pure white marble, laced with veins of silver and gold. It stretches on and on with no end in sight. Twelve archways, each marked with a unique, glowing Zodiac symbol, dot the perimeter. Vines spiral around the pillars and huddle at their bases. It's a Greek wonderland, mapping out the constellations and their signs.

"Oh, my goodness." Mary gapes at the circular arena spanning out in front of us.

"What is this place?"

"Look out!" Mary ducks.

I dive with her. A fireball, the size of a basketball, sizzles past my head, missing me by inches. I check my hair and breathe a sigh of relief. It's all there. "What the heck?"

A stream of water, thick as a hundred-year-old tree trunk, slices in the opposite direction. Huge water droplets fly from it, whacking Mary and me. The ground shakes and the once-smooth marble cracks in several places. Jets of air gush through the cracks, dumping hot gases into the mix.

I leap to the side to avoid getting obliterated by a rush of pressurized steam. "The place is destroying itself."

Mary clamps both hands around my wrist. "Let's get out of here!"

The fog rises again, eclipsing us and blocking our view of anything beyond an arm's length.

"So much for seeing where we're going," I mutter.

"We can't stay here." *Tug, tug, tug.*

We creep along, making sure we step on solid ground with every step. Even though the battle rages on, the mist buffers the sound like noise-cancelling headphones. Flashes of yellow, red, green, and blue highlight the fog like a rainbow of lightning.

An arch solidifies in the mist. The symbol on the keystone looks like two sideways commas, one facing left and the other facing right. Cancer, the crab. It glows an azure blue.

"What're we looking for?" Mary whispers.

"Not sure."

The yellow swirls that guided us earlier re-form in the fog. They unfurl like tendrils ahead of us.

Mary extends a hand to touch one of them. It dissolves around her fingers, retreating like a drop of oil fleeing from water.

"We should follow."

The next arch's symbol—a circle with a winding tail circling around it—glows red. Leo.

Soon, we pass green Virgo.

"The arches follow the Zodiac calendar. We're getting closer," I say.

"Closer to what?"

"The next arch should be Libra."

"And William?"

"I hope so." I could use his calming support right now. I could go for a hug too. And maybe a kiss. Yep. That'd be nice.

"There it is!" Mary shoves me forward.

We cross the threshold of an arch adorned with yellow scales and the smoke turns to grit—a wall of yellow, sparkling sand.

"William!" I shout. "What are the swirls doing? William!"

Mary bangs her fists against the sand. "Why block us? I thought it wanted us to come here."

More swirls curlicue around us. A mixture of amber and gold, the streams head-butt the yellow wall.

"Wait. We must be trespassing on Libra." I knock on the sand. "William is our friend. Can we please enter?"

Our golden and amber swirls delve into the pure yellow. They leave dozens of tunnels in their wake. Soon, the wall looks more like Swiss cheese than a solid glob of sand.

Mary gasps. "I hear footsteps."

"Me too. And they're closing in fast. Let's hide." I duck around one of the arch's pillars and Mary rushes for the other.

A lanky figure emerges from the haze. Dark hair, jeans stained with paint.

"William!" I lunge at him, wrapping my arms around his neck.

He grunts, probably startled, but hugs me back. He twirls me around twice before setting me down and looking at me at arms' length. "I'm so glad you're here." He frowns. "By the way, where *is* here?"

My heart bursts from his embrace. Then again, he's most likely thrilled to see anybody, no matter who it is. I untangle my arms from his neck and pat his chest. Awkwardly. "I'm not sure, but I think it's where Z has sent all her Zodiac signs."

Mary leaps from her hiding place. "William. It's so good to see you. Like, really see you, rather than through Anne's eyes." She tucks her hair behind her ears.

He smiles at her and clasps her shoulder in a friendly greeting. "That was totally wild." He peers through the archway. "Do you know what's going on?"

In reply, a fireball whizzes past and a second later, a geyser of water skims parallel to the ground in the opposite direction. The ground shakes again, loosing another wave of steamy air.

My fists clench. "Earth, wind, rain, and fire."

William and Mary both say, "Huh?"

I smack my forehead. "Z said she collected kids who had invoked their signs. Think about it. All the signs are here and they're all using their signs' power. It makes sense!"

Mary's eyebrows crease. "I'm glad it makes sense to you, but can you explain why everybody's fighting?"

William ushers us behind a pillar. "Good question."

"Where's a wall of sand when you need one?" I mutter.

"Huh?" William frowns.

"Never mind." I face Mary. "Remember when Gamma said we have to work together in order for our power to work? Maybe Z wants us to fight so we don't band together and find a way out."

Mary taps a finger to her mouth, deep in thought. "That's a theory. But won't all this fighting drain the Zodiac power?"

"Maybe only a few are fighting at a time and she's isolating the rest of us. I've been wandering around here forever." William squints at the surrounding mist.

"All this fighting could destroy the place." Mary's logic sobers us.

"What if destroying the place will get us out?" I say.

"Or it might get us killed. We don't know where we are or how to get home," she counters.

My stomach drops.

William snaps his fingers. "We figured out how to combine our signs. All we have to do is get the others to call a truce. Then we'll pool all our Zodiac power and break free."

Mary shakes her head. "Again, a nice theory, but we can't go out there. It's a war zone. We'd be torn apart before we had a chance to talk."

I chew on my cheek. "What about Evan?"

William's mouth curves down. "You think he's here?"

"Z took him. He has to be here."

"We can start with him." William tips his head to the side. "He's Aries, right?"

"Yep, and a Cardinal sign, like you."

"They have more power than the others?" he asks.

"Certainly more influence." I pinch my lower lip with my thumb and forefinger.

William slaps a palm against the pillar. His brows hang low over his eyes. "You think Shequan's memories are here?"

Mary and I glance at one another, then at him.

I suck in a breath. "He doesn't remember who he is. It's like he's an empty shell. His body is there, but his mind isn't. Maybe something went wrong when Z chanted over him. As far as we know, he hasn't invoked his sign and Z mentioned something about needing people who showed *proficiency* at calling on Zodiac power."

"You sound pretty convinced that's what happened. Why would she bother taking him if he wasn't 'proficient'?" William drags his fingers down the pillar.

"I don't know." I cuff my throat with my hand, shivering at the memory of Shequan's hands squeezing, *squeezing*.

"You think Shequan figured out how to get out, but it destroyed his mind?" Mary asks.

I huff. We'll never get out of here.

William swallows. "I wouldn't want my mind and body to be in different places. No wonder he went crazy."

"All the more reason to make sure we know what we're doing," Mary says.

I purse my lips. "Whenever we figure out what to do."

"Z's not going to help us," William puffs out his cheeks.

"I wish Gamma was here." I plant my back against the pillar and fold my arms across my chest. "You hear that, Castor and Pollux? Any way you could shuttle Gamma here?"

Mary redirects us. "So we get Evan on board and we have two Cardinals. Maybe he knows what happened to Shequan, since they share a sign."

"Right. Then we convince Capricorn and Cancer to help us." I list the signs off on my fingers. "William is a Libra. The sign is known for its balance and justice. If you do the talking, it'll go better."

"Fair enough." He peeks around the pillar again. "Aries is directly across from us. How do we get there?"

"We cut across or walk around." I swing my arm around in a mini-demonstration of the plan.

"I vote around." Mary scrunches her nose.

"Agreed." William enters the arena, but sticks close to the edge, and heads counterclockwise. He gestures for us to stay to his right. "Keep over here so I can protect you."

"You don't have to—" I start.

His lips thin.

I shut my mouth and huddle close to Mary at his right side, my modern senses reeling and my romantic heart quivering from his chivalrous I-shall-protect-thee-my-lady stance.

"Do you think the Gemini twins will help us get to Evan?" Mary jumps at a pair of random fireballs and geysers streaking past. They come within inches of William. Mini-tornadoes pirouette around us in an Elizabethan court dance. Earthquakes rattle the ground. Jagged cracks riddle the marble, and columns of gas shoot out the larger holes.

"Good idea." I grab their hands and tip my head back. "Castor and Pollux, we could use your help here!"

The sky—I guess it's sky—flashes with lightning. I squeeze William's and Mary's fingers. "Chant with me." Mary takes William's hand to complete the circle.

I chant:

> "Castor and Pollux,
> Hear my plea,
> Invoke the Scales of Libra.
> Castor and Pollux,
> Support my friend,
> Help us bring this fighting to an end!"

I hold my breath, waiting. Behind William, the smoke converges into the shape of the Scales. Next to them, Castor and Pollux appear, as benign as ever. Amazing they have so much destructive power. Gamma would probably say something like, "Quiet ponds run deep." The symbols advance and compress around us. Electricity surges through me, connecting me even more with Mary and William. Their eyes fly open and their hair whips around their heads.

The Scales shrink down until they're a funnel of mist and dive into William's mouth. Castor does the same to me and Pollux possesses Mary. Fueled by raw Zodiac energy, I spin to face the arch and the war field beyond. I see my target across the arena. Red Aries. Evan.

The moment I think it, I'm there. Mary and William are beside me, with their mouths gaping.

Evan jumps back with a start, his arms flying up over his face. "Yo!"

"Evan. It's you!" Mary leaps at him, much like I had when we found William.

"Mary!" He wraps his arms around her and spins her around. After setting her down, he holds her at arms' length, grinning. "Are you okay?"

"I am now." She blushes.

He cups her face in his hands and leans in, kissing her full on the lips. Mary squeaks, then giggles.

After he kisses her long and good, he hugs her again and finally pays attention to us. "Anne, William. You're here too? Do you guys know what this place is? I got here and everybody was fighting, so I joined in." He hooks an arm around Mary, who's still grinning ear to ear. "But I'm not sure why. It's like...like somebody whispered something in my ear and I just started lobbing these fireballs from my hands. It's so cool. Let me show you."

He extends his free arm to the sky. A fireball bursts from his palm. *Whoosh!* It flies from his hand and disappears into the fog above. Once it's gone, a dissatisfied sigh pushes past his lips. "Wish I was home, though."

"Do you remember being collected by Z?"

He runs his hand over his spiky hair. "Sort of. I remember chanting at your grandmother's house and this big storm coming up. Then everything went dark. A bright light flashed over me and that old woman cornered me. The next thing I know, I'm here."

"Did you see Shequan?"

He shakes his head. "No. He's here? Have you seen him?"

I slump against the Aries pillar. "I saw him at the psych hospital. We think Z spit him out, but we're not sure why."

William locks elbows with me. "He doesn't remember who he is."

"Dude." Evan's eyes widen.

Mary tucks a loose strand of hair behind her ear and pats Evan's chest. "We'll find a way out."

William stuffs his hands in his front pockets. "With our memories intact."

"We have a plan—" I start.

Evan interrupts, "What do I have to do?"

"When we invoke our signs here, they..." I pause and glance at Mary.

"They possess us," she finishes.

"Let's do it." Evan gives a single nod.

His sign, the Ram, materializes as soon as we say the invocation chant (it's the same one we used for Libra, but we substitute in the Ram for Aries). He smiles, flexing his arms when the power of his sign is given to him. "I feel like I can do anything!"

I put my hands up to calm him. Fire symbols are so... fiery. "Easy. I know it's super cool, but we need to get Capricorn and Cancer on board next, okay?"

William nods and slaps Evan's shoulder. "Yeah, dude, chill out."

Evan relaxes, and the flames behind his eyes simmer down. The Scales must have had an effect. Even so, he still has an edge. "How come I was able to shoot fire from my hands before being possessed by the Ram's power?"

I shrug. "Dunno. We'd invoked your sign at Gamma's. That could have something to do with it."

Evan puffs his chest. "I want to test my power. See if it's different."

William's brow shoots toward his hairline.

Mary cuffs Evan's wrist with her fingers. "Be careful."

Evan grins. He twists his hand around so he's holding Mary's and draws her hand to his lips. "Don't worry." He lets her go.

She snatches his collar and plants a solid kiss on his mouth.

William covers his mouth with a fist and coughs. He spins on his toes, turning his back to them, then wags his eyebrows at me.

I sigh. Geez, I need to take some lessons from Mary. I'd never be brave enough to kiss William, slam, bam, just like Spam.

Like before, Evan points his hands to the sky. He stands there for a long time, not moving, like a praying Bible-thumper caught in the bliss of faith.

"Nothing's happening. Why isn't anything happening?" Mary tugs on my sleeve.

An evil cackle floods around us. Mary, William, and Evan huddle near me.

"Keep your backs to me and call your signs." We stand back to back to back to back so Zeena can't sneak up behind us. "Castor!"

Mary yells, "Pollux!"

William barks, "Libra!"

Evan rounds us out. "Aries!"

A dark figure emerges from the fog directly in front of me. I stumble into the backs of my sister, boyfriend, and friend. They turn to face Zeena. William to my left and Mary to my right with Evan on the other side of her. A united line of Zodiac powers.

Zeena tucks her hands into the sleeves of her cloak. "It's amazing how you refuse to give up, Anne Devans. I've collected all the signs. I've defeated you."

"You haven't won yet. We're still able to fight," I counter.

"You're as stubborn as my sister." Zeena swills something in her mouth and spits it on the ground. It sizzles and eats into the marble ground.

Ew.

"Who's your sister, the Wicked Witch of the West?"

"Anne," Mary elbows me in the side. "Don't provoke her."

Zeena smiles, but narrows her eyes. "You should listen to Mary. She's more level-headed than you. Edith is like that too. Thought she could talk me out of collecting the signs. She knew nothing."

Edith. For the first time since I'd arrived in this alternate plane, the air leaves my lungs. "Gamma?"

Mary grips my hand. "She's lying. Don't listen to her."

"Nice try, little girl." Zeena digs into a deep fold of her cloak. She draws out a photo. It's curling and one edge is torn. "Take a look."

The photo levitates above her palm and coasts toward me on a subtle air current. I pluck it from the mini-breeze and hold it for Mary and me to see. The image is blurred, in black and white. Two women sit on a sofa-sized rock. They're wearing matching sundresses and sandals. Broad smiles brighten their faces. Crowns of daisies adorn their heads.

Mary points at the lady on the left. "Grandmother."

Thick-rimmed, cat's-eye-shaped glasses. Strong arch to the eyebrows. A bangle bracelet on each arm. It *is* her.

"And me." Zeena snaps her fingers and the picture flies from my hand to hers. With it, my confidence in Gamma flutters away, tattered by the breeze of doubt. She must know about Zeena...Eneaz...her sister. Didn't she think she should tell us? The ache of her secret burrows into my chest, cinches around my heart, and cuts off my circulation.

"You're Eneaz. Gamma never said what happened to you," I confess.

"That's Great Aunt Eneaz to you," she corrects. "I'm not surprised she didn't tell you about me. We haven't really kept in touch." She shrugs. "Now that the family reunion is over, let's get down to business."

I shake my head, clearing out the lightheadedness from Zeena's "hey, we're family" atom bomb. "What's so important about collecting the signs? You're stealing people, ripping them from their lives, their families, and their friends."

"You've felt the power of an invoked sign. Imagine having all twelve of them coursing through you." She closes her eyes and sways left to right. A contented smile lifts the corners of her lips. Then the smile fades and she sets her cold gaze on me. "I won't let Edith's hot-headed, strong-willed granddaughter steal it away from me."

"Then let us go. And we'll stop fighting you."

"The signs will never grant your freedom. They do as I say. *I* rule them. *Me*. No one else!" she screams.

"Then how was it that we were able to invoke the twins? And Libra? And Aries? The signs may not want you to be their boss," I hiss.

"They're mine! They'll never listen to you!" Zeena's cry shakes the earth, echoes in the sky, and tremors its way down my spine.

"Uh, guys. Get ready." Mary's voice wobbles.

I clasp hands with William.

Zeena steeples her hands and begins chanting.

"We need to get to Cancer. Concentrate on the Crab," William says.

A swirl of red and yellow pours from our bodies, circles us in a tornado of wind and fire, and whisks us away from

Zeena. Heat buffets me, but doesn't burn. Wind slaps my face, but doesn't suffocate me.

William and Mary's hands tighten around mine. We anchor each other. It's the only thing keeping us together.

Evan yelps, "Wahoo!"

At least someone's enjoying himself.

Just when a scream builds up enough pressure in my chest to bust free, we're abruptly plopped onto solid ground. The shock of it reverberates in my legs and my knees buckle. I drag everyone down with me.

I untangle my fingers from William and Mary and push up on my hands and knees.

Standing a few feet away, hands splayed in our direction, is a red-haired, sour-faced kid. Freckles crowd his cheeks and forehead. His clothes are dirty and torn. Steam escapes off his fingers. The last thing I need is a geyser lobbed at me.

"Easy, guy, we're here to help. I'm Anne. This is Mary, Evan, and William. Cancer is your sign, right?" I talk fast.

"Did you make that red and yellow cyclone?" His dark gaze volleys between us.

"Zee—"

I clamp a hand over William's mouth. "Don't say her name."

He says, "Okay," but it's muffled by my hand.

I let go.

William stands slowly and positions himself between Cancer Kid and the rest of us. "We were attacked and needed a fast getaway."

Cancer Kid frowns. "Who's Zee?"

I give a short description. "The old witch. Black cloak, yellow teeth, ugly face."

Recognition lights his face. "I met her at a Renaissance Faire. Her shoppe was in the woods. She asked me about my birthday, if I believed in magick. I laughed, but then she started talking about the constellations and I got totally sucked in. Stupid me for liking astronomy." He pauses to take a couple quick breaths. "She had me repeat a poem with her about my Zodiac sign and before I knew it, she was talking really fast and then this flash of light blinded me and... Man, it hurt really bad, like all my bones were breaking."

"She was sending you here."

"Where are we?" He looks around. "All this fog. I can't see anything. Every time I leave, these blue streaks surround me and push me back here."

Mary and I lock gazes.

"I keep hearing all this yelling and screaming. The ground shakes." His face grows red. "I just want to go home."

The unsteadiness of his voice tears at me. "We all do."

"I'm Libra. The girls are Gemini, and Evan is Aries. If we pool our signs' powers together, we might be able to beat the witch and get out of here." The scales appear behind William and a calming energy floats around us. He touches Cancer Kid's shoulder.

"What if it doesn't work?" The kid asks.

"What other choice do we have?" William replies.

He nods. "All I want is to get out of here. I'm Trevor, by the way."

William shakes the kid's hand. "Nice to meet you, Trevor. Welcome to the team."

Trevor smiles. "Good team to be on, if it gets us home."

I let out a pent-up breath.

He snorts. "I didn't think she could do real magick. I mean, who would? I should've listened to my sister, but I thought it was all a joke."

I wish I'd listened to my sister too. "Z's powerful. It's not your fault."

He wipes his hands on his brightly colored Bermuda shorts. "So what do I have to do?"

I smile. "Hold my hand."

I help him chant to invoke his power. A blue Crab forms over his head, then streams into his mouth.

He drops to his knees, panting. "Whoa. That was weird…but cool."

William grins. "One more Cardinal sign, and we're done."

"Then we get the heck out of here," I say. Should be easy as riding a tornado.

Chapter
Twenty-Six

We crash-land in a heap on Capricorn's territory.

"Whoa! That's wild!" Trevor exclaims.

I have to agree. Adding his power made traveling by whirlwind all the more frenzied.

The tri-color swirls dissipate. We haul each other upright and search for Capricorn, the goat, an earth sign.

"Over there," Mary gestures to a tower of vines piled next to the sign's arch.

A girl, younger than the rest of us, huddles behind the mass of leaves. Her golden hair is soaked, and bits of mud cling to her blue wrap dress and pale limbs. She is shaking. "P-please don't hurt me!"

Mary approaches her slowly, but steadily. "We're here to help. We need the power of your sign to help us escape. Will you join us?"

"How do I know this isn't a trick?" She nestles herself deeper in the foliage.

"Trust me, it's not." William edges closer to her.

I lean toward Evan. "We should keep an eye out for Z."

He nods and promptly pins his back to mine. Trevor does the same, so we form a triangle with a 360-degree view of the swirling fog.

As soon as William touches the girl, her shoulders relax and a grin spreads across her face. "I tried to get one of the other kids to help me, but he threw a fireball and ran."

William hooks an arm around her shoulder in his easy way and guides her over to us. Mary flanks her other side.

She extends a shaky hand to me. "I'm Callie."

I take her hand. "I'm Anne."

"How do you guys know each other? I mean, I can tell you and Mary are twins, but…" her voice trails off.

"We just met Trevor. William and Evan are our friends." Friends? *Friends.* I said William and I are friends. I watch his face for any signs of happiness, disappointment, anxiety, or anything.

He plays it cool, keeping an encouraging smile on his face for Callie. Dang levelheaded Libra.

"You have some good friends," Callie says.

She couldn't be more right.

With Callie on board, we've collected all the Cardinal signs. We walk through the arch, like the cast of a TV legal drama struts down the courthouse's hallway. Except for the slow-motion part.

The mist grows thinner the farther we go. Soon, it's completely gone. We pause.

Giant puddles of water pool in holes blasted out of the marble flooring. Jagged slabs of earth dot across the arena. Smoldering bits of ash fizzle and smoke here and there. Intermittent bursts of wind whack us.

"It's a war zone," I grumble.

One kid darts from behind a mound of dirt and bellyflops to slide behind another. A fireball collides with the spot he just vacated. Another kid yells and shoots a geyser back.

"Now what?" William yells into my ear.

I hesitate, uncertain. "How do you call a cease-fire?"

Mary tugs on a curl. "We need to combine our signs and do something drastic."

"That's a great idea!" Trevor holds up his hand to high-five her.

She obliges him, then grins at Evan.

"Awesome idea." He wraps his arms around her and pecks her on the cheek.

She blushes.

"Did you have something in mind?" I ask.

"Z said the signs would never listen to us. But if enough of us are working together, maybe they will. Plus, we've got the Cardinal signs. The others will have to listen, right?"

"She did say that!"

Evan scratches his chin. "Bet she didn't mean to tell us that, too."

"I bet not." Mary tangles her fingers with his. "Once they're listening, we can ask them to let us out."

"It has to work." I close my eyes and open them again to take in all the people who've helped me. My sister, my best friend, a new friend, and new acquaintances.

Mary brushes my hair with her fingers. "What's wrong?"

"Nothing." I shake my head.

Her mouth puckers. "I know that look. What're you thinking?"

"Gamma should've told us about Z."

"What if she couldn't? We weren't able to talk about her for a while, either." I really hate it when Mary is so reasonable.

I suck on my bottom lip. "And she should've never given me the spellbook."

Mary huffs. "A little late for woulda, coulda, shoulda, isn't it? She gave you the book because she thought you could handle it. She wanted to share it with you. How could she have known Z would show up at the faire? We haven't seen her before."

"Obviously I couldn't handle it. I bet my chanting is what brought her here." I roll my eyes.

She claps both hands on my shoulders. "Hey, we don't know that, so stop moping. Okay, so you've made mistakes, but we all make mistakes. What matters is that we keep trying and that we stick together."

I take a deep breath. "You're right."

"I know. And don't forget it."

I smile. "Okay."

Evan clears his throat. "Sorry to interrupt, but don't we have an alternate plane to escape from?"

Mary nods. "Let's see if the signs listen to us."

I take off my pity pants and straighten my spine. Gamma owes me an explanation, but I have to get home first before we can talk about it. "I'm ready."

William draws a circle in the air. "Gather around and hold hands. Anne, lead us."

I have a hard time focusing on anything but the whirlpool of emotions circling in my gut, so I concentrate instead on the warmth of his skin. I close my eyes and clear my throat. All I have to do is grab the attention of five Zodiac signs. No pressure.

"You can do this. They'll listen to you." William kisses my cheek.

I bite my lip to keep my heart from popping out of my mouth and floating away. "Okay. Here goes nothing."

I chant:

> "Castor and Pollux,
> Hear my plea,
> Gather the following signs to thee.
> The Scales of Libra,
> The Ram of Aries,
> The Crab of Cancer,

The Goat of Capricorn.
Castor and Pollux,
Hear my plea,
Gather the Cardinal signs to thee.
Castor and Pollux,
Hear my plea,
Encourage them to unite,
Show your strength,
So the other signs will yield to thee.
Castor and Pollux,
Hear my plea,
Use the Cardinal signs,
To set us free!"

Energy courses through me like a cascade of falling marbles. My eyes fly open. A golden glow emanates from me, a yellow one from William, and an amber one from Mary. They blend into a brighter yellow while red glows from Evan, blue from Trevor, and green from Callie.

In a flash, the lights we produce shoot from our heads and into the sky. Beams of yellow, red, blue, and green pulse above us. The beams fracture and fly apart, forming a multi-colored "X."

"They must be connecting to their energies—fire, earth, wind, and water." I yell.

Mary nods.

Trevor opens his mouth, but I can't hear what he says.

The ground shakes and we're tossed in different directions.

Lightning bolts course in jagged tracks along each beam of color. They join one another and thicken at the crossroads, then shoot down to the ground directly in the middle of the field. The strike triggers another earthquake, and a plume of smoke and dirt rises from the impact site.

"Wow." William stands. He helps me to my feet while Evan helps Mary and Trevor helps Callie.

Kids stumble out from their hiding places, jaws slack and arms limp at their sides like a horde of dazed zombies.

I take a breath. And another. Then a third. "William. Now's your chance. The others will listen."

He takes his cue and strides toward the group.

One by one, they focus on him and drift in his direction.

"Zodiac signs. Hear us. The Zodiac Collector, has trapped us here and turned us against each other. She wishes to keep us for her own power. If we work together, we can beat her and find a way home." William's voice is clear and strong.

He turns to stare at me and extends a finger in my direction. "Anne knows how to chant. She can help you access your sign's power. Who's with us?"

Seven hands extend into the air.

My heart warms.

"It's working!" Mary squeaks.

William ushers the kids to us.

"Everyone, I need you to line up according to your sign." I count out all twelve, erm, thirteen if I count myself. We stand in a circle, in alignment with our distant arches, and hold hands.

After invoking the remaining signs, we're ready to ask for freedom.

My heart pounds faster than the beat of hummingbird wings.

Four kids separate me from William. He stares at me, squares his jaw and gives a quick nod as if to say, "You got this!"

I try to take a deep breath.

> "Castor and Pollux,
> Hear my plea.
> Zodiac signs,

Gather to me.
Fire, earth, wind, water,
Powers that be,
Bring us all home,
And set us free!"

Colors of the elements surge around us—green for earth, yellow for wind, red for fire, and blue for water—mixing and clashing together, rumbling where they touch.

"Anne!" Mary yelps.

"Hold on!" I cry.

Above us, a dozen tunnels form out of the smoke. The colors mingle, turn darker, and blend into a murky brown. This is different from before. I scream as the funnels rush down to meet us.

I latch onto Mary just as we're pulled into the spinning vortex.

Unlike before, my body doesn't shrink and my bones don't feel like they're being pulverized, but the air is so compressed that it's hard to breathe. When I think my lungs will collapse from the lack of air, everything freezes like a cosmic pause button has been hit. My heart leaps into my throat. Mary slips away from me. I fumble for her ankle, but miss. I scream.

I'm still screaming when I land in a heap on the ground.

Real ground this time. Hard ground.

I groan, lifting my head, despite the dizziness that follows. It's night and damp from a recent rain.

Something soft is next to me. "Anne." It's Mary. "Where are we?"

I sit up and rub the back of my head. "No idea."

We stand and lean on each other for support. I scan the landscape, searching for anything familiar. I see trees, a path, bits of shoppes illuminated by the moon. In the distance, street lamps mark a nearby road.

"We're in the faire grounds."

"Not ours," Mary counters.

"No, we're at the one we transported to," I reply.

Spires of red, blue, yellow, and green impale the earth. They flare to an ultra white on impact and fizzle into a puffs of smoke. All of the kids from the Zodiac plane are left in their wake. They gather nearby, marveling at the grass, trees, buildings—you know, normal earthly plane things.

"Where's William?" I ask.

"And Evan?" Mary whirls, scanning for him.

A thrashing comes from the woods behind us. I whip around in time to see William fighting the underbrush. He stumbles over to us, picking leaves out of his hair. "Hey."

I raise an eyebrow. After everything that's happened, he says "hey"? We survived. We escaped. We beat Zeena. Where's the ultra-romantic moment? Isn't the hero—William—supposed to kiss the heroine—me?

I squeeze some life into my fingers by curling them into fists. Mary went for gold and kissed Evan. I could do the same. "Will—"

He pins me with his gaze. "Yeah?"

I step closer and stare into his eyes. "We did it."

"Yeah." He grins and his dimples blitz out.

I lean close and open my mouth slightly and—

"Guys! There you are." Evan pops out from behind a nearby shoppe and jogs our way.

I clamp my mouth shut and roll from my toes to my heels. "Thanks for your help." I pat William's shoulder.

He blinks away a squint of confusion. "You're welcome."

Mary and Evan embrace. They don't waste any time locking lips.

For goodness sake. I purse my lips, kicking myself for being such a coward and stuffing down the green jealousy monster pawing at my stomach.

There are way too many people around anyway. It'd be too weird to kiss William in front of them. And, he may not even want to.

And that would be too devastating to face.

Out of nowhere, a bolt of lightning punches the ground with a *thwack!*

The old witch pops into view, walking through an invisible door torn into our earthly plane. She locks onto us immediately. "So you thought you'd escape, did you?"

Mary's eyes widen. "She'll never give up, will she?"

I square off with Gamma's sister. "You've lost all your power now. The signs chose us." I nod at William, Evan, Mary, and all the other kids who've joined us. We complete the entire Zodiac.

They all nod back.

I open my mouth to chant. A flash of lightning zings over our heads, zapping away the words I'd planned to say.

The bolt impales the ground between Zeena and us. Dirt sprays and smoke billows from the crater. A hazy figure rises from the hole. There's a familiar hunch and fluff of curly hair.

"Gamma!" I cry.

She climbs out of the hole, grunting with every step. "Eneaz. Stop this at once."

Zeena's dark eyes spark with rage. "Edith. It's been a long time."

They circle each other like heavyweight boxers sizing up their opponents.

"It's foolish of you to pick on my granddaughters. They're your flesh and blood, sister."

Zeena sneers. "If you cared so much about them, you'd have taught them properly."

Gamma shakes her head. "And the other children? How many families have you destroyed in your greed?"

The old witch points a finger at Gamma. "Had you joined with me, we'd have been unstoppable. I'd never have had to go to such lengths to draw the signs' attentions."

"You manipulated the order of things to suit you. I could never agree to such a thing."

A white glow pulses from the tip of Zeena's finger.

"Gamma, look out!" I yelp.

Too late. A light rope lashes out from Zeena and snaps around Gamma's waist like a whip.

Gamma yells and drops to her knees. "Eneaz, stop this madness!"

"Why must you fight me?" She shoots another light rope and pins Gamma's upper body.

Mary claws at my sleeve and whimpers. Evan wraps her in a protective hug.

I grab onto William's shirt and he circles my waist with an arm. "Hold tight, guys."

I step forward. "Great Aunt Eneaz."

Zeena whips her head toward me. Her upper lip is curled back. "Eh?"

"Aunt Eneaz. That's who you are. You aren't a kidnapper. You're a twin. You have a sister and a family."

The wrinkles in her forehead deepen with her frown. "What?"

Mary joins me, shoulder to shoulder. "That's right. Your family misses you. We can be together if you let go of the Zodiac power and join us. Must be lonely being by yourself all the time."

She faces Gamma again.

Gamma lifts her head. "It's true, Eneaz. I searched everywhere for you. I chanted for years. No matter where I looked, I couldn't find you."

"No you didn't. I would've felt it," Zeena snaps.

"Our bond was broken. When I gave the spellbook to Anne, I'd hoped her and Mary's bond would be strong enough to mend the tear. I'd hoped to find you with their help."

My jaw drops. Bone-crushing agony riddles my ribcage, steals my breath, and tears at my heart. "You used us."

Gamma crawls toward us. "I'm sorry, Anne. I never meant for this to happen. We were supposed to do magick together. I was supposed to guide you."

"But I didn't listen." Tears stream down my face. "I screwed it up."

"*I* did, dear. It's my fault. I wanted my sister back. I hope you can forgive me." Gamma collapses to the ground.

"Gamma!" I dash to her and drop to my hands and knees. She's made mistakes, but so have I. And I still love her. She's my Gamma. I guess I understand why she wanted to save her sister.

"Anne!" William cries.

I press the back of my hand to Gamma's cheek. Her skin is cold. I tug at the light ropes binding her. "Zeena, let her go! She's your sister. She loves you."

Zeena's sneer fades. The hardness of her eyes cracks, revealing a soft, creamy center inside. "You're lying."

"Mary." I hold my hand out to her.

She rushes to my side, kneels next to me, and laces her fingers with mine. It gives me the strength to keep talking. "Let us go, Zeena. Don't hurt Gamma. You can't live without your sister. I know I can't live without mine," I say.

I grab Gamma's hand and squeeze Mary's. Mary gestures for Evan and William to join us.

All our energy combines on contact. Our auras glow gold, amber, yellow, and red. Zeena squints and holds an arm in front of her face.

I slide my fingers toward her light ropes. They fizzle and snap apart under my touch.

Freed, Gamma stirs. She moans and opens her eyes. "Anne."

Mary, Evan, William, and I help her sit up. She centers her red glasses on her nose. "Thank you, dears."

"Are you okay, Gamma?"

Gamma nods at us, then addresses Zeena. "You see, Eneaz? Your power is not omnipotent. The bonds of friendship and family overrule it."

Zeena fists her hands and throws her head back to the sky. "Zodiac signs unite! Smite my enemies. Draw on their powers and claim them for me!"

We huddle together, our arms an interlocking knot of unity. Zeena has been so corrupted by power that she's forgotten about love and family. Still, she controls the weather, the stars, and the entire Zodiac and we're defenseless against any smiting. I cringe, swallowing the sticky lump of terror rising in my throat. Whatever happens, at least I'm spending my final moments with my closest friends and family.

Lightning does not flash. Thunder does not boom. Wind does not howl.

Curious, I open one eye, then the other. The night is still. Zeena stands a few feet away from us, arms spread wide, palms facing the universe above.

"Gamma, why isn't anything happening?" I whisper.

"The signs. They're not responding to her."

"Is it because we're all here?" Mary asks.

"I'd say so, dear. You've swayed the Zodiac to listen to you."

"Signs, why have you abandoned me?" Zeena screams.

Gamma tries to stand. "Help me, boys. Girls, keep hold of me."

William and Evan steady her while Mary and I grip her hands tight.

"This is your last chance, sister," she warns.

Zeena lowers her gaze to us. The cold fire burning inside them flares, then hushes, stifled and somber. "I have nothing left. I'm all alone."

"You don't have to be, Eneaz." Gamma reaches out to her sister.

"It is too late for me, Edith. I cannot go back to my old life." She drops to her knees, broken, pitiful, powerless. "Send me away, but be merciful."

Gamma sniffs. Her face glistens with falling tears. "I love you, sister."

"I do not deserve your forgiveness." Zeena folds her arms into her robes and closes her eyes.

Gamma chants:

> "Four elements of life,
> Earth, fire, water, air.
> Four corners of the earth,
> North, South, East, West.
> Elements of the Zodiac,
> Release my sister!
> Four elements of life,
> Earth, fire, water, air.
> Four corners of the earth,
> North, South, East, West.
> Elements of the Zodiac,
> Take Zeena's powers.
> Set them free.
> Elements of the Zodiac,
> Hear our pleas,
> Give my sister, Eneaz, peace!"

Zeena opens her mouth in a silent scream. The four Zodiac colors stream out of her mouth in a rainbow of vomit. She flails and arches.

Mary stuffs her face into my shoulder. Evan cocoons her in an embrace. William presses into my back. I lean against him, but don't look away. Gamma cries. I can only partially understand the agony she's feeling. I'd thought I'd lost Mary once and it almost killed me. I can't imagine being the one to send her away.

The rainbow fades and the world darkens. Zeena—Eneaz—disappears in a blink. An empty void is left in her place.

Gamma releases my hand. "She's gone."

Mary pulls Gamma into a hug. I wrap my arms around her too.

Her body shakes with sobs. She struggles to catch her breath. "Where are the others?"

All the kids from the Zodiac plane crowd around us, somber and quiet.

Gamma's smile is the smile of someone who's lost everything and still is brave enough to set aside her own pain to help others. "Let's send you home."

Callie steps closer. "What'll happen? When we get home, I mean. Will everything be normal?"

Gamma nods. "It'll be as if you've never left." Gamma opens her arms wide. "Gather 'round, kids and hold hands."

She chants:

> "Four elements of life,
> Earth, fire, water, air.
> Four corners of the earth,
> North, South, East, West.
> Elements of the Zodiac,
> Hear our plea,
> Return the signs to where they were
> And set their hosts free!"

Epilogue

The bell rings and Ms. Sutters announces, "Time is up. Please stop working."

A collective sigh escapes all the students in the room. I lean back in my chair and stretch my aching muscles. Sludge fills my skull instead of brains. That's what math does to me—it takes fresh, young, pliable neurons and liquefies them.

Twenty chairs scrape across the floor as the students rise.

Mary files in line behind me. We dribble out of the room half-dead from all the knowledge we just belched out. A whole day of testing. Talk about cruel and unusual punishment.

"How'd you do?" Mary bops my ponytail and hops next to me so we walk side by side.

I shrug. "Uh, well, I answered all the questions."

She hooks pinky fingers with me and swings her arm. "I bet you did great. Once Shequan showed you his trick, you got every practice problem right."

"I wish I had your confidence."

She pauses. Students flow around us like river water breaking over stubborn rocks. Some stare straight ahead with vacant expressions while others toss us annoyed frowns. "*My* confidence? You're the one who always acts so certain of herself."

"That's just it. I'm *acting*. I don't know what I'm doing." I duck my head and start walking again.

"Anne. I'm beyond impressed by how you," she balls her hand into a fist, "go after stuff. You don't let fear stop you."

I clap a palm over her fist. "And I'm impressed by how you always think things through and ace every single test put in front of you."

She smirks.

"We make a pretty good team, though."

"When we work together."

William and Evan crash into us from behind. They both yell, "Huzzah!" William wraps an arm around my shoulder while Evan circles Mary's waist with his. He lifts her up.

She squeals and kicks out. "Put me down!"

He lets go and pecks her on the cheek.

She giggles.

"Time to celebrate." William shakes me.

"Definitely," I reply. A pleasant buzz carries me along the hallway, out the front door. Humid air swirls around us in a sticky, sweat-inducing welcome to summer.

"Okay guys, assume PG positions in 3…2…1…" I nudge Mary and nod toward Dad's truck.

Mary and Evan separate and William unwraps his arm from my neck.

"We'll see you later," William says.

Evan nods and waves. "Later."

They're swallowed up by the crowd before I have a chance to ask them where we'll "see" them and when "later" is.

Dad waves and leans over to unlock the door. Mary slides into the middle while I hop into the passenger seat. "How'd it go, girls?"

"Okay." Mary clicks her belt in place.

"We're still alive," I mumble.

Dad chuckles. He flips on the AC, opens the vents, and merges into traffic. Fifteen minutes later, instead of taking a left at the intersection toward home, he turns the wheel right.

"Where are we going?" I ask.

"Your grandmother's." He smiles and clicks off the AC. "What do you think about spending a couple days there? You know, get out of the house and have some fun. Be kids."

Mary glances at me, then Dad. "Huh?"

"Mom's going through a lot right now. She's very sick, so I'm going to stay home with her and help her get back on her meds." He pulls into Gamma's driveway. "I just think it's best if you guys hang out there and come home when she's feeling better. Besides, your grandmother has a surprise for you."

"A surprise?" I grip my seatbelt.

Dad shifts into park. "Mom packed your bags, and I brought them and the dogs over earlier."

"Mom packed our bags?" God knows what's inside them.

He grips the steering wheel until his knuckles turn white. "She says she's sorry for putting you girls through…hell. I'm sorry too. I know it's too little, too late, but I hope that when Mom is better we can all sit down and talk."

"For real?" Good thing I'm buckled in because if I wasn't I'd probably fall out of the truck.

He splays his fingers and taps the wheel with his palms. "You don't have any reason to believe me, but things will be different. I promise." He swings his arm around Mary's neck and kisses her head while squeezing my shoulder. "I've been a crappy dad and I have no excuse. So I can understand if you don't believe me."

"You can't drink anymore," Mary whispers.

"I know."

"And Mom has to stay on her medicine all the time," I add.

"I know."

"How can you promise us that it'll happen?" Mary picks at a fingernail.

"I can't, Mary, but I can promise to do the best I can."

"Why now?" I twist so he can't keep hold of me. "You've had plenty of chances before this to do something."

His hand flutters through his hair. "I don't have a good answer for you, Anne, except that I've made some bad decisions and I'm trying to make amends."

Mary turns her head to face me. Her brows are low and she's sucking on her lips. I don't envy her, sitting between Dad and me. She has no buffer, no way of escape from his sudden awakening to stepping up to the parenting plate.

"I love you, girls." Dad hits the "unlock" button. "Remember that."

I unclick my buckle and open the door, insides quaking from a clash of anger, fear, and hope—a trifecta of emotions that leaves me speechless. We grab our bags from the truck bed.

After Dad reverses out of the driveway, Mary elbows me. "What do you make of that?"

I shake my head. "Absolutely no idea."

"Could it be magick?"

"Magick doesn't change people."

Mary's eyes darken. "I don't know about that. It changed Eneaz. It changed William and Evan. It changed us."

"Fair enough. The question is, who chanted and what did they say?" I turn and knock on Gamma's screen door.

The dogs bark. I smile at the *click, click click* of their toenails scratching on the floor as they scramble to greet us.

"Maybe Grandmother did."

Gamma pops into view. She's drying her hands on a dish towel. She must've been in the kitchen. "Hello, girls. Come in. I'm cooking up a surprise for you, so why don't you hang out in the living room and watch TV? I'll come get you when it's ready."

"I'm not sure I can handle any more surprises."

Gamma grins. "Oh, you'll like this one."

♐ ♈ ♊ ♏ ♓

Gamma leads Mary and me by our hands, blindfolds pressed against our eyelids. I twist my mouth to the side, fighting the urge to tear the fabric away.

"Can I open my eyes yet, Gamma?" My heart thumps away, pumping excited blood through my veins. Waiting hours for a surprise is not healthy. Neither is passing those hours by debating why Dad claimed he and Mom would change. It has my fingers itching for my inhaler even though I'm not wheezing or short of breath.

"We're almost there." She chuckles and eases us forward a few more steps. "All right, girls. Take off the kerchiefs."

I whip the blindfold off. My jaw drops.

The woods behind Gamma's house are completely transformed. Hundreds of colorful streamers sway in the warm evening breeze. Tied to dozens of tree branches above, they create a squiggly canopy of celebration and fun. Chinese lanterns dot the paper sky in random constellations of pastel light. White Christmas lights are strung along an archway leading to the magickal oasis.

"Come on." Gamma hooks her arm.

We follow her inside. To our left, a harp sits on an oriental rug. To our right is a table full of presents—dozens of them. More tables decorated with white tablecloths, fancy place settings, and hydrangea centerpieces are tucked amongst the trees. The center table has a three-tiered cake centered on it. Silver Zodiac symbols are piped along the lower tier, gold swirls ring the middle one, and silver stars orbit the third level. On the top rests a silver Gemini symbol.

"Grandmother, it's beautiful." Mary clasps her hands and holds them to her chest.

My vision blurs from the shock bursting from me in tears. "It's perfect."

Mary's grin falters. "How many people are coming?"

I do a quick count of chairs. "I'm not sure I know enough people to fill all these seats."

"Turn around, dears." Gamma eases Mary around.

She gasps.

I spin.

Our entire class huddles on the other side of the archway. Shequan stands at the front.

"Shequan." I suck in a breath.

"Hey, Anne. Thanks for inviting me to your party. This is pretty cool." He smiles and traipses inside, releasing the dam. He pauses in front of us while the other guests flood in, *ooh* and *ahh* over the cake, and settle down to pick seats.

The vacant stare he'd sported at the psych ward is gone. "I didn't bring a gift. I figure I can give you guys a couple of riding lessons. What do you think?"

Mary giggles. "That's a great gift."

I'm tempted to ask what he remembers about Zeena, but I don't. What's the point of wrecking the moment? Besides, he's back to normal. We all are. "It's an awesome present. Thanks."

"Cool." He claps my shoulder with his palm and heads off to find a chair.

The harpist from the faire brings up the crowd's rear. She greets us with a bow and smile, then joins her harp and starts plucking a soothing tune.

Mary hugs Gamma. "This is the best birthday party ever, Grandmother."

Gamma chuckles. "I'm glad you like it."

Evan pops through the archway. He scoops Mary into a hug. She giggles and wraps her arms around his neck. They couldn't be more perfect together, really.

With a sigh, I turn from them and wander toward the arch, gaze trained on my sandals. Everyone's here. Except...

I smack directly into someone. My head jerks up.

It's William. He's wearing a blue button-down shirt and black pants. His hair is combed back, except for the rogue strand that flops into his eye. "You should watch where you're going."

I can't resist the cheek-spasm-inducing grin exploding across my face. "William!"

He smiles down at me. "Long time no see. You look nice."

"Me?" I swish the skirt of my green sundress. "You look handsome."

William tangles his fingers in my hair and his smile fades. His gaze falls to my mouth and his fingers linger at the nape of my neck. Definitely *not* a "friend" touch. I want to drag him to a shadowy corner. "You know you're amazing, right?"

"Erm..." My brain sputters and stalls. Friends don't call friends amazing. Not even best friends. Cool, sure. Funny, even. But not amazing.

William's thumb tickles the sensitive part behind my ear and along the edge of my hair. I shiver. More of that this-is-more-than-friendship touching. I like it. A lot.

I glance at him through my eyelashes.

A calmness only he can create washes over me. His blue eyes tell me everything I need to know.

He leans down. I tip my head up. Our lips meld and the stars applaud.

THE END

Acknowledgements

I'd like to thank my fabulous editor, Jennifer Carson, and the team at Spencer Hill Press for taking a chance on *Zodiac* and helping me bring the Renaissance Faire and the stars to life.

As the tiniest Hapenny, a race of little people,
Maewyn Bridgepost spends her
days from breakfast to midnight nibble
scrubbing the hearth, slopping the pigs and
cooking for her guardian, Gelbane. As if life
as a servant isn't bad enough, Maewyn learns
that Gelbane is a troll—and Hapennies
are a troll delicacy!

T. J. Wooldridge

THE
Kelpie

When Heather and Joe decide to be Sleuthy
MacSleuths on the property abutting the castle
Heather's family lives in, neither expected to
discover the real reason children were going
missing:

A Kelpie. A child-eating faerie horse had moved
into the loch "next door."

SPENCER HILL PRESS · spencerhillpress.com

SILENT STARSONG

SILENT STARSONG

by T.J. Wooldridge

Eleven-year-old Kyra is meant to continue the Starbard's proud family legacy of interpreting the future from the stars' songs. Her deafness, incurable by the best medics, breaks her mother's heart and pushes her father to explore anything to help his little girl--including the expensive purchase of a telepathic alien servant to help Kyra communicate on a planet inhospitable to unfixable genetic defects.

About The Author

Laura Diamond is a board certified psychiatrist and author of all things young adult paranormal, dystopian, and horror. Her Young Adult Paranormal Romance novelette, *New Pride*, and novel, *Shifting Pride*, debuted in 2012 from Etopia Press. A spin off short story based on the lions of Tsavo, *Tsavo Pride*, is now available on Kindle. When she's not writing, she is working at the hospital, blogging at Author Laura Diamond—Lucid Dreamer (lbdiamond. wordpress.com), and renovating her 225+ year old fixer-upper mansion. She is also a full-time staff member for her four cats and a Pembroke corgi named Katie.